LIZ

A JACK HANDLER NOVEL OF SUSPENSE

BY MICHAEL CARRIER

Volume Three in the "Jack Unchained" Series

A number of very wonderful people helped me prepare this book for publication. Each of them contributed significantly.

Thank you Evie, Charity, Andy, Steve, John, EmaLee, and all the members of Grand Valley Artists,
Grand Rapids, MI.

LIZ

A JACK HANDLER NOVEL OF SUSPENSE

BY

MICHAEL CARRIER

GREENWICH VILLAGE INK

An imprint of Alistair Rapids Publishing
Grand Rapids, MI

LIZ

Published 2023 by Greenwich Village Ink, an imprint of Alistair Rapids Publishing, Grand Rapids, MI.

Visit the *JACK* website at http:/www.greenwichvillageink.com

For upcoming books by the same author visit www.greenwichvillageink.com.

ISBN: 978-1-936092-17-8 (trade pbk)
Printed in the United States of America

Library of Congress Cataloging-in-Publication Data

Carrier, Michael.
LIZ / by Michael Carrier. 1st ed.
ISBN: 978-1-936092-17-8 (trade pbk. : alk. paper)
1. Drug Dealing 2. Murder 3. Torture 4. Sugar Island 5. San Francisco.

What people are saying about earlier Jack Handler books

"Just finished 'Murder on Sugar Island' and can't wait to get the next in the series! Unfortunately, with the holidays it took me awhile to get to reading. But, I must say, the first time I sat down with it I read over half the book!! Love Jack and Kate, and of course Red and Buddy! Hope Santa brings me several more! Please don't stop writing!!! Happy Holidays!" —Susan M

"I want to let you know that I really enjoyed your book 'Murder on Sugar Island.' So much so that I have just received 'Superior Peril' and 'Superior Intrigue' in today's mail. I read 'Murder on Sugar Island' in 4 days. I enjoy the shorter chapters, allowing me to pick up and put the book down for short, quick reads in between chores. I'm anxious to start the next one. Thanks so much for introducing me to Jack, Kate and Red." —Patti from Escanaba

"I work midnights. I recently started 'Murder on Sugar Island.' ... Twenty four chapters in and I didn't want to put it down to sleep. ... Enjoying it very much. You have a remarkable knack for writing." —Marla S

"Well, my husband took my book before I could even read it! He loved it! I just started it and also love it. He just started book two and wants to know how to get the rest! Thank you so much for taking the time to talk to us!!" — Anastasia K

"My wife and I met you in Valparaiso, IN., at the Shipshewana on the Road event. I purchased 'Murder on Sugar Island' for her and you signed it. However, I read it before she had a chance and have since purchased 'Superior Peril' from Amazon. ... I'm not a reader but I can't put it down!!!!" —Jake K

"I stumbled upon your book at the Frankenmuth Shipshewana vendor show. I just had the opportunity to read it, and absolutely loved it. Could not put it down. ... I will be looking for more of your books to read." —Joan T

"Top Shelf Murder Mystery—Riveting. Being a Murder-Mystery *JUNKIE* this book is definitely a keeper ... can't put it down ... read it again type of book ... and it is very precise to the lifestyles in Upper Michigan. Very well researched. I am a resident of this area. His attention to detail is great. I have to rate this book in the same class or better than authors Michael Connelly, James Patterson, and Steve Hamilton." — Shelldrakeshores

"Move over, Patterson, I now have a new favorite author. Jack Handler and his daughter make a great tag team, great intrigue, and diversions. I have a cabin on Sugar Island and enjoyed the references to the locations. I met the author at Joey's (the real live Joey) coffee shop up on the hill, great writer, good stuff. I don't usually finish a book in the course of a week, but read this one in two sittings so it definitely had my attention. I am looking forward to the next installment. Bravo." — Northland Press

"I enjoyed this book very much. It was very entertaining, and the story unfolded in a believable manner. Jack Handler is a like-able character. But you would not like to be on his wrong side. Handler made that very clear in *Jack and the New York Death Mask*. This book (Murder on Sugar Island) was the first book in the Getting to Know Jack series that I read. After I read *Death Mask*, I discovered just how tough Jack Handler really was." — Deborah M

"I thoroughly enjoyed this book. I could not turn the pages fast enough. I am not sure it was plausible but I love the characters. I highly recommend this book and look forward to reading more by Michael Carrier." — Amazon Reader

"An intense thrill ride!!" — Mario

"Michael Carrier has knocked it out of the park." — John

"Left on the edge of my seat after the last book, I could not wait for the next chapter to unfold and Michael Carrier did not disappoint! I truly feel I know his characters better with each novel and I especially like the can-do/will-do attitude of Jack. Keep up the fine work, Michael, and may your pen never run dry!" — SW

"The Handlers are at it again, with the action starting on Sugar Island, I am really starting to enjoy the way the father/daughter and now Red are working through the mind of Michael Carrier. The entire family, plus a few more are becoming the reason for the new sheriff's increased body count and antacid intake. The twists and turns we have come to expect are all there and then some. I'm looking for the next installment already." — Northland Press

"Finally, there is a new author who will challenge the likes of Michael Connelly and David Baldacci." — Island Books

"If you like James Patterson and Michael Connelly, you'll love Michael Carrier. Carrier has proven that he can hang with the best of them. It has all of the great, edge-of-your-seat action and suspense that you'd expect in a good thriller, and it kept me guessing to the very end. Fantastic read with an awesome detective duo—I couldn't put it down!" — Katie

"Don't read Carrier at the beach or you are sure to get sunburned. I did. I loved the characters. It was so descriptive you feel like you know everyone. Lots of action—always something happening. I love the surprise twists. All my friends are reading it now because I wouldn't talk to them until I finished it so they knew it was good. Carrier is my new favorite author!" — Sue

"Thoroughly enjoyed this read—kept me turning page after page! Good character development and captivating plot. Had theories but couldn't quite solve the mystery without reading to the end. Highly recommended for readers of all ages." — Terry

LIZ

Chapter 1 —

Y ou pathetic, thieving bitch!" Spyder clepted Liz, just as he planted a vicious, closed-fisted backhand solidly across the left side of her face. "You absolutely will tell me what I want to know—I promise you that."

While the punch did not knock Liz unconscious, the impact did momentarily lift her entirely off her feet, while sliding her psyche into a senseless stare and releasing a veritable gusher of blood from her nose and mouth. But, contrary to Spyder's prediction, she did not let a single word escape her crimson lips—at least, not at that time.

These two young women, Liz, twenty-six, and Angel, fourteen, had found themselves entangled in this terribly untenable situation just as they were trying to establish a suitable residence in Michigan's Upper Peninsula. Liz, who for several years had lived and worked in Frisco tending bar, had also developed a very lucrative drug business there boasting a relatively high-end list of young professionals who lived in and around the SoMa (or South of Market) district of the city.

Angel was Liz's newfound best friend, and while she did enjoy hanging out and shooting pool with Liz in their SoMa neighbor-hood, Angel was not at all familiar with that dark side of Liz's "oth-er life." Not only did they have few obvious traits in common, it was doubtful that anyone who had met both of these young ladies would ever have imagined that they could have become embroiled in the sort of seedy situation that was suddenly cascading down upon them on this day.

In fact, up until only a few months ago Angel had lived qui-etly with her mother in Michigan's Upper Peninsula, aka, The UP. There she enjoyed a very simple, sheltered life as the daughter of the now-deceased Millie Star, a very good friend of Sugar Island's well-known private security contractor—Jack Handler. And, quite unlike her friend, Angel would never have dreamed of dealing drugs.

In Angel's eyes, her friend was simply a popular waitress and very personable barmaid. Angel had no inkling that her friend called Liz made most of her real money selling drugs in San Fran-cisco for a very sinister character named Spyder.

Unfortunately, while Angel was steadily growing to appreci-ate the attractive attributes Liz so craftily displayed, she'd been left totally in the dark regarding two game-changing character flaws that were taking over in her friend's life. First, while the only in-come reported by Liz was the typical low minimum-wage earn-ings of a bartender (plus tips, of course), by far her most serious income was derived through the flourishing rewards she produced through her criminal talents as a drug dealer. And second, Angel was also blind to the fact that her friend had just ripped off her boss's brand new shipment of drugs—a stash with the street value of a million dollars, give or take.

On this night at a remote cottage in Michigan's Upper Peninsula, in spite of (or perhaps *because* of) all of her questionable attributes, and an unbridled knack for endless conniving, here Liz was—now an absolutely helpless human being at the mercy of one of the Bay Area's most notoriously powerful and unscrupulous drug dealers. And not only did this scandalous criminal have Liz under his total control, he also had cornered and captured Angel. Because Liz was the older and more mature of the two girls, and because he saw no evidence to the contrary, Spyder was convinced that Angel's only role was that of a passive bystander. And so, he zeroed in on Liz.

Spyder had both of Liz's hands securely tied together at the wrists with a three-foot piece of white ¼ inch Knotrite Nylon Rope. Next, he tied one end of a fifteen-foot length of larger rope to the rope that bound her hands, and then looped the free end of that longer rope one full turn around a cold water pipe that ran through the floor joists directly above her head. After doing that, Spyder yanked firmly on that rope, jerking Liz's hands toward the ceiling with such ferocity that he elevated her body a good inch higher than before. At that point, only Liz's toes were touching the basement floor. Then, keeping that longer piece of rope tight, he tied it off on a twelve-foot length of half-inch conduit that ran parallel to the cold water pipe.

Once secured, Spyder checked his work to be sure the rope was taut enough, and he decided that he could tie the rope off a little tighter. So, he forcibly lifted Liz well off her heels by pulling even harder on the free end of the rope, and then tied it off again on that stretch of conduit.

"The Coach," the street name by which a UP drug dealer, and

Spyder's new associate in this little part of Liz's ordeal, was known, stood nearby watching. "Holy shit!" the Coach said to himself. "I'll be damned if it don't look for all the world like this son-of-bitch has done this a few times before! This is not going to turn out well for these two females. I think it best for me to observe from a distance, and not offer to participate." And so, he did not volunteer to help.

To prevent Liz's screams from being heard outside the house, Spyder had shoved a dishcloth into her mouth, and then kept it there by wrapping a three-foot length of duct tape around her head two times.

And then, if all that wasn't painful enough for the poor girl, he stripped her down to her bra and panties, and then sporadically began pouring cold water onto the bare skin of her dangling body.

"Well, bitch! You ready to tell me where you put my merchandise?" Spyder demanded. She could not talk because of the gag, but she could shake her head and shrug her shoulders as a signal to her antagonist that she did not know where his drugs were. He barked that command over a dozens of times. And every time he did, Liz let it be known that she had no idea what he was talking about.

Spyder could see her body quivering every time he doused it with cold water.

After about the twentieth time he grilled her about the drugs, Spyder decided he needed to put some additional pressure on the young woman he was convinced had ripped him off.

So, using his left hand to keep it taut, Spyder untied the lynch-like rope that was fastened to the conduit. And then, placing his right hand between Liz's hands, he lifted her body another inch or more. At that point her toes were barely touching the concrete at all. Spyder then took up the slack he had just created, and tied the rope off on the conduit yet again.

He then repeated the cycle of cold-water dousing, interrogation, and berating.

After four more rounds of identically administered torture, Spyder took a closer look at Liz's hands and feet and realized that not only were her toes at times no longer even touching the floor, many of her fingers were beginning to turn blue. So, recognizing the futility of cranking Liz's feet any higher into the air, he grabbed the pitcher of cold water and slowly poured all that remained onto her neck and shoulders. He watched as it ran down her back and legs, and finally trickled off her toes and into a towel he had placed on the concrete basement floor beneath where she was hanging.

"I'm telling you, bitch, you're gonna be talking to me sooner or later. I ain't quittin'. … So, I suggest you make it sooner, 'cuz you ain't gonna survive much more of this shit. You and I both know that for a fact. If I don't kill you outright, your hands are gonna develop gangrene, die, and just fall off your arms. And that's gonna hurt real bad while you watch yourself bleed slowly to death.

"So, listen to me *carefully*. I'm tellin' you that an end can be put to this insane pain right now if you want. … You can be my girl again, and we can go about havin' a great life—just like before. You remember how good that was? Right? All you have to do is just talk to me and tell me what I want to know. Simple as that."

Spyder then walked over and grabbed The Coach by the back of his left arm and signaled with his eyes for him to walk upstairs with him. "I want to talk to you for a minute … in private," he whispered to him so that Liz could not hear. "Come upstairs with me. We'll let this bitch stew in her own piss for a while. Eventually, she'll be begging me to hear her out. Guaranteed. … And after I get my merchandise back, I'm gonna kill that slut. I'm gonna kill 'em both. Come upstairs with me."

Once they'd reached the top of the steps, Spyder closed the basement door, and led The Coach into the living room.

"She can't hear us now," Spyder said to The Coach in his regular voice. "We can be sure of that. Why don't you go grab me a beer, I got some shit I wanna run by you. You do have some beer, right?"

"Yeah, I got a beer for you," The Coach said. "Anything else?"

"No, just a cold one. For now."

About three minutes later The Coach came back in carrying two bottles of cold Corona Premier. He handed one to Spyder, who had taken a seat on the living room couch. The Coach took a seat in an adjacent recliner. All the furniture in the house was old and stained. The same was true for the carpet in the living room. In places it was not only threadbare, it actually had holes worn all the way through it, exposing the near-ancient cattle-hair padding beneath.

Seeing the dilapidated condition of all the home's furnishings, Spyder asked, "How's business goin' for you up here? You know, in the Upper Peninsula. You doin' okay?"

"It's alright," The Coach said. "Could be better, though. Can't get enough product. … And it's too damned expensive. Some of my buddies drive downstate where they can do better. I have to drive truck too. Couldn't pay my bills without the second income."

"It's always good to have a job," Spyder added. "Makes you look more legit to the neighbors and the cops—if you're gainfully employed. ... But, it sounds like you're not doin' so good. Is that the case?"

"I do okay," The Coach said. "But I'd really like to make a little more money in ... my other business. Like I said, I got these friends who are driving south to buy their stuff. Most all the way to Chicago. Some even farther—like Mexico."

"Where do you get your shit?" Spyder asked. "I'll bet you get your merchandise through Canada. Right? Ain't that shit expensive as hell?"

"That's right. Could be a lot better, I think."

"Tell me again how that went down," Spyder said, "how the hell you found out about that bitch downstairs. How she'd ripped off my merchandise and shit. What gave her away?"

"Actually," The Coach explained. "I was never sure that she actually did it. Still not positive. This is what happened. One of my buddies from San Francisco tole me last week that there was this gal from out there who was trying to line up some additional sales for this week—out there. Discount sales. Money to help her cover the cost of a trip to Upper Michigan. He couldn't, or wouldn't, give me her name, but he did ask me if I knew anything about some babe from out there coming to the UP for something. To Sugar Island, to be specific. I tole him I hadn't heard anything. And I didn't think much more of it. Not until I heard about you gettin' ripped off by some chick. Then I started puttin' two and two together.

"I called my friend again, and I got your number from him—I think he knows you pretty well. ... But, I never talked to her before I called you. So, I didn't really know anything until tonight. And, I still can't say that I know anything for sure.

"All I know is that this babe called this guy she knew who deals a little in the Soo—out of a bar there. And one of my buddies heard about it and called me to see if I'd be interested in talking to her. I asked where the shit came from, and he said that the chick was from Frisco, but that the shit was from Mexico.

"And then I started puttin' it all together—what I heard about you getting ripped off by some babe, and some girl wantin' to sell a bunch of shit out there, and then this new gal wanting to do some business here in the Soo. ... Like I said, that's when I got your name from a buddy out there, and that's how I ended up giving you a call.

"Sure, I could use some cheaper product. But, I know from experience that it never pays to go behind a person's back, especially if that person happens to be connected. And, my friends out there let me know that you were not a good person to mess around with. So, I called you and let you know what was goin' on ... at least, goin' on as far as I knew. That's the whole story, Mr. Spyder."

The Coach remained silent for a few moments, and then he said, "I understand you know that girl very well. Do you think she's the one who stole your shit?"

"She's definitely the bitch who ripped me off, alright," Spyder stated without any signs of doubt. "She had access to my home. And she knew that the shipment had just arrived. She did it, alright. ... Now, all I have to do is to get her to tell me where she's got it stashed. She'll talk, eventually ... before she dies. I'm sure she will tell me what I want to know."

"What's the deal with the young one?" The Coach asked. "The one in the back of that Toyota. Does she know where your stash is at?"

"My guess is that she doesn't know a damn thing," Spyder replied. "But, I can't be totally sure about that. Maybe she does. Maybe the bitch told her. I just don't know that yet. I can tell you one thing for sure, I'm gonna find out. ... I got a plan. I'm gonna have you bring that young one back in. I'll string her up just like I did the bitch. I can beat that young one as much as I want, because I don't know for sure what she does or does not know. So she might not have anything to tell me. I could kill her right there in front of the bitch—do it for effect.

"Her value is only in the eyes of the bitch. I think the older one likes the young one, and she will not want to see me beat on the kid. ... I'm thinking that the bitch just might start talking if she thinks she can save the young one from some pain. That might work. At least, I think it might be worth a shot.

"And, if the kid kicks off, it ain't the end of the world. ... The bitch is the only one of them that for sure knows where my merchandise is. That I can be quite sure about. But, the kid might know as well. Just can't be sure about it. Smartest approach is to work 'em both, and see what gives."

"So," The Coach asked, "you then want me to bring the kid inside?"

"Yeah," Spyder said. "I'd say so. The bitch is about to lose it. So, I'd better get it done, before she goes out on me. ... Like a light bulb, you know. Poof."

"She's dying? You think she's gonna die?"

"No, I'm not suggesting that. At least not right now," Spyder declared. "But her hands aren't gettin' blood. They're cold and blue. She's in a *lotta* pain, but it's almost like she's turned her body off to it. ... I think she knows that whether she tells me where my shit is, or if she holds out and doesn't, that I'm still gonna have to do her. ... I just can't give in to her. What she took from me was a major shipment. It's paid for, and I can't afford to lose it. Street value, over a mil—give or take. At least out west.

"And I sure as hell can't have dealers ripping me off. Period. Even though the mil wouldn't kill me, I just can't be havin' that shit happen. ... One, I gotta get my property back. That's just gotta happen. And then, I gotta get rid of them—the both of them. Period. Can't leave them out there tellin' about it. Or other people talkin."

"No matter what," The Coach said. "No matter what the outcome, they've both got to go? Is that what you're sayin'?"

"Absolutely," Spyder declared without equivocation. ... "Go ahead and get the kid for me. And bring her on inside the house. But don't bring her downstairs until I call for her. I'll let you know when you should bring her down. ... I'm headed back down right now to get ready for her. But keep her up here until I call for you. Got that?"

"I got it," The Coach replied.

"Okay, go ahead and bring the kid in the house. Bring her into the living room. But be sure to leave her upstairs for now."

Spyder had become exasperated from working with a helper who went by the street-name Cash, and he was beginning to really appreciate the way The Coach paid attention to and carried out his directives. "He ain't an idiot, like Cash," he told himself, sometimes aloud. "I'm really starting to appreciate this new guy. Might want to hang on to him." It had only been hours since Spyder's frustration had placed a 10mm hollow point right through Cash's left temple.

"Right," The Coach replied.

Spyder went to the freezer and pulled out two trays of ice cubes and dumped them in a large plastic bowl that was sitting on the cupboard. He then went down the steps, walked over and placed the bowl down on the small table beside Liz's near-naked body. As he set it down he took a glancing look at the girl's hands. They, of course, were still turning blue, but Liz herself still appeared totally cognizant of what was going on around her.

"I'd say that was a good sign," Spyder said to himself. "Looks like the little bitch still has her senses about her. A very good sign, indeed."

"Liz, baby, give me what I'm after and I can take you down from this stupid gallows. We will cut that damn rope off your hands, and we can get you a nice warm, cozy blanket. You'll be able to get comfortable again, and then everything can start getting back to normal. You know, the way it used to be. ... I understand you better now. I never knew you wanted to be a partner in my enterprise. I like that idea. I can use you for sure. No doubt, it took a lot of guts to challenge me like that. Took a lot of planning, and guts. We could definitely work together."

Spyder then heard his friend upstairs come back into the house, and he detected the sounds of two people walking across the floor. "One of them is barefoot," Spyder said to himself, "that would be the girl. ... I'm pretty sure Liz also heard her young friend. So, now she knows the girl is upstairs as well. I'd better get this last part of the show going."

"Tell me, Liz," Spyder said after he'd walked around so he could address her face to face. "We can do this three ways. You pick one. You can go back to the Bay Area with me, and we can live there. I will put you in charge of all of my coke business in San Francisco.

All of it. I'll run everything else—the fentanyl, and the other shit. That will stay mine. But you can be in charge of all the coke business inside Frisco. You can move in with me, if you want to. And we can even get a larger place to live. …You will be so rich you will have to hire an accountant just to count all your money. … That's one plan.

"Second plan would look like this. If you've got your mind made up to live in the UP, we'll find you a nice house up here, and you can move here for good. You'll be in charge of my entire operation in Michigan. Again, you'll get rich in no time flat. Rich! And I mean really rich. I'll see to it you receive a shipment every month … directly from Mexico. That'll be just like we do it out in California. But you'll be totally in charge. You'll set up your own network of dealers. We'll talk often—probably every day. Especially while you're getting the whole thing set up. But, you'll be your own boss, once up and running. With your talent, it will take you no time at all.

"And then, there can be a third plan. It will look just like the second, except with this one additional option. With this third plan you can live with your friend Angel, in her house, if that's what you ladies want. I understand she's got her own house here, and she can work with you. But, while you will be in charge, you will be totally answerable to me. … So, tell me, which option do you choose? Plan 1, 2, or 3? … Just know, there are no other possibilities. Choose one of them right now, or, I'm sorry, but you will leave me no other choice, I will kill you both—her first, and then you. … What'll it be? I'll give you only a minute to make this decision."

With that having been said, Spyder went to the staircase leading up and said loudly, "Hey, Coach, you can bring the girl down here now."

With that command, Liz turned her head as much as she was able to see if she could get a glimpse of Angel coming down the steps.

During the latter stages of this whole debacle, Liz had become more and more convinced that there did not exist any circumstance under which Spyder would accept terms that included her or Angel remaining alive—that would include any conceivable scenario in which she were to return the drugs to Spyder. *I could giftwrap that shit,* she told herself, *and tie a big red bow on it, and that asshole is still going to kill us. I'm positive about that. We will stay alive only so long as I hold out. … But, it now looks like he's even calling in that last card—that 'Angel Card.'" But, nothin's changed, that bastard's gonna kill both of us, regardless.*

And then down the stairs stumbled Angel. The Coach picked her up at the bottom of the stairs and led her over to where Spyder was standing. Liz had not counted on this. Here, right in front of her, stood her poor quivering fourteen-year-old, pool-shooting buddy. As soon as their eyes met, the young girl broke out in a barrage of uncontrollable weeping. She tried to talk to her older friend, but could not articulate words.

No matter what I do, Liz said to herself. *Spyder is going to kill us both. And it will be right here—right where we are now. He will kill her first, because he thinks that it will scare me into telling him where I've hidden his drugs. And she doesn't know where they are, anyway. … And then I'll have to watch her suffer and die. After he kills Angel, he will come back to me—no matter what I say or do at this point, he's gonna kill me. I will have my best chance of living as long as I keep my mouth shut.*

As soon as Spyder saw Angel fall to her knees in tears, he pulled out an evil-looking knife—a KA-BAR eleven inch US Marine Corps Fighting Knife. He pressed the razor-sharp point through the skin on the back of Angel's neck. Blood began to trickle down her body.

He then looked at Liz, and said, "Where are my drugs, Liz? Tell me now, and put an end to this shit—for both of you."

Liz was surprised to hear him use her name. *So, now I'm Liz,* she said to herself, *not the bitch. … He really is getting ready to kill me!*

"Damn it!" Spyder looked back at Angel and said to himself, "That bitch did not even try to warn the kid to keep her mouth shut. Not at all! That has to mean that the stupid kid doesn't have a clue."

Spyder looked to the side and downward. And then, out of immense frustration, slowly shook his head and uttered one single word: "SHIT!"

TWO MONTHS AND TWO WEEKS EARLIER

Chapter 2 —

While Liz was fond of saying that she was always looking for ways to improve her earning capacity, her life was actually not that bad. She had a regular job working at an upscale casual dining restaurant/bar. On the days she served tables, she spent from 4:30 until 9:00 serving food to a pretty regular group of diners; and then, on those same days, she moved from waitressing to serving drinks at the bar from nine to closing. And, at the bar, she took care of a couple dozen or so very faithful repeat customers.

On the days when she worked the bar exclusively, she came in at 7:30 in the evening. Whether serving tables or tending bar, Liz was very popular among the patrons. If asked, all who had gotten to know her would say that they loved her beautiful eyes and inviting smile. However, even though she did very nicely with tips, she still wanted more.

This is how a person meeting Liz for the first time might size her up. In virtually every instance, the casual observer would think Liz to be a highly independent twenty-six-year-old woman. She always drew positive attention to herself by sporting a thick head of raspberry highlights, and lovely blue eyes, which, when considered thoughtfully, created a striking contrast. As should be expected for a contemporary woman of her age, she sported several visible tattoos on her arms and upper calves, which in her case were a bit larger than average, yet still tasteful and well designed. Those tattoos most likely suggested a sense of individuality and creativity.

As for her personality and demeanor, Liz would strike those who were meeting her for the first time as an interesting and open-minded young woman. And, once that new acquaintance became aware that Liz had lived for several years in San Francisco, and that she worked there in restaurants and bars, that new associate would begin to understand what made her tick. Or, at least they would think that they were figuring her out.

Along with her tattoos and loose, messy updo, one of the more telling of Liz's attributes was her fondness for girly cowgirl boots. Whether wearing shorts, jeans or a skirt, the likelihood that her feet would be artfully adorned in boots was practically one hundred percent. If there was a single sentence that could be offered to describe her boots, it just might be this: "Liz loved to wear the Western-style boots that were often associated with the glitz and glamour of Hollywood." The boots she wore were always made from high-quality leather, and were designed with the sort of intricate detailing and embellishments that made them stand out.

One of her favorite style was that of the Hollywood cowgirl boots decorated with silver. The leather of the boots was a bright shade of pink, giving them a bold and eye-catching appearance. The silver decorations on the boots took several different forms, such as silver stitching, silver studs, or silver conchos. These silver elements were then arranged in various patterns, such as floral or geometric designs. Each in its own way created a visually striking look.

The boots were also typically adorned with other details that added to their charm and character. For example, one of the styles she frequently wore had a leather fringe along the sides and back of the boot, which swayed and moved with her steps. Another of her favorites featured a pointed toe and a stacked heel, which provided more of a classic Western look.

That is exactly how Liz always comported herself.

For probably the past six months Liz had been actively entertaining various possibilities for a new business enterprise. And, in virtually every set of circumstances, she knew that for her new business to be successful, she would have to find an alternative place to live. *Moving would be essential,* she reasoned, *because for me to make serious money, my new business would have to involve the sale of drugs.*

Liz had lived in Northern California for her entire life, and she loved everything about the Bay Area. Nevertheless, she reasoned that Spyder would not allow her to compete with him. "So," she told herself, "even though I love the Bay Area, I will *absolutely* have to relocate. Spyder will kill me if I stayed around here."

The big challenge before Liz was in figuring out where she ought to relocate to. But, that dilemma seemed to resolve itself when she helped a new girl get a job at her San Francisco restaurant.

It was right at that time that Liz developed a friendship with a fourteen-year-old girl who was going through a difficult time in her life—she needed to find a job, but she was too young to qualify for anything. Her name was Angel Star.

After the young girl had presented her entire dilemma in detail to her, Liz began to have an idea.

"Really," Liz said to her, "I just had a thought that might work for you. I have a friend who might be able to fix you up. Sometimes he can make up the paperwork you will need to get a job. Think you might like to talk to him? I'm thinking that if you had the *right* papers, you might be able to get a job at the same restaurant where I work. I could put in a good word for you. ... Interested?"

Liz told Angel that her friend's name was Spyder, and that he had a lot of experience at producing realistic-looking fake credentials. Liz explained to her that it would surely be expensive to engage her friend in such a project on her behalf, but the quality of the documentation he would provide would be the absolute best possible, and that they would work perfectly for her. "His working papers *always* do the trick," Liz told her. "Other friends of mine have told me that several times after they used him."

"Do you think you can get him to help me?" Angel asked. "And, do you know how much he charges?"

Liz knew Spyder *very* well, and she thought that he would want to impress them both. So, she was quite certain that he would take the job. But, she did not know exactly what he charged. "I'm quite sure he will do it for you," she told Angel. "But, I'm not positive what he would charge. I've never hired him myself, so I don't know about that part of the deal—not exactly. ... I do think he would let you work it off. I've heard he does that sometimes. Probably two or three weeks' pay, I'd guess. But, that's only a guess—I'll have to ask him about it."

"So," Angel said after taking a moment to let it all sink in, "if he'd do it that way, he must be pretty sure the papers he'll give me would work. Right?"

"Always have," Liz replied. "At least as far as I know. I've heard that Spyder is the best out there."

After Angel had left, Liz gave Spyder a call and explained to him that she had an underage "girlfriend," and that the girlfriend would like him to make up a set of papers so that she could get a job at the same restaurant where she (Liz) worked.

"I think she'd really like to work with me," she told Spyder, "but she's too young. She's absolutely amazing at a pool table. She's even better at it than I am. ... But, right now, hustling pool is actually how she's making a living. Never seen anything like it. That fourteen-year-old girl is actually feeding herself by hustling drunks at a pool table. Isn't that somethin'?"

"Shooting pool don't mean shit," Spyder said. "So, be totally honest with me. Okay? How old is this girl? Tell me straight."

"She looks like she's eighteen," Liz told him, "but she's only fifteen. Actually, she's still fourteen—has a birthday coming up. But she really does look a lot older. I guess you could say she's been around the block a time or two. Think you could help her out?"

"Hell," Spyder said, "I might get her set up for sixteen, but it would be foolhardy to go beyond that. If she's only fourteen. She could wash dishes where you work, maybe. Wait tables perhaps, if there ain't no alcohol. ... That's probably the best anyone could do. ... How would she pay for it? It ain't cheap, you know. ... My going price is one thousand cash, or two months' paychecks signed over to me."

"Wow!" Liz said with a gasp. "I didn't know it cost that much. Could you think about it and let me call you back tomorrow morning? And I'll run it past her when I see her later."

It was obvious that Spyder was a bit pissed that Liz would ask him to do that—to think about it. "Who the hell does she think she is?" he asked himself.

"Goodnight," he said as he abruptly disconnected the call.

"He did not actually agree to think about it," Liz mumbled softly, as she slid her cell into her pocket. "But he didn't say that he wouldn't, either."

It was at that point Liz realized that she was going to have to kick in her charms.

The next morning she called him back as she'd promised. And she did go out of her way to flirt with him, hoping to soften him up a bit. She wanted to ask him outright if he had reconsidered the offer that she had made him—that Angel could pay for the new papers by providing her earnings for the two weeks' pay after she'd landed a job. But, she didn't have to. Liz was, after all, at that time Spyder's favorite pillow-mate.

"Oh, screw it," Spyder said, after making small talk with Liz for a few minutes. "Have the girl meet me at the restaurant Thursday—that's tomorrow. I am going to have to get a good look at her before I can make a final determination. If it looks like I can work with her, I'll give it a shot. And, when she gets a job, if she works the maximum number of hours allowed for her age, and agrees to sign all her checks over to me for three weeks, I'll see what I can do. But no promises. None!"

That's all Liz was after, and so she immediately agreed to arrange for the meeting between Angel and Spyder at the restaurant where she worked, and she said that she would come in early to join them.

Ironically, it was that meeting the very next evening that turned out to be the arena in which Liz hatched her very own plan to steal Spyder's next drug shipment, and to relocate herself to Michigan's Upper Peninsula—to Sugar Island, to be more specific. "That is how I start my own business," she confided to herself.

With the price of and timeframe for his work successfully negotiated, Spyder's mind for a time took him in a totally different direction. "You need to explain somethin' to me," Spyder said, mocking her. "Earlier, when you first told me about this Angel girl, you called her your *girlfriend*. You called that *underage* Angel girl your girlfriend. Tell me again, just how young is this underage 'girlfriend' of yours? Aren't you afraid of getting yourself arrested?"

"Go to hell, Spyder," Liz grumbled, realizing that she was being made fun of. "You know what I meant. She's a female friend of mine and she's too young to work in a restaurant, or probably anyplace else. If you helped her with necessary papers, I think I could get her in working where I work. She looks to be over sixteen, and that's what she would have to be, I think. ... At that age, sixteen, she couldn't serve alcohol, but she could wash dishes, or something. If I'm right, she just has to be sixteen or older."

"Now," he said, still mocking her, "how old is she? Really?"

"She is fourteen, but she looks to be *at least sixteen*. You'll see for yourself tomorrow."

"Fourteen!" Spyder repeated. "I still say that's awfully young, even to wash dishes in a restaurant, unless your parents own the place. ... I'm gonna have to take a real careful look at your underage girlfriend. ... Like I said, I'll make the final determination at the restaurant on Thursday—tomorrow. I'll buy you girls a Coke or something. But I really gotta see what I'm dealing with."

Liz could read into the tone of Spyder's voice that he was interested in impressing the girls, and that's how she expressed the results of her inquiry to Angel the next morning. She felt like both of them were growing impatient to get the process started.

While presenting her case to Spyder, Liz had been most eager to make it clear that when she referred to Angel as her "underage girlfriend," no sexual undertones should be assumed; but, had the nature of the friendship been described by the younger girl, her natural innocence might have left some doubts regarding the matter. Therefore, Liz concluded that it was best if she were the one to describe the nature of the girls' relationship.

In fact, it could be said that Angel was not actually interested in any sort of an inappropriate relationship. Her only driving desire was to get on her feet financially. With the recent murder of her mother, Angel was not only left with no family, but also without a regular source of income. While she did receive a small stipend from her mother's estate, up until very recently most of the cost of living came from the money provided by her friend and roommate. But, things were changing. As of a month ago that friend, with whom she had originally ventured out to California, had packed up and moved down to Florida. While the friend did offer to take Angel with her, the young girl did not wish to move to strange surroundings yet again.

The afternoon before the meeting with Spyder, Liz had Angel meet her at their favorite club/pool hall for a few games before she started work.

"I'm pretty sure my friend Spyder is gonna help you," Liz excitedly told her immediately upon exchanging greetings. "I need you to meet with him tomorrow evening. I've made arrangements with my work so I can be there with you. If he agrees to help you, he's gonna get you fixed up with a fantastic birth certificate, and all the rest of the shit you're gonna need to get a real job. You can't survive very long shooting pool for money. There's always gonna be somebody who's better than you, and can out-bluff you. It's always that way. You're pretty good, but not good enough to make a living at it."

"I know that," Angel said. "I don't shoot for money unless the guy's drunk. And if he's flirting with me. I take his serious money only once. Otherwise he gets mad. I know there's no future in it. But, for right now, it helps buy me food. That's it.

"But, tell me, this friend of yours—this Spyder guy. What's he gonna want from me in return? I don't do crazy stuff for anybody. It's just not my style."

"Nothing like that," Liz said. "Spyder and I are a bit of a thing. Have been for several months, now. He's going want you to give him your next three weeks' pay, but that's it. No special favors."

"Really?" Angel said. "And you say that he is pretty good at that stuff?"

"He's a real pro," Liz confidently responded. "He's done it for a hundred guys, and never failed. You're not going to be able to sell alcoholic drinks, but you can serve food, or wash dishes. I'm pretty sure I can get you a job where I work. It would be washing dishes, cleaning up, or stuff like that. Maybe serving food. I just don't know about that for sure. ... Spyder says he's gonna make you old enough to work, just not to serve alcohol. But, he wants to see you first. He wasn't so sure about it ... whether, at fourteen you could pass for a sixteen-year-old. I told him you could, but he still wants to see you before he makes any commitment. I think it makes sense."

Visibly shaken, Angel said, "Where are we going to have this meeting? At his place? Or yours? I'm not comfortable going to his house. Can't we do it in some public place? I'd like that better."

"We're gonna do it right in the restaurant where I work," Liz said.

"Right here?" Angel asked. "Won't they see me? And know that my papers are fake? How can that work?"

"Oh," Liz said through a smile. "It will work just fine. They want somebody who will work hard and do the job. I don't think they much give a damn if your papers are real or phony. They want warm bodies—ones who look good and are willing to work like hell. If that's you, and I believe it is, then I don't think that they will even give a shit what your bona fides look like.

"Spyder comes to my restaurant every Thursday at 7:00. I'll meet you there, tomorrow, at 6:30," Liz assured her. "You'll do just fine. We'll have burgers, a Coke or something, and you two can figure out your work papers deal. … Sound good?"

Angel did not respond to her friend's question, but not because she was against having the meeting. She failed to answer because she was so incredibly scared. She wanted to get a job, but she was worried about the process that might be suggested. Even though she was only fourteen, she knew enough about adults to be wary of them.

Liz was so excited that she barely slept at all that night. Instead, she lay in bed for hours contemplating the next steps in the plan she was developing.

"First," she said to herself, "I'll have to find a place to locate my business. Can't be very close to the Bay Area, because, if I set it up anywhere around here, Spyder will just find me and slit my throat—just like that. Or find some other way to kill me. I've gotta find someplace far away from here, and set up there. New York, Philadelphia, or maybe Chicago. Someplace far away from here, and with a lot of people.

"Now, I know Spyder gets a new shipment in every three weeks. On a Thursday. Always. I need to start spending Thursday nights here. He received a shipment two weeks ago, So, I know that in seven days from now he will be receiving a new one. I know where he stores it. When we leave here and go to his place, I'll slip him a sleeping pill in his drink—strong enough to put him to sleep. When I'm sure he's passed out, I'll clean him out. If his schedule doesn't change, and it *never* does, I'll be all set. And I can use his little hand truck. I'll load it in my car and haul it to the airport.

"Damn, I think they've got drug-sniffing dogs at the airport—so that can't work. I will have to get someone to fly me private. ... I won't have cash for that. So, I'll just have to drive. ... Could sure use somebody to help me drive—"

"Oh hell," she said out loud, "I'll figure all that stuff out later."

"But," she then went on talking silently to herself, "I first have to find the right place to live. ... Damn, that's not going to be easy. I gotta go someplace where there's gonna to be a good market for my products. Wherever I decide to go, I gotta be able to sell my shit."

She turned over in bed, but did not fall asleep. For the next three hours she just lay there silently, but with her eyes open. She was considering all the possible places she could move to, but could not determine what the perfect location might be. All during that N-1 cycle, random thoughts kept popping into her mind, some waking her up entirely.

Finally, some time after three A.M., she actually drifted off into the real thing, and she did not awaken until her cell rang at 8.59 that morning.

"Yeah, who is this?" she said, slurring her words while trying to get her bearings.

"This is Angel," said the voice on the other end. "Liz, you sound like you're just waking up. I'm sorry if I'm calling too early. I just wanted to ask some questions about our meeting this afternoon … or, actually this evening. I'm still a little nervous about it. Shall I call back later?"

Liz thought about it for a few seconds, and then said, "Let me use the little girls' room. And I'll call you back in a few. Okay?"

"Sure," Angel said. "Talk to you in a bit."

Liz disconnected the call, slowly slid out of her bed and stumbled into the bathroom. As she sat there relieving herself, which she was fond of doing first thing in the mornings, she had another fresh thought. *I wonder where it was that Angel used to live? She always speaks so highly of it, maybe that would be a good place for me to move to? I'll have to find out from her after our meeting later today.*

A few minutes later Liz sat down on the edge of her bed and called Angel back.

"Hey, girl," she said when her friend answered. "What's on your mind this early in the morning?"

"It's not really that early, is it?" Angel said. "It's a little after nine. … Anyway, I'm scared about meeting with that man today. You know, your friend, the one who creates my new identity. Think you can make me feel a little better about that whole thing?

Like I said, I'm scared."

"Trust me, girl," Liz said, in an effort to reassure her friend. "You have absolutely nothing to worry about. Spyder has done this plenty of times. Early on, this stuff was all he did. ... Before he got into his other businesses. But, I promise you, he has done this many, many times. And he's always successful. Always."

"I believe you," Angel said. "I know you wouldn't guide me wrong. I trust you a lot. I just needed to hear you say that, I guess. ... And, tell me this, what is he going to ask me? Can you tell me that?"

"Sure," Liz said. "He's going to ask you for your birthday. He'll keep that the same to make it easier for you on down the road. The year will change, of course. And he'll ask you where you were born—you know, like the city and state, and the hospital. He'll keep that the same too, I think. ... But, like I said, he will change the year. And there's some other stuff that he works with—not sure what all that is, but it's no big deal. I think he improvises as he creates it. At least to some degree. ... Where were you born, by the way? You can practice on me a little bit.

"You see, employers are only interested in covering their asses with who they hire. As long as you show up sober and on time, look good, and do the job, they couldn't care less about your credentials. Just so that if the state challenges them on an employee's credentials ... as long as they have something to protect them—that's all they really care about. That's it."

Angel thought about what Liz had offered, and found that it made sense. And then, after a few moments, she repeated the last question that Liz had asked her: "Where was I born? What has that got to do with anything?"

"Well," Liz said. "When creating a history, it helps Spyder if he can understand where you've been. Then he can incorporate that info into the story he's creating."

"I was born in Cleveland, Ohio," Angel replied, after thinking about it for several seconds. "But, my mom and me moved to Curtis, Michigan when I was just a baby. It's kind of a resort community, in Michigan's Upper Peninsula. She ran an ice cream shop there for years. And then we came into some money—not too sure about where it all came from, but Mom and me then moved into a house in Sault Ste. Marie—that's also in the UP. We lived there until she died. That was only earlier this past year. She was murdered. That's when I came out here to California. It would have been hard for me to move back into her house after she was gone—at least right afterward. ... And besides, the law wouldn't have let me move in there without a responsible adult."

"Your mom was murdered?! You gotta be kiddin'. How'd that happen?"

"I don't want to talk about it," Angel admitted. "That's why I left and came out here. ... I had a wonderful mom. ... It would have been too hard for me to stay in Michigan after that. Even if they would have let me move into the house."

"Then, you have family in Michigan?" Liz asked.

"Well, sort of," Angel answered. "I guess you could say they were family. Jack and Kate Handler were very close to my mom. And they had two foster boys they were raising—Red and Robby. Same age as me. They were all great. I loved them all like family. The boys, Red and Robby, they were truly like my brothers. We went to school together and everything. Same grade as I was. And Jack and Kate were like parents. They loved me back the same way parents do. But, they weren't my mom and dad. … I just felt like I had to get away. … My mom and I were close—*very* close. And when she was murdered … I just couldn't handle it."

"Wouldn't you like to visit them sometime?" Liz asked. "That Jack and Kate couple. They sound like real nice people—the whole family sounds like they cared for you. What did you say their last name was?"

"Handler," Angel said, "Jack and Kate Handler. And, they did care for me. They were very kind to me and my mother. In fact, I think that if Mom had lived, Uncle Jack would have married my mom. They were very close."

"But, wasn't he already married—to Kate?" Liz asked as she wrote their names down so she could check them out later.

"No," Angel answered through a big smile. "Aunt Kate was Uncle Jack's *daughter*. He was way older than my mom. But, I think they had feelings for each other. In fact, I know they did. Mom told me how much she cared about him. … But, it was one of those things—her getting murdered and all. I think it had to do with some of the stuff Uncle Jack does. He does stuff for people—important, rich people. And I think it might have been one of those deals that got my mom killed. Don't know much about it, but I do know that my mother was a wonderful lady, and never hurt anyone. … Anyway, that's me. Do you think your friend can make me sixteen? Can he make me older so I can get a job? And drive a car. … I already know how to drive. But I need a license. Can he get me a driver's license, and a work permit?"

"I'm sure he can," Liz said. "But, let me ask you something. Do you think you could stay with that family—the Handlers—if you wanted to? Long enough to get a job up there, in Michigan's Upper

Peninsula?"

"Yeah," Angel replied, "I'm quite sure I could stay with them for a while. They are really special people. But, there might not be a reason to stay with them—at least not for very long. I actually own a house in the UP. ... At least, I think I own a house up there. Mom left it to me. Aunt Kate sends me rent checks every month. She's got my house rented out to some people. I don't make enough to live on it, though. Not out here in San Francisco. But it helps a lot. I didn't really check out the lease papers, but I think the renters have the house for the rest of this year. ... I just know that I can't move into the house yet, because I'm fourteen. And, it is still legally rented."

"But you could rent the house out, right?" Liz asked. "They would let you do that, wouldn't they?"

"No, not really. I can't rent it out because I'm not considered an adult. It's rented out now only because Jack and Kate oversee the whole thing. I can't actually be on the paperwork.

"And, if the house was empty, and I showed up there to move in, the cops would be on my case, and they would haul me in. It's kinda working out okay because Jack and Kate are as honest as people can be. They look out for me. ... And the cops don't mess around with Jack. They're actually afraid of him. He's just that kind of guy. Nobody questions anything he says."

That got Liz to thinking. "What if Angel and I *both* moved to Michigan?" she asked herself. "And, what if she rented her house out to me? That would work, I think—at least it could. And then, I could let her live with me. Why wouldn't that work out just fine?"

Angel and Liz continued with small talk for the next fifteen or twenty minutes, and then Liz suggested that they meet at their favorite pool place for a few games before they sat down with Spyder to discuss the final plans regarding Angel's new papers.

"Anything else we come up with won't mean anything if Spyder doesn't want to help you out," Liz told her. "So, let's not get ahead of ourselves. Okay? … But, I can tell you what I think right now. I am very confident that he will get you all set up if you talk to him as openly as you just talked to me. Be honest with him, and don't object to paying him what we talked about. Stick with that, and I'm almost positive it will all work out. Like I told you, he's done this hundreds of times before, and he's very good at it."

That all registered well with Angel, and so she agreed to meet Liz to shoot some pool. And that's what they did.

Angel got there first, and Liz arrived ten minutes later. While they both carried enough cash on them to cover the cost of their games and incidentals, after listening to all of Angel's sad stories, Liz insisted on picking up the tab for their Diet Cokes.

"Whereabouts is this house you were talking about?" Liz asked, after they'd got their game underway. "The one you own? Is it a big house? Like more than one bedroom?"

"It's not a huge house," Angel said. "Not at all. Actually, I think that half of the houses in the Soo are probably bigger than ours. But it's quite nice. And, yes, it has three bedrooms on the second floor. It's a two-story house. And one bedroom on the main level. That's where my mom sleeps—slept. But there is also a finished attic, and it could be used for one or two more bedrooms, if somebody wanted more bedrooms. I don't know why anyone would do that, but it's quite a nice attic. Mom was thinking about putting a bathroom up there, but she got killed. … It's finished off nicely, except for there not being a bathroom. And, the basement is even finished off as well, with a full-size pool table. That's how I learned to shoot. There is a bath down there, and there could be two rooms that could be used as bedrooms, but I'd rather keep them for games and stuff. Only need so many bedrooms."

"Sounds really great," Liz said. "You're a very lucky girl to have a house like that."

Angel stared silently at Liz for several seconds, and then she said, "Maybe, if my mom hadn't been killed. I don't feel too lucky about that."

Liz had no comeback for that statement. She knew that there were no words available to her that could compensate for Angel's loss, nor her insensitivity to it. So, she let the young girl's grief-laden comment close that discussion.

For the next nearly three hours, the two girls simply let their mutually-loved game of pool fill their minds and conversation. Finally, after Liz called and dropped the eight-ball to win her first out of six games, she said, "Thanks for letting me win one … Do you think you're ready to meet Spyder? I think it's about that time."

"Yeah," Angel said, still obviously more than a little apprehensive about that part of the project. "Any further advice for me?"

"Just that, while Spyder won't go back on his word, he will not bend, either. As long as you're okay with signing over all of your paychecks for the next three weeks, you will do just fine. Just be sure you don't try to screw around with him—you know, like take advantage of him. He's not above anything. If you even thought about cheating him in any way, it would not be good for you."

"I wouldn't do that," Angel said. "I'm good with the deal, and I'll stick to it. I'll do the work, and he'll get his money."

"Then you're good," Liz told her.

"And," Angel asked, "your friend won't be looking to me for any special favors? I'm sure you know what I mean. … He won't be expecting any funny business on the side. Right?"

"Right," Liz assured her.

The two girls left the pool hall and headed directly to the dinner meeting with Spyder. The trip was not far—out of the parlor, down the street for two and a half blocks, and into the restaurant. Together they did not speak a dozen words during the walk. Angel was quiet because she was intimidated, and Liz was equally silent because she was deeply engaged in contemplative planning.

Spyder had arrived early, as always. He had himself all set up and was ready to conduct business.

As they walked in Liz's eyes carefully surveyed the dining area, and quickly spotted Spyder at a corner booth. "This way," she said to Angel, and then she led the way.

"Spyder, this is my friend Angel," she said as they approached where he was seated, "the girl that I told you about."

Spyder, who did not stand, said to Angel, "Young ladies, have a seat." With his hand he signaled for them to sit across from him. Liz waited for Angel to slide in next to the wall, and then she sat down on the outside.

At first Angel was a little apprehensive about being trapped in the booth, but soon lost most of her fear.

"Liz explained to me what you are after," Spyder said, wasting no time with small talk. "You want credentials proving that you are sixteen—papers that would allow you to get a work permit, and a driver's license. Am I right?"

"Yes, sir," Angel responded in a shaky voice, "That's right. I need to get a job at a restaurant."

"We can do that," he said, "but, you must understand, you won't be serving alcohol. Not at all—no exceptions. Do you understand that?"

"Yes," she said. "Completely."

"Do you also know that you will be working the maximum hours that they will allow?" he asked in a commanding voice, "and that you will sign your entire paychecks over to me? And you will do that for the first month?"

"I thought we agreed that she would do that for three weeks," Liz said, jumping in before Angel could respond.

"The terms are one month," he said without looking over at Liz. "One month or four weeks. Maximum hours permitted. Do you understand?"

Angel realized that Liz had told her that the man would do it for three weeks' pay. She looked over at her friend, but Liz refused to make eye contact with her, and Angel knew what that meant.

"Yes," Angel said. "I will do that. Do you promise that I will be able to get a driver's license with this deal?"

"I don't promise you shit," he growled. "The papers I provide will get you in the door, but you are the one who has to pass the written test, and the road test. All that shit's on you—*totally* on you. Period. Do you understand what I am telling you?"

"Yes," she said. Angel, being an intelligent teenager, could see that this Spyder guy was not interested in conversation. So, she decided she would be better off responding to these preliminary questions with single-word answers. And she understood that single word would need to be in the affirmative—every time.

"Do you have any other questions about this?" Spyder asked.

"What do you need from me?"

"I will need a few things. I need your mailing address," he said.

Seeing that she was not writing anything down, he slid a napkin in front of her, along with a ballpoint pen.

"Here, you stupid little shit," he said, clearly agitated. "Don't be wasting my time here. Write down what I tell you, and don't screw around with me. I'm givin' you a great deal. Take advantage of it, and don't let me down. Or it's off, and you will still owe me a month's wages ... or more, if you keep messin' up. ... So, take notes! Understand?!"

Angel again looked over at Liz, but found her overtures continued to be overlooked. So, she looked Spyder in the eye and said, "Yes, I understand completely."

And she then started writing down what he was telling her.

"Okay," he said. "Now I've got some questions for you. Don't tell me anything that's not one hundred percent true. Got it? You lie to me at all and the deal's off. And you still have to pay me. Understand?"

"Yes."

"Where were you born? Was it in the US? And what city? ... I don't give a shit what year, only where. I'm gonna make you sixteen. So, I don't give a damn what year you think it was."

"I was born in Cleveland, Ohio."

"Hospital?"

"Cleveland Clinic."

"I thought you lived in the Upper Peninsula of Michigan? You better not be lying to me!"

"I did live in the Upper Peninsula. My mom moved from Cleveland to Curtis while I was still a baby. Curtis is in Michigan's Upper Peninsula."

"Never heard of it," Spyder said. "Where is it, exactly?"

"Sort of center of the UP," she replied.

"And you moved from there to the Bay Area earlier this year?"

"I lived in Curtis for over ten years. My mom owned an ice cream shop in Curtis. She sold the shop and we moved to the Soo—that's Sault Ste. Marie—last year. Then moved from the Soo out to San Francisco a few months ago."

"I've heard of Sault Ste. Marie," Spyder said, somewhat excited. "Have you ever heard of Sugar Island?"

"Yeah," Angel said, with a big smile capturing her face. "My best friends live on Sugar Island. Been there many times."

"S-H-I-T," Spyder said, enunciating the word slowly. "Ever heard of a town called Barbeau?"

"Heard of it, but never been there."

Liz was now being drawn into their conversation. She'd never heard of Barbeau, but was becoming quite interested.

"Barbeau," Angel said, "that was located about forty-five minutes to an hour directly south of my house, I think."

"*Your* house?" Spyder asked. "You have a house in the Upper Peninsula?"

"I do. My mom left it to me in her will. She died a few months ago."

"And *you* own the house?"

"Yeah, but I'm too young to live there by myself. I need to be older."

"Think you will ever move back?"

Angel caught herself thinking about what she had not dared think about for some time. She waited until she had got her mind just a bit wrapped around her future, and then answered Spyder's question.

"Someday, I imagine," she said. "I'm not ready for that yet."

Spyder did not respond to her comment for several uneasy seconds, and then he said, "Liz was right about one thing, young lady. You do look older than fourteen, that's—"

"I'm almost fifteen right now. And when I lived in the UP, I used to drive everywhere … especially when I was visiting my friends on Sugar Island. I know how to drive just fine. I know I can pass all the tests, if I can just be sixteen."

"Well," Spyder said, as he retrieved his cell phone from his jacket pocket. "I would like to snap a few pictures of you now, for your driver's license, and other shit. Hold still and look directly at the camera. Like I said, we'll shoot a few shots."

Liz took a look at the back of the booth to see what was behind Angel, and Spyder noticed what she was doing and said, "We don't have to worry about the background. I use Photoshop. I can put any background in there that I want to. No problem."

Liz did not understand what Photoshop was, but she knew better than to open her mouth right then. Instead, she shut her brain down to what was going on and being said around her, and instead began contemplating what she might do with her new-found friend from Northern Michigan.

"I will keep a close eye on shipments coming into Spyder's apartment," Liz said silently to herself. "I need to make sure I can count on them being on time. I'm thinking that they arrive every third Thursday. Late afternoon—like clockwork. I'll make sure nothing changes with that schedule. And then, after Angel gets her debt paid off to Spyder, maybe six weeks down the road, she and I will load up Spyder's shipment, and we will take off and go to her house in the Upper Peninsula of Michigan. And I will set up shop there. What a great plan!"

Every time she laid out her scheme in her mind, she got stuck with the part that had her transporting the drugs to Michigan from San Francisco. "Can't take a chance of trying to get them on a plane," she said to herself. "The luggage handlers use machines that can actually see through a suitcase, and see what's inside. And dogs—like I was thinking before, some airports can even have dogs to sniff out what's in a suitcase. We are gonna have to drive it. No other way to get it where I want it. We'll just have to drive it all the way. … And, when we get to Michigan, we'll stay with Angel's people until—"

"Damn it, Liz!" Spyder barked, trying to get her attention. "Will you pay attention to me? What the hell's goin' on with you? You in some kinda trance, or something crazy like that? … Pay attention, damn it, I'm talking to you."

Spyder's first "damn it" totally got her attention. She snapped her head around to see what was going on, and she spotted Angel staring at her.

"Oh!" Liz exclaimed. "I'm sorry. I must not of got enough sleep last night. Maybe I should get a cup of coffee to wake me up."

"You can do that on your own damn nickel," Spyder complained as he slid out to stand up. "I gotta be gettin' outta here."

"What were you doin', Liz?" Angel asked after Spyder walked out of earshot. "Were you actually sleepin'?"

"I guess I must have been," she confessed, flashing a "please forgive me smile" at her friend. But, in truth, her mind was so far from repose that in a totally creative fashion she could have described in detail what it felt like to have the north wind off Lake

Superior blowing her now wildly messy hair straight back, or what it would be like to be standing in a wooded patch of ripened wild blueberries in Paradise. She was ready to move that moment.

Now to devise and implement the perfect plan, she told herself.

Chapter 3 —

D ad," Kate asked, glancing over toward her father as she began clearing the table after breakfast. "Just how sure are we that Angel is actually on her way back to the island? I think you talked to her after I did. Any ideas on that?"

Jack did not respond immediately. Instead, he simply assumed a blank expression, which suggested to her that he really had no solid opinion on the subject. He then began pouring himself a second cup of coffee. Kate had seen him do that a thousand times before, and she knew exactly what he was silently saying.

Jack's two fourteen-year-old foster boys, Red and Robby, while they had finished eating, remained at the table and were furtively paying very close attention to every nuance of the conversation— especially to the non-verbal aspects of it.

The Angel to whom Kate was referring was, of course, Angel Star—the fourteen-year-old daughter of the family's now deceased friend, Millie Star. Not only had it become obvious to friends and family that Angel had grown to become one of the boys' very best friends during the short time they had known one another, but it was also clear that Jack and Millie had themselves become regarded almost as an *item* on Sugar Island. Jack had let it be known that he harbored some very special feelings for the attractive young woman.

And, now that she had been murdered, Jack let it be known to those closest to him that he privately concealed more than a little self-imposed guilt for her death. "Were it not for me," he'd frequently told himself (and those closest to him), "the beautiful Millie Star would still be around, raising and influencing that young daughter of hers, were it not for me."

While he never discussed those pangs of guilt with anyone outside his immediate circle, he remained totally convinced that those self-accusations were based on solid fact. And, he had a great deal of difficulty dealing with what he called "that incontrovertible truth."

Finally, Jack turned back toward the table with his coffee, and sat down.

Kate also knew what that meant. It told her that her father was ready to respond to her question.

"Well, Dad. What do you think? Have you formed an opinion?"

He took a long sip on his hot coffee, and said, "Angel is a very special young lady. I know you feel that way about her as well. And, we both know how much she meant—means—to our two boys. Angel was always one of their very best friends. ... I certainly hope to hell that she finds herself willing to step back into our lives—if even for just a short visit. Nothing would make me happier than that. But, I just don't know how to answer your question. … Whether or not she is ready to come back to Sugar Island. And, if so, for how long or under what conditions? … or terms? She must have her reasons for reaching out to us in the first place. We're just going to have to find out more when … if, she actually shows up here. … What are you thinking?"

Kate was expecting to have her father kick the question back to her, so she was ready for it.

"I'm thoroughly expecting to see her knock on the door one of these mornings," Kate said. "And sooner than later, if you ask me."

"Really?" Jack replied. "Why's that?"

"It was never her practice to play games," she said. "Even when dealing with the boys, she always came off in a sincere way. … And that business about you being somehow responsible for the death of her mother—I don't think you're being fair to yourself, or Angel, by going there. I'm sure she doesn't blame you a bit for her mom's murder. She knows your heart just as well as the rest of us do."

Kate gave her father some time to absorb the thoughts she had just shared with him. After nearly five minutes of silence, Jack spoke up: "What do you know about that friend of hers—the one she's supposed to be bringing up with her? Have you ever heard Angel talk about her before? I think the friend's name is Liz."

"Aside from the name," Kate replied, "I am totally unaware of Angel's new friends. None of us have ever heard about any of the people in her life since she moved out to Oregon."

"Oregon?" Jack queried. "I don't think that's the case? I heard California."

"She started out in California," Kate answered. "But I think that's where she met this new friend of hers—*Liz*. In San Francisco, I think. And, this Liz girl stayed in something like a commune outside of Portland."

"How did she manage that?" Jack asked, now very much interested in more of the finer details. "Angel was only fourteen years old. A kid can't live in a commune at that age, can they? ... And, all I heard was San Francisco. That's where you send her rent checks. Right? San Francisco?"

"Right," Kate replied. "I did always question that. It was like she didn't want us to know enough to set out to find her. We both assumed at the time that she had to have been flying under the radar. To get away with that age issue. But, we agreed at the time that we needed to give her some space, or she would totally alienate herself from us. We wanted to be there for her if and when she decided to reach out to us. ... And, that appears to be what's happening. Isn't that how you see it?"

Jack did not verbally respond to his daughter's last question. Instead, he just slowly nodded his head in agreement, and continued to cradle his coffee between his hands, as he slowly sipped away on the hot, black elixir. All the while his eyes remained unfocused.

He could recall the events they were discussing as vividly as though they had taken place the night before—that's how clearly they were etched in his psyche.

Kate had seen her father drift off in deep thought many times before, and so she knew this to be the time to keep quiet and allow his spirit to wander freely.

"How could I not be held accountable for Millie's death," he finally muttered. "At least to a sizeable measure? Had it not been for her relationship with me, she would most certainly be alive and well, and actively engaging in the raising of that precious daughter."

Jack had been on his own ever since his wife Beth had been murdered while walking with him on the streets of Chicago. That was way back in his life—when Kate was but a toddler. For all of those years following, Jack had refused even to consider another woman in his life. That's how much Beth had meant to him.

In fact, it was not until he had met and grown close to Millie that he even entertained the possibility that there might come along a woman with whom he would even consider forming any type of close relationship. And now, she too was gone. Worst of all, Millie had met her end following Jack's directive. *Had it not been for my sending her out east*, he told himself, *she would still be alive. What is it with me? Why do I always have a hand in killing the ones closest to me?*

Still, Jack remained silent as he relived his earlier years, and entertained those devastating pangs of guilt surrounding the death of the only two significant women during the course of his entire life.

"I don't know anything for sure right now," Jack said. "But my guess remains fairly solid. I think Angel is still living in San Francisco. … We might be able to get to the bottom of that dilemma pretty soon if she shows up at our door. Don't you think?"

"I don't know anything for sure right now," Jack said. "But my guess remains fairly solid. I think Angel is now living in San Francisco. … But, whether it be the Bay Area, or Portland, I suspect we just might be getting to the bottom of that dilemma pretty soon— if and when she actually shows up at our door. … Don't you think?"

Chapter 4 —

How sure are you that we'll both have a place to stay once we get there—on Sugar Island?" Liz asked. "These people don't know me at all. What makes you think that they're gonna welcome me with open arms?"

"That's just the way they are," Angel replied. "You're a friend of mine, that makes you a friend of theirs. ... By the way, I'm not sure if I told you this before, but Jack's a former Chicago homicide detective, and he now works as a private security contractor. I'm not real sure what all he does, but he makes a lot of money. ... And Kate's a cop right now. A New York City homicide detective. I'm—"

"Homicide?!" Liz blurted out, interrupting her friend. "What the hell you getting me into?! You never told me that they are cops!"

"He's not a cop, he's a *former* cop. He's been retired from that for a long time. I said he was now a private security contractor. That's way different. His daughter's the homicide detective. I told you all about that before. She works in New York. ... They'll be good with you as long as you don't kill anyone. You weren't planning on doing that, were you?

"They're really great people. Good friends to have, too. I'm sure that they will welcome you because you're with me. And as long as Kate's good with our visit, her dad will be good with it as well. ... And, of course, the two boys will be eager to see me. They're my age—or were my age. We just have to be upfront with Kate. Even about that age thing. ... We gotta be upfront with the whole family, actually."

"I think that I should just sleep in the car," Liz said. "And you can go to the house. That would be safest, I think—"

"Nonsense!" Angel interrupted. "That's not the way they do business. If you tried that with Kate, she'd be out to get you within the first minute. And she'd be dragging you in whether or not you wanted her to. ... They're gonna want to see what you're all about, and get to know you a bit. Whatever you do, do not lie to them. Like I said, Kate's dad is, was, a Chicago homicide detective. He's a living, breathing lie detector. That's how he describes it. That's kinda what he does for a living. ... I'm not too sure exactly what he does, but one of his good friends is former President Robert Fulbright. He has him out to the house quite a lot."

"A former president? To the house on Sugar Island?" Liz said in near disbelief. "Really? Are you shittin' me?"

"No," Angel replied, an element of boasting discernible in her tone. "I've actually met him out on the island ... Secret Service and everything."

"Think I'll get a chance to meet him—the former president?"

"Unlikely," Angel said. "But anything's possible, I suppose. I'd say, though, it'd be unlikely that he'll be visiting right at this time. And, if that were the case, then they would not be entertaining us at the same time. I think they'd have let me know if they were having other houseguests. And Kate said nothing about anything like that when I talked to her. So, I'm pretty sure they're all good with having us. Kate would have let me know if there was a problem."

Angel was driving. They were just entering Sault Ste. Marie from the south on I-75. Both of them were totally exhausted from their twenty-five-hundred-mile trip. They had left the Bay Area in the middle of the night on Thursday, and driven an average of ten hours a day, for four days. Had Angel a little more experience behind the wheel, they might have attempted to cover the geography a little more quickly, but she had just been granted her driver's license, and neither of the girls were comfortable pushing her contribution too hard.

The first three nights they satisfied their need for sleep by pulling off the highway at rest stops and stretching out as much as possible in their rented white 2022 Toyota Corolla. On their fourth night on the road they found themselves in need of a hot shower. They were in Appleton, WI. Appleton seemed the logical choice to spend the night because, even though it was in a different time zone, Sugar Island would be easily reachable from there at a reasonable time. So that's what they did.

They were both getting psyched up for their arrival at the Handlers'. Angel was very confident that they would be welcomed at their destination, but Liz was, for several reasons, a bit more apprehensive about what lay ahead. So, it was Liz's uneasiness that rubbed off on Angel, causing her to also be a bit more nervous than she ought to have been about dropping in at the Handler house.

Initially, their plans had them leaving Appleton by 7 A.M., which would put them into the Soo by one or two, allowing for the different time zone. However, lingering fatigue delayed their embarking for almost an hour. Even though they were arriving a little later than hoped, they still thought it prudent to switch vehicles before going to the island. And, they were able to do that because Millie's estate (through Jack Handler) had left a late-model silver Chevy Traverse in a storage facility in the Soo. Jack had then provided keys for the Traverse and the storage room overhead door, and a gate card—all that would be required to grant her access to her vehicle and many of her mom's belongings.

And then, in order to further facilitate readiness, he filled the fuel tank with 94 octane gasoline, and connected a trickle charger to the battery. Plus, while he did not announce it to Angel, nor even make his family aware of it, he was intending every six months to pay a visit to the Traverse in order to give it a brief ride around the block.

"Where are we going?" Liz inquired. Angel could tell by the tone of her voice that she was at least a little agitated. "My GPS tells me Sugar Island is right off a street called East Portage. That's not where you're going. What's up?"

"I never explained that, did I?" Angel said.

"Explained? Explained what?"

"I have a car in storage here in the Soo," Angel told her. "Mom left it for me. We gotta pick it up before we head over on the ferry."

"Ferry?"

"Right," Angel said through a smile. "There's no bridge here. We gotta take a ferry to get on the island. ... We'll quickly switch cars, and then get on the ferry."

"Holy shit!" Liz complained. "How long is that gonna take? Are we gonna be able to get there before dinner?"

"It won't take long," Angel replied. "If for some reason Mom's Traverse won't run for me, we'll just stick with the rental. But this car is costing us every day we have it. … And, you're on the ticket for the rental. So, the sooner we get it back, the more money you will save. It'll all be fine. Won't take long at all."

Millie and Angel lived only a quarter of a mile from the ferry dock, and so the storage facility that Jack found for Millie's things was close by—just west and south of the approach to Sugar Island. While Angel had never physically been there, she had the address, and was familiar with the neighborhood.

"We're almost there," Angel said, reassuring Liz. "Can't be more than a block or two. … Straight up ahead. I can see the sign from here."

"Yeah," Liz said. "I see it now too. … Want me to take it from here? Or are you good to drive in these tight quarters?"

"I'm good," Angel replied. "I'll take it on in. After we make the switch, you can take the Toyota rental on in. Not sure where the rental return is, but we've got GPS. We'll plug in the address, and I'll follow you there."

"Sounds good to me," Liz agreed. "I just want to find myself a hot cup of coffee, and get into some fresh clothes. I am pretty damn sick of the road. I'll bet you're tired of driving. Right?"

"I'm good and ready to wind this thing up," Angel agreed. … "And I am very eager to have you meet Kate, and Jack. I really love those guys. At first I was a little angry with Jack, because I blamed him for the death of my mom. But, I know her death was not his fault. I know that. He loved my mom. I think they would have eventually got married if she'd lived. Then he'd have been my dad. … That would have been okay. … You know, I never had a dad— not really. My real dad ran off when I was still a baby. … And now, I don't even remember him. He must have been an okay guy, cuz my mom was in love with him. At least, at one time. … I don't know, really. I guess that's the way life goes.

"What I'm quite sure of is that Jack and Kate were good friends to my mom. They both truly cared about her. And she loved them. … We were all truly fortunate to have known each other. And Red and Robby. I can't wait to have you meet those guys. You're going to really like them too."

"Well, that worked pretty good," Liz said as the gate opened for Angel's card. "Hope the lock on the door works as well as the card worked on the gate. One down …"

"Yeah," Angel said. "That's pretty cool. So far so good."

"What all your mom got packed away in here?" Liz asked. "They look like good-sized storage rooms."

"I have absolutely no idea what got packed away in this room," Angel explained. "Uncle Jack and Aunt Kate packed it all up. I never set foot in our house before I headed west. I couldn't do it. That whole business just hurt me way too much. I had Kate pack up some clothes, and I was outta here. … She was my mom, and I loved her a lot. But she was dead, and I didn't even know what death was. … I never said a word to any of them. I was angry, confused, and hurt. … Jack has a man who works with him. A Native American named Henry. Like I said, he works with Uncle Jack, but he's more than just an employee. He's Uncle Jack's good friend. I told him to have Kate pack me up what I'll need to take with me, and that I was moving to California.

"And when I got out there, I called Henry and gave him my mailing address. Kate shipped my stuff to me. She did a pretty good job, too. ... I really love that whole family. I was too hurt to talk to them at that time, though. ... Until now. I'm sure I can talk to them okay now.

"Henry told me that they left most of the furniture in the house, and that the people renting the house are using it. He said that Uncle Jack thought that was a better idea than trying to store it, or to sell it. At least, I suppose I'm making a little money on the lease—for the furniture. It helped pay my bills when I lived in Frisco. ... I sure didn't make enough shooting pool."

"Sounds to me like they had a good plan," Liz agreed. "... Are you a little excited to take a look at all your stuff? Bet it will bring back memories."

"Don't dare let it," Angel said. "I know it's gonna be real hard."

"Well," Liz said, "I have to say that I'm gonna find it exciting. Even though it's your stuff and not mine, I still think it will be a little intoxicating, even for a casual observer like me. ... Anyway, if your key gets us in, I think we should make it quick. Switch vehicles, and get across the channel, then on to Sugar Island."

"I agree," Angel said. "Let's do it like that—in and out."

Angel checked the paperwork once in, and saw that the garage Jack had rented for her was located in the section of the facility where they had the largest storage areas.

"There it is!" Liz declared, pointing down a drive housing the units large enough to store a vehicle in. "182. Your storage garage is number 182. And that's it right there."

"Yes," Angel said. "I see it too."

Just as Liz predicted, Angel was beginning to grow a little more excited as each minute passed.

"I better not block it in," Angel said. "We have to be able to back the Traverse out of here if it will start for me, so I don't want to stop right in front of the door. Let's just leave it here for now, and go check it out—see if this key works."

"Leave it running," Liz said. "You can see if your car starts."

"Can't," Angel said, turning off the rental and jumping out of it. "I've put the Traverse keys on the same keychain as the Toyota. … It'll take me a minute, but I'll get it. Let's see if we can get in this place."

It took her only seconds to unlock the padlock Jack had used to secure the storage room door, and it took Liz even less time to open the basically flimsy overhead door.

"Holy shit!" Liz exclaimed when she switched on the light and glanced around the neatly packed storage room. "Whoever packed this place up did a really nice job. Very tidy. … Do you think it will start? Your car? Do you think the battery will even turn it over? It hasn't been run in a while."

"I think it probably will," Angel replied. "Henry said they put it on a trickle charger to keep it ready to go. … I'll give it a try. If it does, I'll unlock the back hatch. And maybe you can start switching our stuff over to my car? Then we can take the rental back, and save you some money."

"Sure," Liz said. "Give it a shot and let's see what we got here."

Angel removed the keys for the Toyota and handed them over to Liz, and she jumped behind the wheel of the Traverse. … And, happily, Angel was able to start the Traverse on her first try.

"I'll pull the charger off and shut the hood," Liz announced with a smile. "And then I'm gonna grab my shit from the rental. I'll get your stuff too."

Angel looked over at Liz and flashed a thumbs-up to signal her approval.

Liz opened the rear hatch and began transporting their luggage. She first slid Angel's two bags into the vehicle, and then she retrieved her own bags, of which there were three. She loaded two of them into the Traverse, but one of them—the heaviest of the lot—she dragged over to the right rear corner of the storage garage, and there found a box that she determined would be large enough to store that one single bag in, and still have a little space left over. As one might have guessed, that one bag that she wished to hide contained virtually all the coke that she had stolen from Spyder.

With Angel totally preoccupied with relearning all the intricacies involved with gearing up to drive a different vehicle, Liz rapidly removed all the contents of the oversized box, and transferred all the coke to that box. Since she was left with some empty space in that box, she filled the container the rest of the way with some of what she had just placed on the floor. After fitting as much as she was able to back into the box, Liz sealed it back up. She then neatly stacked the materials that did not fit within it, on top of that same box.

When finished, Liz glanced back at Angel to see if the girl had observed what she'd been up to, and was convinced that her repacking efforts had gone unnoticed.

"I'll be damned," Liz said to herself. "I'm pretty sure that the kid has no idea that we just transported a million dollars' worth of shit across seven or eight state lines. Damn! And now she's got a small fortune worth of drugs in her little storage barn—packed away with her dead mom's vinyls. I wonder what Michigan law would say about that. ... Hell, I wonder what AC/DC would think about it!"

When Angel realized that Liz had their luggage all squared away, she jumped out of the Traverse and began surveying all the boxes that Jack had stored in the garage.

"You wanna go through this stuff now?" Liz asked her, using a tone she was hoping would dissuade her young friend from wishing to pursue that endeavor at this time.

Angel thought about what Liz was suggesting for about half a second, and then emphatically said, "No! I don't want to get into all of this right now. I'm not ready to start with it. If I begin opening boxes and crates, I won't stop. ... It would bring back too many memories—not all happy. I'll save that for another day."

"Then, shall we get this rental returned?" Liz asked. "You ready to find that ferry? ... You got the address for that rental place?"

"Yeah," Angel said. "I'll get it on my GPS. Don't think it's exactly nearby, but it should not take too long."

And it didn't.

"Yeah," Liz announced. "I got it here. Looks like we head west toward I-75, then turn left on a street called Ashmun. Have you heard of that one? ... And we follow Ashmun south to 3 Mile Road. It looks like it's not too far from there. ... Shall I lead the way, or do you want to?"

"You got it on your cell already," Angel said. "That's good. I'll just follow you there."

And that's what they did, and they had no problem finding their check-in station. After a brief physical inspection, checking for damage and verifying mileage and fuel level, even though the fuel was not topped off, those running the service approved it, and the two girls both got in the Traverse. "I should take it from here," Angel announced. "I know the way from here, and I should be driving my own car when we get there. Right?"

And, again, they were able to pull off this phase of their adventure flawlessly. Angel hopped back on Ashmun and headed north toward the Canadian border.

"How far on this do we go?" Liz asked. "You said that you do know the way from here, right?"

"Yes, of course," Angel reassured her. "We turn right up here on Portage—that's well before the border. You actually can't cross the border ... not from this street, anyway. The shipping channel runs between the US and Canada. We'll turn on Portage up here, and then we can take that all the way to the ferry. ... Actually, we're almost there already. Sault Ste. Marie is not a huge city. We'll be at the ferry in no time."

"Are you scared about this whole thing?" Liz asked her. "Not having seen your friends for such a long time, and everything? You know what I mean?"

"I'm a little nervous," Angel said, "But not scared. Like I said, I really like that whole family. And they've always liked me, and my mom. We'll be fine."

Liz, expecting Angel to provide a few more details, waited politely without commenting.

Angel, however, for several minutes just drove and kept silent. Finally, she spoke up, but not on the topic Liz anticipated: "I can't believe how strange this all looks to me," she said. "It hasn't been that long since I've been here. Yet, almost nothing looks familiar.

... Probably because I wasn't driving much when I was here before. And when I did, it was always on Sugar Island. No cops on the island. ... Out here, where there are so many cars, everything looks much different now—especially from behind the wheel."

From the moment they turned onto Ashmun, until they reached West Portage, Liz did all the talking, as Angel's full attention was glued on taking in her surroundings.

Once she had successfully maneuvered the turn onto Portage, Angel again spoke up: "We didn't live very far from the ferry dock—Mom and me. ... We used to visit the Handlers a lot. I think I've probably been over on Sugar Island twenty or thirty times—probably more. Back when Mom was alive.

"But, I think there's a good reason why it feels so strange now. Back then, before I met you, I never drove much this side of the ferry. So, now I'm seeing things very differently. Everything looks strange from behind the steering wheel. It's just a little weird."

"Before you met Spyder, you mean," Liz corrected her. "Spyder is the one who fixed you up with a driver's license."

With that thought each of the girls retired a little more deeply within their private worlds—Angel, to the land of memories, of the time when her mother was around to ward off the sort of threats and negative influences that now seem to dominate too much of her thought life, and Liz, to her mysterious little world of fear that she hid from everyone. What will I do, she asked herself, if Angel's friends get too personal with their questions? They are, after all, cops. And, oh my God, cops never trust nobody. They especially won't trust me. I just know they won't.

"How far did you say it is to the ferry?" Liz asked. "We are pretty close? You said we were—close, that is. I'm guessing we can make it to their house before dark? The Handler house, that is."

"For sure," Angel said with a chuckle. "Trust me, we really are almost there right now."

"Is this where we turn?" Liz asked. "It's Portage. That's where you turn. Right?"

"Yup."

"Now how far?" Liz asked.

"A couple miles, maybe," Angel replied.

The "two mile" report from Angel set very well with Liz. It was what she needed to hear. With those words she was able to sit back in her seat a bit and relax. *I can handle that*, she was thinking. *Two miles means we will be at the ferry in less than ten minutes—regardless of traffic.*

"Very cool," she said aloud.

Angel just smiled, and remained silent. She could tell that her passenger was very apprehensive about what awaited them. She, on the other hand, was looking forward to seeing her old friends.

While Angel's arrival prognosis struck Liz in an agreeable yet frightening fashion, there was another situation secretly awaiting them that was to prove itself anything but agreeable. Totally unbeknownst to the two girls there existed a surprise of immense potential for harm. Parked in a white Toyota rental car were two very unhappy, shady-looking characters … and they were lying in wait specifically for those two girls. The names of those loathsome reptiles: Spyder and Cash.

As soon as the word reached Spyder that there was a good possibility that the woman who had stolen his entire drug shipment might be planning to hide out on Sugar Island with her young friend, he set about plotting the recovery of his merchandise, and

66 *Michael Carrier*

the two females' demise.

Spyder had brought Cash, one of his lowlife drug dealer associates, along with him as backup, in the event that a situation requiring some help might develop. The two of them had flown out of San Francisco International almost immediately after Spyder became convinced that Liz was the thief he would have to catch up with, and that she would almost certainly be headed to Michigan's Sugar Island. And since the nearest airport servicing Michigan's Upper Peninsula would be Chippewa County International Airport (located just south of Sugar Island), that's where he decided they should go.

So, as it turned out, the two men landed at CCIA almost two full days before Liz and Angel drove into the Soo. To add irony to the story, upon landing Spyder hired a taxi to take him and Cash to the same car rental service that had cleaned out and inspected for use the white Toyota the girls had driven from Northern California to the UP.

And now the two men were here, after spending two days awkwardly moving from one parking place to another in and around Clyde's Restaurant parking area. It was from that area that they were able to monitor all the vehicles taking the ferry over to Sugar Island. It is an understatement to say that both of the men were getting very sick of being stuck together for that extended period of time. While nothing would have felt much better to them than a soft bed and a warm shower, they were determined.

Actually, Spyder was the one who was determined. The simple fact was, he possessed more than enough of that powerfully enabling elixir to have sufficed for the two of them. While both had suffered through far more discomfort than either of them would have cared to, neither of them was even slightly tempted to give up—Spyder, due to two powerfully enabling defense mechanisms. First, the enormous financial burden it placed on him. The value of what was stolen was literally more than what his business could absorb easily. And, second, his immense anger at being so callously deceived by his principal "love interest" drove an emotional dagger through both his heart, and his pride.

And, as for Cash, he was emboldened to act decisively by the fact that he was very confident that if he were to fail at this juncture, his boss would most certainly kill him. Had he the opportunity over, Cash was certain that he would not have accepted Spyder's invitation to work this job. "Damn it all," he said to himself many times since embarking. "If only I had passed on Spyder's offer. I'm afraid I might not survive the trip. I'm afraid that this bastard just might put a bullet in my brain before it's over!"

What all that meant at this point in time, was that they were both totally wired as far as keeping watch for any vehicle transporting one or two women to Sugar Island. And if one of those women were to even remotely resemble Spyder's former girlfriend Liz, then they would be prepared to swing into action.

It would be safe to say that it would not take a very vivid imagination to conjure up what the inside of that white Toyota had begun to smell like.

"Well," Liz said, obviously a little stressed, "I will be happy to get the first part of this over with. That's the part where you introduce me to your friends, and I get to see just who these folks are, and start to get a feel on whether or not they're gonna be accepting me. … Yeah, I guess you could say that I'm a bit on edge."

Angel did not respond to her friend's comment. All Liz accomplished with her expressions of insecurity was to dull her young friend's sensitivities to certain potential threats, with one of them being a very real thing—the fact that as of less than one minute ago they truly did have the occupants of a nearby car taking careful notice of them, and in another few minutes, it would be following them with bad intentions. This part of her trip to Sugar Island was not anticipated. And, it was not in any way going to be easy or fun.

Chapter 5 —

Again, exactly how did you leave it with them?" Liz asked. "With your friends, Kate and Jack, that is?"

Angel weighed her words. She knew better than to lie to Liz. Still, she did not wish to respond in any way that could be deemed 'out of turn,' so to speak.

"I talked only to Kate," Angel said. "And I did not lay too much at her feet. She is a cop, you know."

"Okay," Liz said. "I get it. But what all did you tell her? Did you relay the warning as Spyder put out there?"

"Not exactly," Angel said. "I just told her that we had a man out west who might like to hurt you. Actually, that he might want to hurt the both of us, because we are friends."

"Did you tell her that he was quite motivated? That he just might be following us to Michigan?"

"I didn't get into it like that," Angel said. "I didn't think that Spyder had any idea that we were in Michigan. So I didn't tell her anything that specific. ... Like I said. She is a cop. A detective. It's her job to chase down the bad guys, and toss them in jail. If she knows that Spyder wants to kill us, and has even attempted to ... do it—to kill you. Then, she might think she has to go after him, and put him in jail. I don't know how she might view her role in this thing. I think we'll just have to sit down with her and feel her out. To see how she thinks this ought to get resolved."

"Then," Liz followed up, "Kate does not know what Spyder's got against me in particular. Right? You must have told her something."

"I told her that we had some friends that had a little business selling drugs," Angel said. "That's true. I didn't lie to her. I told her that one of those men was named Spyder, and that he was older. That he had asked you out on a date, and you didn't want to go out with him because he sold drugs. I said he didn't handle rejection well, and that he threatened to hurt you, and that you think he might even have followed us. ... That you think he is kind of crazy, and that he might want to hurt us. ... Isn't that—"

"Might want to hurt us?" Liz interrupted. "Then your friends do not know that Spyder might be hot on our trail to Michigan? Because I can promise you that he's crazy, and that if he gets something in his head, he doesn't stop. I'd bet that he's coming after me right now."

"No," Angel admitted. "I did not go there. When I talked to her I truthfully had no idea that he knew you were coming to Michigan. ... Dang, all you did is refuse to go out on a date with him. Just how mean and vindictive can he be? Talk about being possessive. He must think he owns you. Can't he take no for an answer? ... I figured that we could go out to the island—Sugar Island. Sit down over breakfast with Kate. Let her, or her and Uncle Jack, meet you, and get to know you a little bit, and then you can explain what has gone down, and the threat we think it might pose."

Liz just sat in silence for a few moments. And then she finally spoke: "I've seen it before, how guys like this operate. I know for a fact that Spyder has people he sells to in Chicago, Detroit, and probably other cities in Michigan. Spyder is not going to accept this threat to his pride lightly. He's gonna do something. I know more than a little bit about how he thinks, and how he deals with what he regards as threats like me. ... And, that's exactly what I am to him now—a threat."

"There!" Spyder shouted to Cash. "Check that out! I think. ... Well, I'll be damned if that ain't Liz! Sure as shit, it is her! It absolutely is!"

With very few exceptions during their vigil had Spyder ever shut the engine off, so he was ready to pounce when he spotted his prey. All he had to was shift into drive and pull around Clyde's. As swiftly as possible he slid in the line behind the Traverse. Even though he had reacted quickly, by the time he had actually pulled fully into the boarding line for the ferry, two other vehicles had already squeezed in behind Angel's Traverse.

"Do you think we're gonna make it on same ferry run with 'em?" Cash asked in a concerned tone. "Think that's gonna be a problem—if that's how it works out and we end up missing this ferry?"

"We're gonna fit on it fine," Spyder groused at Cash. "Those ferries are really much bigger than they look. There's barely even a dozen on the approach. That's total vehicles. And even these little boats hold way more than that. ... Who the hell do you suppose it could it be that those girls are visiting, or maybe even movin' in with? There's gotta be somebody there that one of them's been in contact with. I don't know one damn thing about any of all that shit ... nothin' at all!"

Cash could not tell if Spyder was actually seeking his opinion, or was just complaining rhetorically. But, he felt that he should offer some sort of verbalization: "No idea at all as to how it's goin' down," Cash said. "All I know is that a few weeks ago I heard Liz say somethin' about Angel having friends that lived on Sugar Island. … And that might even have been a month ago. But, that info appears to be right on. This is the *Sugar Island Ferry*."

"Bein' right about that doesn't get me my shit back," Spyder grumbled. "But, at least it gives us an idea of where they're gonna be workin' from. That's a hell of a lot better than havin' nothin'."

"Whaddya gonna do once we find out where your shit is?" Cash asked. "Get it and ship it back to Frisco? How's that gonna work?"

Spyder did not answer immediately. He thought about it for a few moments, and then he said, "Haven't got all that figured out yet. One thing I can say for sure—two things. I have to get my shit back. And quick. We need it on the street. Right now! My business is going to suffer big if we don't. That's just a simple fact. I still owe fifty percent on that shit. We've got to get our hands on it, and get it out the door."

Both men waxed silent for a few moments. Finally, Cash looked over at his boss and said, "You said there were two things that you could say for sure. But you only told me one thing. What's the other?"

By that time they had pulled fully onto the ferry loading dock and were waiting for the ferry to empty. Spyder shifted into Park, and then looked over at Cash and said, "Once I get my hands on my shit, I can promise you that those two bitches—I get my shit, and they're both dead. … And, as far as their friends are concerned, I don't care if I have to kill them too. They'd better just keep out of my way or they'll all be dead. I just want to get my shit and get the hell outta this stupid state. ... I have no idea what got into Liz's head that made her think she could pull this off. ... And get away with it. I'm fairly sure that it was all Liz's doin'. That other little bitch, Angel. She's too young and naive. I'm pretty damn sure that she's got no idea what's goin' on. In fact, I'm a little surprised that Liz even brought her along. That was stupid. Anyway, I doubt that the kid's even got a clue. It's all on that Liz bitch. ... All I can say is that those two stupid little bitches are gonna pay big time for what they've done to me. And their friends too, if they get in the way. ... First, I'll get my shit back, and then anyone around when I get it—they're dead."

Both men then faced the front and began watching the vehicles file off the ferry.

"Thirteen," Cash said after the last vehicle coming off the island had passed them. "And I don't think it was completely loaded. There were a total of thirteen cars and trucks on that boat. Where do they put them all? Didn't look like they had room for that many cars on that little boat. But that's what was on it."

"Thirteen *four-by-fours* you mean," Spyder said. "Every single vehicle that I saw get off it was four-wheel-drive—pickups and SUVs. What does that tell ya? ... And most of those ahead of us waiting to get on are four-wheelers. All except us, it looks like to me."

No one really knew what Spyder's real name was. Everyone that knew him always referred to him by that one-word appellative—Spyder. That was it.

Furthermore, he never talked about his age. He looked to be in his thirties. That would make him ten or so years older than his assistant seated beside him, and likely about ten years older than Liz as well.

Everyone who knew him acknowledged as absolute fact that he was not a man to be taken lightly. For one thing, even though he never talked about it either, it was commonly known that he had served several years in prison for killing a rival drug dealer in the Tenderloin section of San Francisco. He had originally been charged with Murder One, but he successfully had it pled down to negligent homicide. Most of his time he was able to serve in county lockup under the realignment provisions of California's 1170(h). This law allows the possibility for criminals convicted for certain crimes, and under certain circumstances, to serve their time in one of the state's fifty-eight different county custody facilities, rather than in one that is part of the state prison system.

He also never talked about his time in prison, but others did.

As mentioned earlier, Spyder's helper on this mission was best known by his street name—Cash. However, to refer to him as Spyder's 'friend' would be a bit of an inaccuracy. Cash was not a real friend to anyone, and he was certainly not regarded as such by Spyder. The boss viewed Cash as a man who would follow any order that might be barked in his direction—even should that command call for the death of or damage to any other human being on planet Earth. That is to say, Spyder viewed the man he had invited along on this trip as nothing more than a useful tool, regardless of the task.

And that was appearing to be what this Northern Michigan outing was going to require.

Chapter 6 —

"Exactly how did Angel leave it with you?" Jack asked Kate. "I know you've already explained it to me before. But, please humor me, and do it one more time. Did she in any way specify what she was looking to accomplish with this visit? Was there anything special? Like, did she indicate a particular problem that had her troubled? Something specific that she thought we could help her with? … You know, she would not be seeking us out like this if she regarded us as ordinary neighbors. Here she is, travelling all the way across the country just to pay us a visit. Why is it that she wants to get out of San Francisco, anyway? How did she leave that? Did she explain her thinking here to you?"

"Well," Kate explained, "you already know that she is travelling with a friend. A female named Liz. Angel had told me that one of their mutual associates developed an agenda against this friend of hers—against this Liz girl. Not so sure she's a girl, exactly. She sounds more like a young woman. That is, I think that she's at least somewhat older than our Angel.

"But, the fact remains that this Liz is a friend of hers, and it sounds to me like Liz would not go out with this older man. And apparently he became a little belligerent, or at least persistent. … So, there does seem to be a bit of a problem between Liz and this fellow. I really don't know any more than what I just explained to you. Could be a major problem, or something minor. Don't know. But, I'm sure she will get into it in more detail once she walks through that door, and gets to talking to us, and the boys. And greets Buddy, of course. I have no doubt that she has her reasons for concern. … I'm sure you'd agree with me that my kind smile was not the only factor motivating her to take this pilgrimage east. I just know that when she first called me to feel me out, I did not want to scare her off by slapping some arbitrary restrictions on her—or by asking too many personal questions. I just knew that all of us are really interested in finding out what she's been up to over the past several months. … Especially given the fact that she left us so abruptly when the news of her mother's murder reached her. I don't think she has even glanced in our direction since that day. That is, not until now.

"I completely understand what you're trying to find out, Dad. And I'm right there too. Just realize that I don't have a good answer to your questions right now. I really don't know what she's up to, or what she's thinking."

Red and Robby had stopped eating altogether, and both were paying total attention to the adults' conversation. Jack had picked up on the vibes the boys were sending out, and flashed a wink and a nod in Kate's direction to make her aware of the boys' silent concern. Jack and his daughter ended that discussion right there in order to spare the boys.

Only seconds later, Kate's cell ringer sounded.

"Angel," she said excitedly, making sure she had her dad's attention by turning the speaker on. "Where are you?"

"We're just getting on the ferry," Angel replied. "Is it still okay if we stop in and see you guys?"

"Of course it's okay, you silly girl," Kate said, flashing two fingers toward her father. He read the code and realized that, indeed, Angel was not alone. "In fact, you'll be in big trouble with me if you decide to take a pass on us. You must spend some serious time with us. Dad, me and the boys are all really looking forward to seeing you. … We've got clean sheets on the beds in the guest room. How many of you are there? Will you need more than two guest rooms?"

"It's just me and my friend Liz."

"Are you taking a taxi?" Kate asked. "Or an Uber?"

"Actually," Angel said, "I'm driving my mom's car. Thanks to Uncle Jack I can do that. He had it in storage right by our house. And you, or maybe he, sent me the keys. So, I just unplugged the battery charger, and it started right up. … I hope I can still find your house. You're still living in the same place, I hope."

"Yeah," Kate said, as she placed her cell in the middle of the table so the boys could join into the conversation if they wished. "We fixed the house up a lot, so don't think you've got the wrong place just because it might look a little different. Look for the two new bears out front. They're sculpted out of wood, and are real tall. … Dad and I, and Red and Robby, of course, we're all very eager to see you. Nothing else has changed around here. Even Buddy's all excited to see you. When he heard your voice over the phone, his ears popped to attention, he looked over toward the phone, and his paws started pounding out a rhythm on the dining room floor. I'm sure he's eager to see you too. You're still on the ferry? Right?"

"Actually," Angel said, "We're not quite on the ferry yet. It just pulled into the dock, and cars from the island are moving past us right now. We're just about next to drive on. I thought that I should give you a quick call to be sure it was still okay, and that you're home and looking for us. You're sure it's okay with both you and Uncle Jack?"

"Angel," Kate assured the girl, "we could not be more eager to see you. We have all missed you a ton. Believe me, if you backed out of this visit now, Dad would come after you."

With that last comment Jack flashed his daughter a feigned smirk and shook his head.

"Well, that's not entirely true," Kate said, correcting herself. "But, we would all be hugely disappointed. Both Red and Robby have already run over to the front windows so they can be the first to welcome you. And, yes, Buddy is right behind them. Are you guys hungry? Or do you need to get some sleep first? Traveling long distances takes its toll. Would you like a soft pillow before you start your day?"

"Already started our day," Angel said. "I don't think either one of us could sleep right now. We got a good night's sleep in Appleton. Liz is a little bit nervous about meeting you and Uncle Jack. But, we're not needing to stay there. We can just get a hotel in the Soo—"

"No you can't stay anywhere but with us!" Kate emphatically interrupted. "We wouldn't hear of it."

Even though Angel did not have her speaker on, Liz could hear Kate's response, and, staring straight ahead, she smiled her approval.

Chapter 7 —

Spyder and Cash watched as the whole line began to move slowly forward. Lying on Spyder's lap was a 10mm Glock with an extended magazine. He reached down and opened the center console to temporarily store the weapon out of sight.

"Stick yours in here too," he commanded. "No point raising eyebrows now. I assume that there is only one way on and off this island. I know I can't swim for shit, and I've heard that water's awfully damn cold."

"And deep," Cash replied. "At least on the western side—it's a major shipping channel, I've heard. How deep do you suppose it has to be for that? One hundred feet? Two hundred feet? I'm just guessing. Whatever, I assume that it is way too deep for me to swim in, I know that for damn sure."

"Sometimes you should just keep your stupid mouth shut," Spyder said through his regular smirk. "All you do is show the world just how ignorant you are."

"I'm not stupid," Cash countered. "Do those freighters need more or less water? I think that two hundred feet's pretty close. Right?"

"Their hull's only fifty or sixty feet—and that's *total*, you idiot," Spyder told him. "I'd say that they draw less than thirty feet fully loaded. ... But, that's not really the point, is it? Any damn fool can drown in a mud puddle if he works hard enough at it. I'm no expert, but I'd bet that the channel is about fifty feet deep—more or less. ... But, like I said, any damn fool can drown in a two-inch mud puddle."

The two men were both worn out. However, even though Spyder was immensely fatigued, he could not attribute his belligerent attitude toward Cash to his just being overly exhausted. He always treated Cash in a consistently demeaning fashion—it was just his way with him. While sometimes he was downright ornery with underlings, seldom if ever did he treat those working for him with even a smattering of genuine respect ... not unless they were female, and he was trying to get something out of them—such as sexual favors.

On this day, Spyder's horribly bad attitude was even worse than usual. In this case, it was brought on largely by his total lack of sleep. For three days he had not been able to get any bed rest whatsoever. The reason for that was because he was convinced that Liz was on her way to Michigan's Upper Peninsula with a whole shipment of his drugs. While he was convinced that would be the case, he had no idea as to how she would be making the 2,500-mile trip from San Francisco to Sault Ste. Marie. He could not understand how she would be able to fly with all those illegal drugs, but he could not take a chance on it. So, he and Cash had flown commercial into Sault Ste. Marie, and there rented a car. And then he and Cash had posted watch at the ferry waiting for the two females to try to drive onto the island.

"I'm pretty damn sure that the little bitch is headed to Sugar Island," he had explained several times to Cash, "but I just do not know how she's going to get there. We've got to be diligent until we catch her. So, we will take turns sleeping until we get a good look at her. … Just remember, if you screw up and miss her when it's your turn, I'll pistol-whip your ass until you plead with me to kill you. You got that?!"

Cash was pissed whenever Spyder put him down. That meant that he was severely annoyed at his leader most of the time. However, he dared not respond in a manner even slightly reflecting that anger. Instead, he fought the urge by squeezing harder on the handgrip of his Ruger as he squeezed it into the center console and tried to force the cover closed.

"Never squeeze a loaded gun into a tight place!" Spyder barked, knocking Cash's hands away using a quasi-formed fist. "That's never a good way to treat a gun … or any weapon, for that matter. It'll do nothin' but jam 'em up, or worse. And when you need it, it won't work right. Or you'll blow your own stupid hand off doin' it! … Mine's in there already. That's enough. Stick yours under the seat. It'll be fine down there. Just need to get it outta sight for right now. … Besides, you know as well as I do that both of these guns are stolen. We have no idea what they've been involved with before we got them. I explained all that to you before he dropped them off. We just can't get caught with a gun."

Spyder was absolutely correct in his assessment of the situation. He had called ahead of his trip to have two semi-autos dropped off for his use when he was parked in the lot beside the ferry dock, and that is exactly what had happened when they first got there two days before. But the man delivering the weapons warned him that both of the guns were stolen, and that he should not get caught with them.

Even though he understood that he had acted inappropriately, Cash was still furious with the callous way his leader disrespected

him only minutes earlier. But, he knew better than to object even
a little. So, he lifted his semi-auto out of the console and closed the
cover. He then angrily shoved it under his seat. He stewed silently
for several minutes. Spyder sensed that he had touched a nerve,
so even though he did not appreciate his passenger's attitude, he
knew it was best to keep his mouth shut as he slowly inched toward the ferry.

"Oh shit," Spyder muttered when he saw where the girls ended
up on the boat. "I hope to hell that asshole doesn't put us next to
them. Damn it all! You don't have any choice at all where they
stick you on these damn things! She-it!"

"Try this," Cash said, handing his boss a cap he had packed in
his bag. "I brought two. Thought something like this might come
up. I've got sunglasses too. And so do you, I think. They might
help. … I'll just slide down in my seat a little, they won't suspect
a thing."

Spyder grabbed the cap and pulled it down nearly covering his
eyes. And then he snatched his own sunglasses out of his pocket
and prepared to pay the ferry toll. He lowered his window and
waited his turn. The girls were two vehicles ahead of him getting
on, but he knew that he had no power over where he was ordered
to park on the boat. So he paid the fee silently and waited for directions.

"Twenty dollars please," the large muscular attendant requested as he stood outside Spyder's window.

"Holy shit!" Spyder responded in shock. "You mean it's gonna
cost me twenty bucks every time I drive onto your boat?"

The attendant just glared at him for a short moment, and then
said, "The fee is twenty dollars to ride the ferry over to Sugar Is-

land. It doesn't cost anything to come back to the Soo. ... So, what do you think? Do you want to pay me, or shall I get you off?" Spyder was angry, but he successfully struggled to keep his mouth shut. He opened a rather stuffed, zippered cowhide wallet.

"No problem, sir," Spyder said, as he took a long, labored breath, and pulled a nearly uncirculated twenty-dollar bill from his wallet. After making sure it was a single bill, he forced a smile and handed it to the attendant. "So, I can just drive onto your boat when I'm ready to come back to Michigan?"

"When you're ready to come back to the Soo, you can just drive down the ramp from Sugar Island, and you can get right on the ferry. And, like I said, the return won't cost anything. ... I take it that this is your first time on Sugar Island?"

"Yes it is," Spyder said through the same strained smile. "This is my first time on your beautiful little island. ... We're meeting some friends here."

"Oh, so you've got friends who live here," the attendant said in an effort to be friendly. He had detected the brief episode of animus in Spyder's voice. "What are their names—your friends? I think I know most everyone. I probably know them."

Spyder was taken aback for a second or two. So, he thought for a moment, and then he said, "Oh, our friends don't live on the island. Our friends are actually from Chicago. It'll be their first visit too. They just know some people who do live on the island, and it's their friends who have some riverfront property for sale. But, I don't know their names—the property owners, that is. ... We're all just supposed to meet up a little later at a place called the *Hilltop Bar.* Have you ever heard of it? The Hilltop? Supposed to be straight ahead off the ferry—up the big hill, and then on the left side of the main road. That would be the north side, I think. Does that sound about right to you? … Maybe you could tell me a little bit about that bar?"

The attendant thought about the request a few seconds, and then said, "I think I could. Just give me a few to make my rounds, and I should be able to get back to you. Okay?"

"Great," Spyder said. "If you think you can manage it. Otherwise, that would be fine, too."

"If I'm not able to get back to you, I can tell you that your directions are right on the money," the now-smiling big man said. "It is located just off the ferry and right up the hill. I'm pretty sure you'll like it a lot. But, there's not a lot to choose from. It is the only bar on the island. … I would be happy to tell you a little bit about it, once I collect the fees. I should be able to get back to you—but we'll just have to see. My name is Glen, by the way."

"Fantastic, Glen," Spyder said, now offering up a broad, nearly sincere smile. "But, like I said, I'll understand if you don't have time. It'll all be cool."

The attendant then smiled, and set about completing his task.

The ferry had barely shoved off when Glen walked back up to Spyder's car and tapped on the glass. It made Spyder jerk his head around as though someone had fired a gun at him.

"Great," Spyder said, gaining control of his nerves and lowering the window. "Then you are gonna have a few minutes?"

"Better than that," he said. "We had this little card in the control room. You can just keep it. I'm not sure where it came from, or just how accurate it might be. But, from what I've seen, it looks pretty much on target to me. You can just have it."

"Thanks for that," Spyder said. "I really appreciate your help."

"No problem," Glen said. "Happy to be of help. Hope you enjoy your visit."

The card the attendant had given Spyder was something that had been printed up and used to promote the bar some time ago, and Glen had simply recalled having seen it lying around in the ferry's cockpit. It read:

> The Hilltop Bar is a decades-old, cozy and welcoming establishment located atop a large hill about a mile north of the ferry landing on Sugar Island. That island, Sugar Island, is itself a tiny isle found just east of Sault Ste. Marie on Michigan's Upper Peninsula. As the only place to eat or drink on the island, the Hilltop Bar is a popular spot for both locals and visitors alike.

> Nestled atop a gentle rise, the bar offers a breathtaking view of the surrounding landscape. The rustic wooden exterior and charming patio seating provide an inviting atmosphere to sit and enjoy a cold beer or a refreshing cocktail while taking in the view, or enjoying a fine, casual meal.

> Inside, the bar is simple but charming, with wooden floors, walls, and a high ceiling with exposed beams. The décor is minimal, with vintage signs and pictures of the local area adorning the walls. Several tables and chairs are arranged around the room, inviting patrons to sit and relax.

> The staff is friendly and welcoming, making you feel right at home from the moment you walk in the door. They are knowledgeable about the local area and always happy to share tips and recommendations for things to do and see during your stay on Sugar Island.

The menu at the Hilltop Bar is simple but satisfying, offering a variety of classic casual pub fare such as burgers, sandwiches, and fried foods. The ingredients are fresh (locally sourced when possible), and prepared with tender care.

All in all, the Hilltop Bar is a friendly, unpretentious, and relaxing place in which to unwind after a day of exploring on the island. Whether you're looking for a casual lunch or a place to enjoy a drink with friends, this charming establishment is the perfect spot to do just that.

"Great!" Spyder said after taking a quick glance at it. "Thanks!" Spyder then feigned a sincere smile, nodded his approval, and pretended to quick read all the words on the card. Feeling that he had already revealed too much, he made sure his facial expression signaled that he was definitely finished talking, and he looked into the attendant's eyes and said with a smile, "We're really looking forward to our Hilltop experience." He then turned his face toward the windshield to confirm his signal of finality.

And so, at that point, Big Man Glen took the hint and excused himself.

"You didn't tell me nothin' about no Hilltop Bar," Cash said, not having to feign his frustration at having been kept in the dark about there being a great restaurant on the island—particularly since it was also a bar.

Spyder sneered in disgust, looked down and said slowly, "Keep your damn head down, you idiot. Those bitches might get out of their car to get a better look at the island from the railing. People do that, you know. We don't need them getting a look at us. ... So, just shut the hell up and don't look their way. Not at all!"

Spyder raised his head a bit and took a better look at the dock on the island. "This is one helluva short-ass ride for twenty damn bucks," he griped. "Won't last very long. You should be able to handle using your brain and not your mouth for that long."

Again, Cash was furious. He did not like Spyder to begin with, but now he was getting more and more angry with nearly every word his boss uttered. He always felt inadequate when in the presence of Spyder—and this was proving to be no exception. So, Cash didn't verbally respond. He simply jerked his body around toward the dash, and lowered his head so that the brim of his Los Angeles Lakers cap blocked out his face. And there he sat silently and virtually motionless.

By the time the ferry had pulled away from the dock and was fully in motion, Spyder turned his head a bit and fixed his eyes in the direction of Angel and Liz. "Looks like the bitches are not getting out of their car," he said. "Looks like nobody on the whole boat's getting out. Passengers probably not permitted to. … Can't be more than a half-mile or so—dock to dock. Total. Be no point to get out anyway, I suppose. Maybe they don't let us. Don't matter, nobody's gettin' out. So we don't have to worry about that right now. Just sit still without attracting attention, and stare at your boots … until after they drive off the boat. Can you handle that?"

"Yeah," Cash responded. "I can handle that."

Spyder's observation regarding the length of the ride, while not intended to be so, was actually exaggerated—the distance between docks was closer to eight hundred feet, launch to launch. Plus, because the western dock lay about five hundred feet upstream from the eastern, it meant that the time required to reach the island from the mainland would be substantially less than that required for the return trip.

No matter how hard Cash struggled to control it, he remained fuming at the way his boss had been treating him. And Spyder could tell that there was a major problem.

"Damn it all!" Spyder growled silently in his mind. "Why can't that basic bastard just sit there and keep his stupid mouth shut. I just don't need any more of his idiotic comments right now. Damn him! … But … I suppose I might as well suck it up and be a bit nicer to him. Or at least make an effort. I can't have him staying mad at me like this. I might need him to take out some of these asshole-friends of Liz…. Damn it all! I just have no idea who they are, or what they're capable of. I have no notion as to what I'm dealing with. Guess it's possible that some of them really might be some very bad dudes. Have no idea what they might be capable of."

"Hey, man," Spyder finally said to his less-than-respected sidekick, "Looks like we made it through the first round okay. So far, so good. Now, if we can follow them without being detected, maybe we can find out where they are going—where their friends live on the island, and who they are. You know what I mean—all that kind of shit. … And then, maybe, we can hit that bar I was talking about, and get a beer. How does that sound to ya? And we can come up with some sort of game plan—something that will work—without killing too many of these assholes. And without getting ourselves hurt. Problem is, right now we have no idea who they might be. Can't ask Google a question like that—know what I mean?"

"Yeah," Cash said, clearly appreciating the fact that his leader was beginning to acknowledge him in a quasi–respectful fashion, "Maybe we can figure that out at the bar. What was the name of that place? The bar? Do you know where it is? Think we can find it?"

"Hilltop," Spyder threw out abruptly. He did not like Cash's again demonstrating his ignorance and lack of understanding, but he had made up his mind to tread lightly on his helper. Or, at least an effort in that direction. "Looks to me like it is on the road that leads right directly off this boat dock. They—Liz and her friend— might turn off that road before we actually pass the bar, but that's where it's supposed to be. Obviously, we're gonna have to follow them. But, once we know where they are staying, I'm sure GPS can help us find our way back to the ferry; and it ought to be able to tell us where the bar is. At least in general terms. … But, we still need to find out exactly where the bitch is staying on the island. That's got to be our first job."

"Yeah," Cash agreed. "We'll just follow them from here. Right? And then go have a beer."

"That's how I see it," Spyder replied.

One by one the vehicles drove over the off ramp and headed east down Sugar Island Road. There were now three vehicles between the Toyota Spyder was driving, and the Chevy Traverse with the girls in it.

"Do we need to get in closer behind them?" Cash asked. "Or are we okay back here?"

"We're fine," Spyder replied. "If we go passing cars here they'll notice and get suspicious. We're good for now."

"Right," Cash said.

He wanted to make a comment about how all the vehicles

from the ferry were still heading east on Sugar Island Road, but thought better of it. "That asshole insults me every time I open my mouth," he said to himself. "Just gonna sit here and shut the hell up. I'm sick of him putting me down."

That was probably a wise decision, as he turned to look back just in time to see the pickup directly behind them turn south down Westshore Drive. South Westshore Drive was the first street they passed.

"Did you see that sign back there?" Spyder asked. "The one advertising the Hilltop Bar up ahead? Looks like it's just up here a bit. Right on this road. … This must be the hill that gave the bar its name."

"No," Cash replied, "I didn't see the sign. Where's it supposed to be?"

"Sign said the bar's straight ahead," Spyder said. "Probably at the top of this hill. … Glen, the guy on the ferry, he said it was on the left side of this road, just at the top of the hill."

Spyder's comment about the bar totally captured Cash's attention. From that point on all he was interested in was the bar. For a full minute they continued east up the hill on Sugar Island Road.

"There!" Cash blurted out loudly. "There it is! The bar! That's it on the left!"

His eyes were glued on the bar as they passed it, while Spyder's full attention was fixed on the Chevy Traverse that had already crested the hill and was now nearly a quarter mile ahead of them.

As the girls progressed, Angel's full attention was on the road ahead, and on her limited memory of geographic details; while Liz occupied herself with nervous small talk, and frequent head turns to see if they were being followed.

Chapter 8 —

D o you still remember where they live?" Liz asked. "Your friends, that is. It's been a while since you've visited them. Right? I know I keep asking you that same dumb shit. But, you're not going to get us lost on this little island, are you?"

"I can find it, okay?" Angel replied. "I'm just gonna take my time and be careful. And you're gonna make sure nobody's following us. Right?"

Liz immediately turned around and looked back. "You're paranoid, girl," she said, laughing at her younger friend. "Ain't *nobody* gonna be following us here. ... I'll tell you what I think you should do. I think we should just pull off the road and wait to see if anyone stops behind us—to wait for us to keep going."

"We're gonna be turning up here in a bit, anyway," Angel said. "I don't want to make us a target by stopping right here on the side of the road. ... Take a look back. Ain't nobody following us. Right? If they were, they'd be right up close. Ain't nobody following us. I'm just gonna find Uncle Jack's house. I gotta get changed out of these boots. They're beginning to kill my feet. ... I'm sick of driving, I just want to kick back and have a Coke."

"Do your friends drink?" Liz asked. "They gonna have a beer for me?"

"They do drink some," Angel replied. "But I can promise you they won't be offering us any. In their eyes, we're minors, and they won't be serving us alcohol."

"Oh," Liz said. "So it's like that. They some kind of prudes, sound like. I sure as hell ain't no minor."

Her friend's using that demeaning of a term to define Angel's highly admired near-family friends immediately drew her attention away from any efforts toward caution, and she countered, "Jack and Kate are not prudes. They are absolutely wonderful people. Had my poor mom not been murdered, I think that she and Jack might have got married by now. And I would be calling him 'Dad' by now. … I know my mom loved him. … She even told me she did. He was always kind and caring, to both Mom and me. … And Kate, she was like a big sister. Do not call them names. I won't put up with it."

"S-o-r-r-y," Liz said, stretching the word out to serve for an apology. "I truly did not mean to make you mad. I knew you liked them, but I guess I never considered that your mom might have had feelings for this Jack fellow. I won't do it again. Okay?"

Angel did not reply. She was still a little angry. And, she was crying. Liz realized the emotional impact of her words, and would have liked to have had them back. So, she just shut her mouth about the Handlers and waited out her friend.

It took Angel a while to bridle up the grief for her mother and focus on her driving. But with substantial effort on her part, she was finally able to stop crying. She blew her nose twice, and blotted out her tears, on tissues handed to her by her passenger.

Then, after drying her bloodshot eyes one final time, Angel surveyed their location and said, "I may have missed the turn. But this will work just fine too. … And, no, I am not gonna forget how to find their house. I spent a lot of time at their place on the island—I can find their house. No problem."

Angel's mind was now beginning to race even faster. "They have two really terrific boys," she said. "I went to school with them. And we hung out a lot just messing around on the island. They really knew how to have fun. … I'm sure I can find the Handler resort. That's where they live—it's their house, but it's also a resort. I'll just turn down South Town Hall, and then circle back." Clearly Angel had not mouthed the name of that street by memory—she had simply read it off of the street sign. "We'll be just fine. I'll find it. The only challenge is that when Mom was alive—back when she and I were living in the Soo, she would never let me drive. But, here I am now, behind the wheel. … But, we'll be just fine. I'm positive."

Sometimes we discover that the game life sets on the table before us is one based more on serendipity than on the rules of logic and predictability. Such was the case in this instance. Had Liz not fired off the comment about Angel's not being able to find Jack's house, the odds are great that the young, inexperienced driver would actually not have doubted herself, and consequently actually been able to steer her car along a more direct path, and right up the Handlers' driveway. She most likely would have accomplished the task quite automatically. However, that's not how it worked this time.

This time Liz's innocent suggestion that Angel could be in over her head, and that the two young females might be getting lost, was more than Angel could grapple with and still remain confidently competent. Her friend's comment distracted her to the point that she inadvertently did drive past Brassar, the road she had intended to take, and instead led her east all the way to Town Hall Road.

Now, her observation that they would still be fine turning down South Town Hall was correct—provided, of course, that they paid critical attention as to where they must go, they most certainly would be able to circle back west and find the Handler house. The critical factor about the distraction Liz's comment caused was that it seized Angel's attention away from what might be going on around her by forcing her to devote her entire thinking process into solving the puzzle that lie ahead—finding Jack's house.

What she missed was the significance of that white Toyota also turning south behind them onto Town Hall Road. After Angel missed making her turn down Brassar she had unintentionally sped up a little, reaching the slightly excessive speed of sixty mph. That meant that when she did approach Town Hall, she was forced to brake rather abruptly, making Spyder do the same. While he did not even come close to rear-ending the girls, by the time he began cranking the wheel to the right, he was right up on the Chevy's bumper.

Had Angel been paying any attention at all to the Toyota behind her, the transpiring course of events would have at least startled her. Instead, not only did it not arouse her curiosity, she did not even notice it.

It was that fact, Angel's and Liz's complete oblivion to Spyder and Cash, which proved to be a lucky break for those men. Instead of having his cover blown, Spyder was able to slow down considerably, complete the turn in a reasonably acceptable fashion, and then to successfully fall into line far enough behind the girls so as not to draw their attention. The men were able to accomplish all of this because the girls were so thoroughly preoccupied with the task before them—finding their improvised route to the Handler house. They remained totally blind to the something amiss transpiring in their rearview mirror.

"So," Liz said, doing the best she could in her effort not to again offend or in any way irritate her young friend, "how far do we go on this—what did that sign say—Town Hall Road? That's what it's called? Right? ... I think you told me they lived on the channel—right on the St. Marys River. Isn't that what you had said? That they lived right on the river?"

"Yes," Angel replied. "We'll just go down here for a bit. Maybe a mile or so, I think. And then cut over back toward the river—to the west. Don't remember the name of that street, though. The one that goes south. It might be the only one. Pretty sure it's about a mile."

They drove about a mile and a half, and they approached what appeared to be a fairly well-traveled road that led off to the right.

"What's that sign say?" Liz asked. "Is that it? The sign says it is Lecoy Road. Does that sound right to you?"

"Has to be," Angel said. "I told you I don't remember the names of these streets. But, we are getting pretty far down here. We really need to cut back to the west. I'll give it a shot. Probably the right street. Or road—whatever."

Unfortunately, the girls were so preoccupied with geography

that they were still not paying any attention to the white Toyota that was now making every effort to hang back far enough so as not to be readily spotted by them.

"Aren't you afraid that they are gonna be turning off, and we'll miss them?" Cash asked Spyder. There were a few times that, even though Lecoy was very straight, because of its sizeable hills they would lose sight of the girls' Traverse.

"Then, you do your job!" Spyder barked. "You should be doin' your damnedest not to lose sight of them! So, just keep your stupid eyes open, and your mouth shut. Think you can handle that, Dumbscum?"

Again Spyder had demeaned his helper by appropriating to him another insulting moniker. And, again, Cash struggled his best to avoid losing his temper. Instead of responding to the intemperate question, he squared himself around in the seat, and fixed his eyes straight ahead.

And then, after taking a moment to realize that Cash's suggestion had merit, Spyder stepped on the gas and closed the gap a little. He did not, however, offer anything like an apology.

After driving about a mile on Lecoy, Angel spotted a crossroad coming up. "This might be our road. … In fact, I think it is," she said.

When they got close enough she read the sign aloud. "Brassar," she voiced. "That's it. That's the street I missed earlier. That's what we wanted."

"Turn left I would guess," Liz said.

"Yes, we turn left."

"What do we look for next?" Liz asked. "I'd say it'd be a mailbox with the Handler name painted on it. Right?"

"Sure," Angel said, realizing that she was being mocked. "You look for the mailbox. And tell me when you find it."

"I'll do that," Liz said, as Angel steered the car south on Brassar Road. "How far do we go on this now?"

"We have to turn right again," Angel said. "Have to get over further to the west. The St. Marys is directly west of here. Their house is right on the river, so we turn into their drive just before we hit the water. Have to find Westshore Drive. That's where we turn. I remember that."

Both girls remained speechless for the next couple of minutes.

"It's a couple miles at least," Angel finally said, breaking the silence. "Looks like Brassar ends up here in a bit, and we will turn right. Whatever that street is. It will take us to South Westshore Drive, and then we just follow that pretty much. ... Even I can't get lost from here. At least I don't think I could."

Both girls had their attention glued to the prospects of the road ahead, and neither of them bothered to look backward to see that they were being followed.

"There!" Angel exclaimed as they approached the road they were looking for, "I totally remember this street. Don't remember the name—Six Mile, or something like that. Starts with a number, that's all I remember for sure."

As they got closer, Liz read the street sign, "*S. 6 Mile Rd.*, that sound familiar?"

"Yeah!" Angel responded excitedly. "That's exactly how I remembered it. ... And, right now, I'd say victory tastes pretty sweet to me."

"So," Liz smiled and asked, "you don't really know how far we go on this. Is that the case? It's just that we got the river up there someplace. I suppose we'll have gone too far when we run into an ore carrier, or some other big boat. Is that how we do it?"

"Not when I'm behind the wheel," Angel retorted. "There'll be a Catholic church up here. On the left. That's where we turn."

"We turn right, right?" Liz inquired. "And I think we already passed that Catholic church—won't likely be another one around here, I'd say."

"South Westshore Road—Drive," Angel answered, clearly anticipating their arrival with considerable distress. Even though Kate had assured her that the whole family would welcome her visit, and while she was thoroughly convinced that Red and Robby, the Handlers' two foster boys, would greet her with sincere open arms, she was still a bit ill at ease with the thought of seeing all of them after so long. "Yes, we turn north for a little bit. The St. Marys is up just ahead. We did it. We're here."

After only a relatively short distance on Westshore, they found and turned left on the little street that thoroughly fit Angel's description.

"Well," Liz jested, "I'm not seeing any marching band. Not even a float. Are you sure they're looking for your visit?"

"There you are, Liz," Angel said, pointing to the side of the road. "You asked me about a mailbox with the name 'Handler' painted on it … So, tell me, what does that look like to you?"

"Well, it's a sign, not a mailbox," Liz said, articulating the syllables slowly as she followed her friend's finger with her eyes. "But, I'll be damned, would you look at that. Let's see now, what does it say? If I'm not mistaken, I'm reading: 'Jack Handler, Private Security Contractor'. I'm guessing that would be your Uncle Jack Handler. Am I right about that?"

Angel, correctly perceiving that Liz was toying with her again, did not respond. Instead she concentrated on sizing up the house, yard and vehicles to determine if there had been any significant changes made since she lived nearby with her mother.

"Holy crap!" she marveled. "Would you look at the size of those bears at the door. Aunt Kate said they were huge, but I've never seen anything like that before. ... I can promise you one thing for sure—we are definitely at the right house."

Liz was also thoroughly engaged in studying the house. "You did not describe their house to me like this," she said in a baiting fashion. "This house is a virtual mansion. You didn't tell me it was this fancy. Ho-ly shit!"

Liz's excitement was not wasted on Angel, for while they both knew that they had found the right house, much about it even caught the younger one by surprise. Not only did it look 'fancy' to Angel—more fancy than she had remembered—but it even seemed to her to almost take on an aura of the spectacular beyond what she had remembered.

It was a fact that, as Michigan log cabins go, the Handlers' abode was truly one of the more striking. In fact, it stood out in many aspects even for high-end log cabin constructs anywhere in the country. "Kate was definitely right about the house," Angel said, virtually repeating herself. "There's much about this house that seems very different from what I remember."

While the first cottage Jack had built for the resort on Sugar Island was fine by any standard, he spared nothing when designing a new one after his return from his highly successful clandestine adventure with the Navy SEALs in the China Sea. Because he wanted it to be near perfect in design and implementation, Jack decided to take a few months off so that he could personally over-see the whole huge project there at the Handler family resort.

As log cabins go, no one would argue against the fact that some of them that have been built in Michigan provide the objective observer an absolutely magnificent sight to behold. And Jack, being fully cognizant of the veracity of that statement, determined even before contacting his architect that he would create one of the truly outstanding examples of beautiful log cabin construction in the state. Let me tell you about the result of his effort:

As you approach the cabin from the south, which is the only access accessible, the first things that catch your eye are the two absolutely massive carved bear sculptures standing guard at the entrance. They are Jack's two twelve-foot-tall bears—tagged Bungle and Baloo by Kate. To create them, Jack contracted the Portuguese artist named Rafael, and presented to him images he had shot of the sort of sculptures he had in mind. Rafael then expertly crafted Bungle and Baloo using huge, virtually knot-free walnut logs, to look incredibly lifelike, with piercing eyes and intricately detailed fur.

The closer the visitor gets to the pair of bears standing guard at the door, the more he marvels at the impressive size of these sculptures. They each stand twelve feet in height, and measure over three feet in diameter at their bases.

The cabin itself is a grand, two-story home with a spacious wraparound porch that provides plenty of space for outdoor relaxation and entertainment. Sturdy wooden posts and railings that add to the rustic charm of the cabin support the two-story porch roof.

The front door of the structure is splendidly designed, standing a little over eight feet in height and is constructed of thick, solid wood. Large windows that allow natural light to flood into the home's living area flank the door.

The logs used to construct the cabin are massively thick, providing both structural support and insulation from the harsh, near Canadian elements. The exterior of the cabin is a warm, golden brown color, giving it a surprisingly cozy, inviting feel.

As you step inside, you're greeted with a warm and welcoming interior, featuring a large stone fireplace and exposed wooden beams. The ceilings do not appear to be so, but they stand over nine feet in height. The furniture Jack and Kate chose when they designed the home's interior strikes the first-time visitor as cozy and comfortable, while still tastefully modern. Words that are commonly articulated by first-time visitors describing the décor are "distinctly charming and unique."

Overall, log cabin homes in Michigan are known to serve as examples of traditional cabin architecture. This is especially so when these log homes are complete with all the amenities one might desire to experience for a comfortable and relaxing stay. The Handler cabin aptly fits that bill.

Inside, the cabin is decorated in a stylish and minimalist manner, with clean lines and a monochromatic color scheme that emphasizes the natural textures of the carefully chosen pinewood walls and stone fireplace. The silver interior accents add a subtle metallic shine and serve to further modernize the space.

In keeping with the cabin's natural setting, Jack and Kate had selected a tasteful assortment of artwork and décor, featuring wildlife such as bears, moose and forest-borne waterfalls, always portrayed in snowy landscapes. For the most part, these pieces were presented in the form of large canvas prints or sculptures, creating a focal point in each room.

While the Handler log cabin served as the principal residence for Jack and the boys, it provided for Kate a luxurious retreat in the heart of nature, combining the timeless charm of a cabin with the comfort and style of contemporary design. She was progressively growing addicted to the sense of cascading peace and serenity that swept over her entire being every time she arrived from Manhattan and walked between the two giant bears that stood guard over her family's castle. She always greeted them with a phrase such as this: "And, Bungle and Baloo, tell me, how have you boys been since I saw you last?"

And then, as she walked past him, she would smile and pat Bungle on his rear end.

While both of the girls were so taken aback by the striking appearance of the Handler residence, they were totally oblivious to the two men who turned onto South Westshore Drive behind them. Further, by the time the girls had slowed to read the *Jack Handler* sign, Spyder and Cash were in direct sight of their car, and they also had stopped to watch exactly what the girls were now up to, and where they might go.

Had either Liz or Angel have turned and looked back in their direction, they could have easily spotted them, and possibly even have identified them. But, that did not happen. Instead, Angel was transfixed on what sort of greeting might await her and her friend. She was just too busy dealing with her anxiety to give any mind to very real dangers that were closing in behind their car.

Spyder waited on the road until Angel had pulled totally onto the Handler driveway, and then on up to the house. Once the girls had disappeared from their sight by parking well off the road, the men slowly proceeded to motor on past the drive where they had seen the girls turn. As they did, Spyder declared, "The sign out front said Jack Handler lived there. And that was a dead end drive they turned down. I could make out the river in the background. That would be the channel, I suppose. … And the big house back there—that would be the Handler house, or resort, or whatever the hell it is. That's where the girls are going to be staying."

Spyder then drove further up Sandpiper Lane and looked for a place to turn around.

"You gonna go take care of her now?" Cash asked. "Or we gonna come back after dark?"

"Would you just shut the hell up!" Spyder barked, slamming on the brakes after spinning around and into a drive. He then turned to face Cash with his full attention. Sticking an extended index finger right to the nose of this most disrespected of scullions, he spoke slowly, carefully articulating every syllable: "Pal, you would do much better if you didn't speak at all. But, if you ever feel it absolutely necessary to open your mouth, you should think over your words before you spit them out. I can't even begin to tell you how irritating I find your conversation. So just shut the hell up!"

He then paused for a moment, and took a deep breath before continuing, "Okay? Can you do that for me?"

"Yeah," Cash mumbled, clearly again angered, and nearly provoked to action. "I'll do that."

Spyder saw what his attack had accomplished and struggled to mellow it out a bit. "I will work up a plan, and when I've got one, I'll fill you in on your part. Until then, I need to clear my head and think. … For me to think best, I need silence from you. That's all

I'm saying here. Can you do that for me?"

"Yeah," Cash replied, turning his face away from his antagonist as he answered. "I get what you're tellin' me."

Spyder momentarily considered making an attempt to further mellow out the anxiety level in the Toyota, but after taking another look at the absolute back of Cash's head, thought better of it. So instead, he shifted into reverse and backed out of the drive just in time to see the right rear quarter panel of a Chippewa County Sheriff's vehicle.

"What the livin' shit is he doin' here?" Spyder growled, his words causing his passenger to swing his head around to see what was prompting the sudden exasperation.

Cash opened his mouth to offer his thoughts, but immediately thought better of it.

Spyder then slowly squared the car into the traffic lane of Westshore Drive, and even more slowly slid past the Handler driveway.

Cash started to talk, but again caught himself just in time.

As soon as they were past the Handler house, Spyder sped up until he reached 6 Mile. There he turned east, until reaching Brassar Road. "We're gonna get the hell outta here for now. Need to come up with a masterplan. I wasn't countin' on having to deal with the cops. At least, not at this point."

Cash had managed to keep his mouth shut all through this. But, his mind was racing. As he sat there silently as Spyder picked up speed heading north on Brassar Road, he envisioned himself stealing the drugs that they were after, and then pushing his knife into Spyder's back. "I gotta be done putting up with this asshole's insults," he said to himself. "This shit has got to end. And I've got the perfect shiv to get the job done!"

Chapter 9 —

I guess you really do remember where they live!" Liz nervously commented as she leaned forward to get a better look. "It's been a while since you've been here, but you did a pretty good job finding it. ... Are you scared?"

"Yeah," Angel replied after waiting a few moments to consider her words, "you could say that. I don't worry about the boys at all. They will be happy to see me. And they will welcome you, too. But Jack and Kate. Not sure how they're gonna react. ... Oh! Shit! Don't look now, but we've got a cop on our butt! What the hell could they want?"

Liz stared at their unexpected guests until Angel had parked and turned off the engine.

"Not sure how well my phony driver's license will work on these local cops," Angel said. "Some of them will remember me, maybe. They might know how old I am."

"You're okay for now," Liz said. "You're on private property. They won't ticket you on private property. ... Anyway, we'll soon know, won't we? Here they come. ... Whatever you do, do not look scared. Remember that!"

As the girls got out of the car, the two officers walked over to where Angel was standing.

"Good day, ladies," the officer who had been driving said to them. "This is Deputy Donald Crandle here with me, and my name is Sergeant William Blake. We're here to see Jack Handler. I'd guess that's what you're here for as well. Do you live on the island?"

Angel at first started to introduce herself as a friend of Red's and Robby's, but thought better of it, as it would make the fact that she was driving look questionable to them. So, she said, "No, we don't live on Sugar Island. We're just visiting Kate and Jack. I used to live in the Soo, but now I live out west—in California."

Sgt. Blake glanced briefly at the deputy, and then smiled at Angel. "Hope you don't mind if we walk you to the door. Like I said, we're just here to see Jack for a minute."

"That's cool," Liz said. "We're gettin' an official police escort and all. How often does that happen?"

"I'm sorry, officers," Angel apologized. "This is my friend Liz. She's from California too."

"Hello, Liz," the sergeant said with a smile. "Nice to meet the both of you."

The girls smiled, but did not verbally respond, as they led the way to the front door.

"Oh my God," Sgt. Blake declared with a big smile. "Would you look at the size of those bears. I'd heard about them, but I never imagined that they were as big as that. They're absolute monsters."

"And they've got names," Angel told him. "Aunt Kate told me their names are Bungle and Baloo. That's what she calls them."

Sgt. Blake chuckled and replied, "Knowing Jack, I figured he must have put them there to guard his house."

Buddy had heard them drive up, and he had gone to 'his' window and jumped up to get a good look at his visitors.

While he would most certainly have announced the arrival of the two girls, the sheriff's vehicle and uniformed officers triggered a vociferously alerting series of barks.

Both Red and Robby scurried over to another window, and they were equally alarmed.

"Uncle Jack," Robby said, "Angel and her friend are here, but so are the cops. We've got two cops coming up to the door with them. Come see."

Jack did slowly walk over behind them and took a look for himself.

"There she is," Jack declared upon spotting Angel walking up to the door. "Damn, she's looking more and more like her mother. ... Quite the young lady, that one. ... Wonder why Blake and Crandle are escorting them."

Jack immediately walked over to the door and opened it. "So," he said to Sgt. Blake, "which of your banks did you catch these young ladies robbing?"

Angel knew to expect just such a witty remark from the man she knew best as "Uncle Jack." She merely smiled and walked up to give him a hug.

Liz, on the other hand, was on the verge of a full-blown state of panic. Not only was she highly agitated at the prospect of meeting Jack Handler for the first time, but the fact that two law enforcement officers had showed up at that very moment nearly pushed her over the edge. But, when she saw Angel handling the whole matter so well, she found herself almost able to control her heavy breathing. She was not, however, about to throw her arms around the neck of anyone so fearsome as Jack Handler. Jack did observe her distress, and sought to put her at ease.

As Angel released him from her embrace, he said, "I assume that the young lady with you is your friend Liz. Am I right about that, or did I guess wrong? Kate said you were bringing a friend with you. Maybe you should introduce us."

"Yes," Angel said, turning to face Liz. "This is my friend I told Kate about. This is Liz. And, Liz, this is Kate's father—this is Jack Handler."

Just as Jack's and Liz's eyes met, Buddy came bursting out of the house with Red and Robby.

"Nice to meet you, Liz," Jack said, reaching out to give her a hug. Even though she was a bit hesitant to embrace Jack, she did so anyway.

And then, just as Jack and Liz terminated their brief greeting, Buddy ran up to Angel, tail wagging so hard that it dictated the motions of his entire hindquarters. Red and Robby were right behind Buddy. As soon as Buddy reached Angel, she dropped to both knees and planted a kiss on his nose.

"This is Buddy," she said to Liz. "I told you about him. He is absolutely the most special dog in the world. Everyone just loves him."

This felt to Liz like her opportunity, so she fell to her knees beside Angel and said, "I just love dogs. … And, I see what you mean about special. He is just the best dog ever. He didn't even jump up on you. What a great fellow he is!"

Both of the girls continued loving on Buddy. But, when the boys reached Angel, she stood up and hugged each of them with all the energy she could muster—Red first. She then put her hand on Liz's shoulder, and said to her, "These are my friends. The ones I told you about. This is Red. He's the one with the red hair, obviously. And the one standing behind Red—that's Robby. And, boys, this is my good friend, Liz."

"Hi, guys," Liz said. "Angel told me all about you. And all the fun you guys had. Sounds like you lead an exciting life."

Robby greeted her by name, and Red smiled broadly and reached out to shake hands. It was obvious that the two boys were both a little ill at ease with meeting a new girl.

Just then Angel, who was becoming more relaxed by the second, spotted Kate emerging from the house drying her hands on a towel.

"Kate!" Angel called out, as she turned and hurried over toward where Kate was standing. "Liz, come over here with me. I want to introduce you to Kate."

Kate tossed the towel on the floor inside the door and quick-stepped in Angel's direction.

The two met at the top of the porch steps, and shared a sincere, unhurried hug.

"I missed you a lot," Angel said to Kate, not quick to let up on their hug. Both struggled to restrain tears.

"I know," Kate said, "I've missed you too. How have you been? Really? We've been thinking about you every day. It was sure good to hear from you. Tell me about yourself. How are you doing? Are you in school?"

Angel did not answer Kate's questions. Instead, she changed the subject by saying, "Aunt Kate, this is the friend I told you about. This is Liz. She's from San Francisco. So am I, actually. Now. I live in San Francisco, now, too. You remember? I told you about Liz?"

"Yes, of course," Kate said, releasing Angel from her arms, and engaging Liz in a brief but sincere hug.

"Liz," Kate said, "I am so glad that Angel brought you with her. It is a real pleasure to meet you. Angel hasn't told us much at all about you, but what she has said has all been good. So we have a lot of 'getting to know one another' to do. ... Angel has been like a member of our family. And, I am sure that if she likes you, so will we."

"Angel is a great friend," Liz said. "And, she has had so many nice things to say about you and your father, and the two boys, Red and Robby, I believe. I'm really eager to get to know the family."

"I just want you to know that you are very welcome here," Kate said. "You girls can stay as long as you want. Feel free to treat this as your home while you're here."

"That is so nice of you," Liz said. "I'm not sure exactly what Angel has in mind, but I don't think we will be staying that long."

"Well, just so you know, you're very welcome here. Okay?"

"Thanks for all your hospitality," Liz replied. "I truly appreciate it."

"Kate speaks for me in that respect," Jack said, looking directly at Liz. "I'm Jack, Kate's father. ... And, I have to say that I am still wondering, however, what you young ladies did to attract the law. If you didn't rob a Chase bank, what exactly is it that you did do to get their attention? Care to spell it out for me?"

Both uniformed officers looked at Jack and smiled. Liz took him somewhat seriously, but Angel knew that he was kidding with them.

"Jack," Sgt. Blake said through a large grin, "I'm sure you remember our appointment out here at your house. Right? To discuss that matter ... the issue we talked about last week. These young ladies have nothing to do with our visit."

Liz was clearly shaken by Jack's comment. And now, even though Sgt. Blake's explanation helped relax her a little, Jack saw through her theatrical façade that she was hiding something; and that whatever that something might be, it was above all immensely powerful in her mind.

"Of course," Jack said to Sgt. Blake. "I asked you men to stop out and see me. Must have slipped my mind for a minute. Maybe we should handle it like this. We can step into the house. I'll pour us a cup of coffee, and we can sneak up to my office. And these young folks can get reacquainted. It's been a long time since they've had a chance to talk. ... What do you think? Kate. That sound okay to you?"

"I think that would be perfect," she agreed. "I know I'm eager to hear all about what Angel's been up to. And I'm sure the boys feel the same way. ... I know I've got some absolutely wonderful sourdough donuts in the freezer. I can slip them into the oven, and bring them up to you. How does that sound? Ready in probably twenty minutes or so. Sound good? ... Coffee is all set right now. I had just put a pot on after these young ladies called to let us know they'd be stopping in."

"I won't fight a cup of coffee right now," Jack said. "And I'm sure my friends here wouldn't object either. That would be great. Just knock on the door when they're ready. And thank you."

With that the three men went up the steps to Jack's private office, and closed the door.

Kate set about preparing the sweet treat for their guests—for the two girls and the uniforms. As she set about preparing the snack, she came up with an idea.

"Boys," she said. "Why don't you take the ladies out to the garage and show them the car you've been working on. Go ahead and start it up and let them hear it, but I don't recommend your driving it yet, because it doesn't have a legal plate, and these are officers of the law that your Uncle Jack has up in his office. I'm sure you know what I'm getting at. I'll call you in when the donuts are ready. Sound good?"

Robby looked over at Red to get his thoughts. Red was nodding his agreement, and so Robby replied, "Sounds good to us. How about it, Angel? Want to see our new car?"

Red then hit Robby on the arm with the back of his hand, and motioned with his other hand with a pointing motion at the driveway.

"Yeah," Robby said. "I'll ask Kate."

"Kate, Red and I think we'd like to take the girls up and down the driveway. That should be alright, shouldn't it? As long as we don't take it on the road. Nothin' illegal about that, right?"

Kate looked directly at Red and said, "Nothing illegal about that. You're right. But, do not do anything crazy that gets their attention. Stay on private property, and off the road. If you get their attention, we could have a problem. Just be sensible—totally sensible. Got that?"

Robby quickly opened up the broom closet off the kitchen hall and plucked the key to the garage from its hook. He searched for a moment for the car's key, but Red let out a soft yet discernable utterance, and pointed at the garage when Robby looked at him.

"Ah," Robby said. "The key's in it?"

Red nodded.

"Ready to check it out?" Robby said to Angel and Liz.

Angel was closest to the outside door, so she opened it and said, "Let's go do it."

Angel was the first out, followed by Liz, Robby, and then Red.

As they walked toward the garage, Robby asked Angel, "Red and I noticed that you were driving a car. Where you livin' now? California? Right? They let you drive at fourteen out in California?"

"I've got a driver's license," Angel said. "A real one. Want to see it?"

Robby did not answer her verbally, but he did hold out his hand to receive it. When she removed it from her billfold and handed it to him, Red slid in closely and examined it over his shoulder. Immediately he, Red, pointed to the recorded birthdate, and mumbled a noise.

"Your driver's license says that you are sixteen. You're the same as us. Right? Fourteen? We're fourteen, and you're still fourteen. … How'd you get that? Can you get one for us?"

"We know a man, out in California, who can get these printed up," Angel said. "I needed to get a job, and I couldn't do that at fourteen. I had to be sixteen. … And, no, we can't get one for you. They're all legal and everything. At least, kinda legal. But, we still can't order a beer or anything like that. Not in California, and not here. Still too young for that. But I can drive, legally. … If I want a beer, Liz has to get it for me."

Angel's last comment did not reflect reality. Liz had never bought alcohol for Angel. And, in fact, Liz had never drunk alcohol when with her younger friend.

Red and Robby did a quick look at each other, and Robby said, "Liz is twenty-one? Really?"

"Yeah," Liz chimed in. "I'm *at least* twenty-one."

"Liz," Angel clarified, "Liz is more *twenty-one* than I am *sixteen*, if you know what I mean."

"I don't want to talk about that," Liz said, jumping into the conversation. "Show us your car. When did you guys get a car?"

"Three months ago, I think," Robby said as he unlocked the garage. "Uncle Jack took it as payment from a client that couldn't pay him. It's a *great* car. He gave it to us if we can get it running. … Well, we got it running, but now we're tuning it up, and fixing some rust on the body. And, there's some stuff that needs work on the interior. It's gonna be a monster, when we're done."

"Oh my gosh!" Angel gasped. "It is beautiful. What is it? Looks like a Mustang. Is that what it is?"

"Exactly," Robby said. "You hit it right. It's a 1965 Mustang. I think it was their second year of production."

Red hit him on the arm and shook his head. And then he held up his index finger.

"Red's saying that it was the first production year," Robby said. "He's probably right. I thought it was introduced in1964, but he's saying that it was '65. Whatever it is, when we get it done, it's gonna be worth a pretty penny." .

"You gonna sell it when you get it fixed up?" Angel asked, looking a little surprised.

"Never!" Robby said emphatically. "We ain't never gonna want to sell it. … Uncle Jack said that when we turn sixteen he'll sign it over to us. … We can't wait for that day."

The 1965 Mustang is, of course, an iconic car from the classic American muscle car era. It was known not only for its sporty and stylish design, but also for its buyer-friendly sticker price.

Jack had told the boys that the vibrant and eye-catching buttercup yellow exterior of this Mustang would make it stand out on the road, and that if they fixed it up nicely, and then took care of it properly, their "Stanger" (that's the name Jack gave it) would hold its value for many years to come.

The exquisite black interior of Stanger provided a striking contrast to the dazzling exterior, giving this car an elegantly classic look.

While evidencing some minor signs of wear and tear, the interior was truly impeccable, arraying all of the original hardware and features in a very well-preserved condition. It was quite evident that all of the utilitarian features (such as the seats, dashboard, steering wheel, etc.) had been well-maintained, so that the overall look of the interior was already clean and nearly pristine.

In addition to the original hardware, Stanger was also equipped with an upgraded music system. In fact, both and Angel and Liz marveled at the fact that the specific sound system installed by the previous owner had been carefully chosen not only to provide high-quality audio, but also because it genuinely graced the appearance of the automobile—it literally integrated so perfectly with Stanger's original design that it provided a modern touch while still regaining a genuine vintage look and feel.

"That's *absolutely* great," Angel said. "But I think I can just see it now. You two are going to be fighting to see who gets to drive it. And it's gonna turn out to be one big, ongoing battle."

"Maybe not," Robby objected. "We might share it pretty good."

"No way," Liz said. "Angel's right. I can tell you exactly how this is gonna work out. One of you will get caught speeding, or driving without a license, or, God forbid, get a DUI. … And he will get a ticket. When that happens, your Uncle Jack will tell the one who didn't get the ticket, that, from that point on, he—the one without the ticket—he's gonna be the designated driver. And then that one will get a ticket. Then, neither one of you will be able to drive it. When that happens, one or both of you will be sneaking around and driving it without permission. And I don't think your Uncle Jack puts up with very much shit. So, when that bad boy gets caught driving, he'll snatch up the key. And that will be the end of your driving. … Maybe for a long time. Years, perhaps. Maybe forever."

"That sounds just about like him," Angel agreed with a chuckle. "Now, what is this? Is that a four-on-the-floor? … Is that what that is?"

"Sure is," Robby said proudly. "Four-on-the-floor. And it's got the biggest engine the 1965 came with—it's the 289 cubic inch, with a four-barrel carb, putting out 271 horsepower."

Angel noticed that Robby had all the brag-worthy facts about the engine memorized, which made her skeptical as to whether he actually understood what they all meant.

"I really don't understand what *cubic inch* stands for," Angel confessed. "So, a lot of that stuff is wasted on me. And a 'four-barrel carb'? I doubt that has much to do with your diet. Does it? You know—carbs. … Speaking of *carbs*—I wonder if Aunt Kate's got those donuts ready yet. I remember having her donuts when Mom and I visited. They are pretty damn good."

With the use of that pejorative (which she had offered specifically for the boys' benefit), Angel triggered a reaction from both Red and Robby, causing each of the boys to toss a curious glance at one another. They were not used to hearing Angel use any depreciating terms of slang beyond pedestrian words like *darn, gosh, dang*, etc. Angel immediately realized that what she had done was a mistake, and she determined to force herself not to go there again.

"Speaking of food," Angel continued, "we really have not had anything to eat since getting to town. Think we could head back up to the house and see if Aunt Kate's got those donuts ready yet?"

"Sure, we could do that," Robby said. "But we had hoped that you could take us out for a drive. Don't you want to get behind the wheel of a real 1965 Mustang?"

"Yeah, we'd really like to do that," Angel said. "But I'm not so sure that it would be a good idea to do with those two cops in the house talking to your dad. Even though I've got a license, they might remember me and know that I'm your age. ... Maybe after they leave—like tomorrow—we can try it. Right now, Liz and I are starving, and nothing would taste better than one of Kate's fresh-baked donuts. Right, Liz?"

"I totally agree with you on that one," Liz said, as she turned and started walking toward the garage door.

The other three followed her lead and they all headed toward the house. Red left last, after he made certain that all the lights had been turned off, and the garage door had been properly secured.

"I see that the Chevy Traverse you young ladies arrived in is registered to one *Millie Star*," Sgt. Blake said to the girls as they walked in. "May I ask how you ladies know Millie Star?"

"She's my ... " Angel started to say. "She was my mother. ...

She passed on a few months ago, and she left the car to me. I just haven't transferred it yet to my name. I've been living out west."

"That's how Mr. Handler explained it to me," Sgt. Blake said. "But, I should tell you that it could save you a lot of aggravation if you took care of that A.S.A.P. Not likely that Mr. Handler will always be around to clarify matters on down the road. … I think that all of us in my office know him personally, and he can be a big help, if you know what I mean. He asked me not to cite you ladies this time. So, just get that paperwork squared away soon. Okay?"

"I'll take care of it right away," Angel said nervously. "I promise."

Sgt. Blake immediately picked up on Angel's agitation, but thought better of making a point out of it. *What good would it do right now for me to pursue this issue with the girls?* he asked himself. *I'm sure Jack will get to the bottom of it when we leave. … Besides, we will most certainly be back on the island after a bit.*

The law enforcement warning totally escaped the attention of the two boys, as they were now already planning their entire week. While Kate had earlier shared with them some of what she knew about the girls' visit, she too was missing most of the details of what Angel had in mind. Angel's revelation provided Red and Robby with substantial fodder for *excitement planning*—now that they knew for a fact that the girls would be staying for at least one more day. That piece of information had provided for them all the hope they needed to begin planning their playground for fun, and it incorporated a plethora of teenage activities that could take a full week or more to fully appreciate.

But then, Red had a thought that ran counter to the emotional rush that Robby seemed to be experiencing.

"Angel didn't come all the way from California just to drive our '65 Mustang around the island," he told himself. "That's a long ways to travel for no good reason. Besides, she knew nothing about *Stanger* until Kate told her. ... She and Liz have a problem. ... Something is very important to her—and it's bothering the both of them. I can see it on Angel's face when I talk to her. She's wanting some help with something. I just don't know what it could be—not yet."

"Good timing, you guys," Kate said as she took the final tray of donuts out of the oven. Both of the officers were already sitting at the table with Jack, and at least the deputy appeared to be on his second sweet treat.

"Why don't you kids wash your hands," Kate instructed, "and then grab however many that you can eat, and find a seat at the table. I've got milk and orange juice set out already. If you'd prefer coffee, help yourself. ... Do either of you girls drink coffee? I know the boys don't drink it. Yet, at least. Thank God! But, I won't assume anything about you young ladies. And, there's water, of course. Just make yourself at home."

"I think I will have coffee," Angel said. "And, I know Liz drinks coffee. I think we both tanked out on it driving here."

"That's interesting," Jack said to himself. "I wonder why they would want to drive all the way from California? That would be a terribly long, hard drive. Seems like they would choose to fly. Wonder why they did it that way?"

Each girl set a single pastry down on the table, and both poured themselves a cup of steaming caffeine.

The boys each had a glass of milk—and they did so with no deliberation, as they weren't actually given a choice.

"Well, Jack," Sgt. Blake said, after drinking the last of his brew, "Be sure to get back to me about that issue we talked about earlier. I'm certain it will prove very important to the both of us. I trust you know what I'm getting at."

The "earlier" to which the sergeant was alluding was that twenty minutes or so they spent with him in his office, while the four younger ones were out flirting with the boys' 1965 yellow Mustang. The adult conversation in question had to do with a report from Drug Enforcement that a reputable confidential informant had provided information about a possible effort underway to expand a drug cartel's operation to sell fentanyl in Michigan's Upper Peninsula, and that the organization which that CI was discussing operated largely out of the San Francisco Bay Area.

The part of the whole story that had piqued Jack's attention the most was that the warning had been issued by a *San Francisco* branch of the DEA. Given that the two girls visiting with them were currently living in San Francisco Bay Area, and given the fact that neither he nor Kate had any solid information regarding what had prompted their surprise visit, Jack was not comfortable enough to relax about his new visitors. No matter how badly he would have liked to simply accept Angel and Liz into his home without any hesitation, his many years as a detective were making it difficult to open his arms too widely at this point.

Jack had informed the officers that he had not heard a word about any such effort. "But," he told them, "if and when I hear anything that might relate to this type of activity, I'll get right on it and reach out to your office."

"The warning appeared credible to Drug Enforcement," Sgt. Drake had said, "because it suggested that this same organization would also be supplying heroin and cocaine. Quite often those three drugs are sold together. And while the CI could not provide specific dates or names, he did tell the DEA that Sugar Island was specifically mentioned.

"Apparently," Sgt. Drake continued, "the reason Sugar Island was selected was because of its proximity and accessibility to the Canadian border. We all know that almost all the water that now flows past Sugar Island, does so through the part of St. Marys River that passes on the southern side of the island—through the shipping channel."

"That's what you'd expect," Jack had thrown in, "because the Army Corps has to keep that branch of the river cleaned out for the big boats. It's only obvious that the navigability of the northern channel would begin to atrophy ... especially over time."

"Well," Sgt. Drake picked up, "as it stands right now, a man could wade all the way across sizeable parts of the northern leg of the channel. If a smuggler is wearing thermal clothing, and works at night, he could likely be successful bringing the drugs onto Sugar Island undetected. ... And, that's how we think the smuggling will eventually take place.

"But," Sgt. Drake continued, "for right now, it appears that this leg of the network is still in the developmental stage. That's why we're—I'm talking about officers out of my office—that's why they're a little surprised to see the drugs entering this market from the south. Over the ferry. Seems a little skewed to some of our guys. But, what do you do? The word is that the CI has a great history for accuracy."

Once the officers had finished their coffee, and after they had delivered their warning to Jack, they were ready to head back off the island.

"Ladies," Sgt. Blake said to Angel and Liz as he stood to leave, "it was a pleasure meeting you two. We trust you will have a fun visit ... and safe travels back to California—or wherever you go from here. If Jack fails to show you a good time, give me a call. Or, even better, just let Kate know about it. I've heard she keeps him on a pretty short leash."

Immediately after he'd said that, Deputy Crandle flashed a purposed glance at Jack to capture his reaction to what seemed to him a seriously cavalier comment. But, all he caught was a muffled chuckle emanating from Jack as he stood to walk his two county officer friends to the door.

After the officers expressed their gratitude to Kate, and excused themselves, Jack walked them through the door and out toward their vehicle.

"So," Jack asked, "what do you make of our two house guests? Do you fellows have any questions for them, or issues *with* them? Are they why you boys came by to pay me this little visit?"

"Jack," Sgt. Blake replied, stopping and turning to face his inquisitor, "I was totally square with you. We came out here for exactly the reason I stated. We had no idea that those young ladies were going to be here. We honestly do not suspect anything. ... Yes, we are now aware that they are visiting from the Bay Area. But, as far as we know, that means nothing whatsoever."

Jack was about to respond, but Sgt. Drake was not finished.

"You, Jack my friend, have more experience as a detective than anyone I've ever known. And, you're also better at it than anyone I've ever known as well—by far. In fact, you'd be the absolute last person in the world I would ever think of trying to mislead. So, if those girls are trying to put something over on you, I have no doubt that you will get to the bottom of it. And then you would contact my office, if you believed it necessary."

"Well," Jack said through a broad smile, "enough said about that. Time to move on. ... But, you are absolutely right. I will assure you that you can count on my cooperation. Should I turn up anything that gets my attention, yours will be the first bell I ring."

Just as Jack approached the door on his way back into the house, he met Liz coming out.

"Taking off already?" Jack asked.

"No," she replied. "Kate invited us to spend a few days here, and I was just grabbing some of my stuff from the car—toothpaste and the like."

"Need a hand with anything?" Jack offered.

"I'm good," she said. "Nothing heavy. I'll be right back in."

Jack accepted her response and re-entered the house. Liz continued on to Angel's Chevy Traverse, and popped open the rear hatch. Inside were three bags: a very large check-in type bag, and two small overnight cases. Two of the three belonged to Liz.

The first thing she did was to set the two overnight cases out of the vehicle and onto the drive. She looked around to see if there were any eyes on her. Detecting none, she removed a key from her jean pocket, and unlocked a small padlock from a huge zippered suitcase. She then surveyed her surroundings once more, and then removed the two small locks that secured the nylon straps that passed around the entire unit. But, before she unzipped the bag, she scrutinized her surroundings yet once more.

Finally confident that no one was watching or approaching, she slipped on a pair of surgical gloves, and then unzipped the bag a bit and quickly examined the contents. While it was not yet totally accessible, she was able to peel back the cover enough to do a quick examination of some of the contents. What she was admiring was that without even getting into that bag deeply, she was still able to spot over a dozen large sealed plastic bags containing a huge quantity of pale blue pills, and several kilo bags filled with white powder. "I wonder how many bags of coke I've got here. Damn, this is a fortune. And still most of the big bucks is back in the storage facility where I left it."

She did only a cursory examination of the contents. Finding the merchandise secure and undamaged, she then quickly re-secured the large suitcase, discarded the surgical gloves, closed the hatch and locked the Traverse back up. It was with a great sense of satisfaction, and a large smile on her face, that she retrieved the two small overnight bags from the driveway and headed back toward the house.

Jack, on the other hand, was not experiencing anything similar to her euphoric reaction. Upon entering the house he had immediately retreated into the bathroom and locked the door behind him. Liz was totally unaware of the video camera above and to the right of Angel's parked Chevy Traverse. She never heard, or even sensed that there could be, a miniature zoom lens focusing in on her as she inventoried her small fortune in drugs.

"Oh shit!" he mumbled quietly as he watched what transpired on his cell. "This puts a whole different wrinkle on what the next few days are going to look like around here."

Chapter 10 —

S pyder had nervously watched as the patrol car pulled into the Handler drive. And he waited there until he had witnessed the cops entering Jack's house. As soon as the uniforms had passed the two bears and disappeared inside, he quickly slid out of his parking spot and rapidly headed back to 6 Mile. He then followed that east to Brassar, which he followed back toward Sugar Island Road. Up until this point neither man talked.

"We headed off the island?" Cash finally ventured to ask.

"We're going to the bar," Spyder barked. "Thought you wanted a beer."

"I do. That sounds good to me."

After their earlier exchange, Cash was hesitant to engage his boss in any conversation at all, particularly if it involved any ideas of his own that he might venture to put forth. Nevertheless, because his curiosity was beginning to get the best of him, he'd decided to take a chance.

"You figure they've got the drugs in their car?" he finally asked.

Spyder took a deep, disgusted breath and said, "We don't use that word. If you must bring it up at all, you should refer to it as 'merchandise.' Or, you can call it the 'shit.' I'll know what you're talking about. ... Got it?!"

Cash grimaced and turned his eyes toward the windshield. "Here we go again," he said to himself.

"Look, Cash," Spyder said. "You never know who is listening to what you say. You just *can't* know. So, you just *never* allow yourself to utter that word. ... Just always remember, if it is a word or a concept that can get you in trouble later, then don't let it slip out of your mouth. That is a good rule to live by."

"I can do that," Cash said. "But we're just riding around in a rented Toyota—in a strange state. No one knows us here. How could *anyone* be listening in on what we say?"

As soon as Cash had completed his sentence, he wished he could reel it all back in.

"Every human being with blood flowing through his brain knows that the law can activate our cell phones to record and transmit," Spyder explained, while clearly showing his disgust. "We would not even know that it was happening. They could do that even here in Michigan's Upper Peninsula. ... We'll go in the bar, and ... What was the name of that bar?"

"The Hilltop Bar," Cash responded.

"We'll go into the Hilltop and get a beer," Spyder said, after several silent minutes. "But, before we go in, we'll power down our cell phones, and leave them in the car. ... You're not expecting a call from your girlfriend up here on Sugar Island, are you?"

"Hell no," Cash said. "You know better than that. I don't know nobody in Michigan. I don't think I ever said a word to anyone from this place. And I got no girlfriends outside California. ... None outside the Bay Area, actually."

"Then, that's what we'll do," Cash said. "We'll turn our phones off and leave them in the car. And then we'll get ourselves a beer and make some plans."

Cash then pulled his cell out and powered it down.

"Your cell turned off?" he asked.

"Yeah, I'm good," Spyder replied.

"Then," Cash asked, "are we safe to talk about the ... the merchandise?"

"Can't say we're ever totally safe to talk about it, but I'd say our odds are pretty good. We still need to exercise caution."

"Okay, then," Cash ventured to ask, "Do you know where the merchandise is right now? Or where it might be?"

"That's pretty simple," Spyder offered. "I would have to say that it is likely to be in one of two places—either they've stashed it in that storage building, or house, wherever it was that the girl had her car stored. Or, they have the merchandise with them. Now, while it is possible that they may have taken the merchandise in the house with them, I would think that to be highly unlikely. You don't just go taking that sort of shit into the house of a person you just met. ... So, odds are that those little bitches are just planning to leave it in their car, or, they did drop it off where it was that they had that Traverse stored. They would have pulled off the transfer when they picked up the Traverse. Cash, it is simply just a game of deduction."

Cash gave it a minute to think about it, and then said, "What the hell 'storage area' are you talking about?"

Spyder did not wish to discuss the topic at that time, but decided to give Cash a brief answer. "Look at it like this," he said. "The Traverse they were just now driving had a Michigan license plate on it. Right? In case you didn't look, it *did* have a Michigan plate. That's how we know that they handled a switch with the cars—might have switched the merchandise at the same time. ... Enough of that shit! Just drop it!"

As they walked into the bar, Spyder surveyed the seating possibilities and spotted a table in the southeast corner that looked like it had a window that might afford them a fair view of Sugar Island Road.

"Can we have that booth over there?" he asked, pointing at the corner table.

"Sure," the gal seating guests replied as she led the way in that direction. "Don't see why not. Wanna keep an eye out for traffic, right? Nothin' wrong with that. ... Can't be too careful, you know. Somebody might be following you."

While that was not the reaction Spyder might have hoped for, he opted not to respond. Cash followed his lead and kept his mouth shut as well. Spyder was surprised at his helper's restraint. "I just hope that asshole can just keep his big mouth shut for a change," he said to himself.

The same gal that seated them then said, "And I'll be your waitress today. My name is Billie. What'll it be for you boys?"

"Whaddya got on tap?" Spyder asked.

"Oh, we got just about everything in a can—Bud, Miller—"

"Miller Lite," Spyder interrupted. "I think Miller Lites would be perfect—that'll do us just fine. Two Miller Lites, please. ... And maybe a couple menus. That'd be perfect. Can you do that for us?"

"Two Miller Lites comin' up," she said. "Menus are already on the tables. Anything else right now?"

"Nope," Spyder said, "that'll do it for now."

As soon as the waitress had walked away, Cash looked across the table and said, "Do you think she suspects something?"

"What the hell you talkin' about?" Spyder asked him, impatient if not actually perturbed.

"That shit about someone following us," Cash replied. "Think she's a problem?"

"That girl was just making simple conversation," Spyder replied as he flipped his menu open.

Cash correctly determined to drop that line of conversation, even though it went against his inclination.

"Shit!" Spyder complained. "All I got are trees and bushes outta this window. Can't see over a damn thing! I guess we'll just have to give them a little time—till the cops leave. And then we'll take a drive back and see if the girls are still there. I'm guessing that's the house they're staying in … would figure. Those damned cops sure as hell will put a new wrinkle in this whole bowl of shit. … Damn 'em. They always make everything more difficult."

"You boys know what you'd like to have with these beers?" the waitress asked as she set two frosty mugs down with the cans of Miller Lite. "Or, would you like a little more time to look at the menus?"

"Let's try one of these," Spyder replied as he pointed at a picture of a cheeseburger on the menu. "You can bring me this. With some fries. … Cook it medium—if that means pink."

"Perfect," she said, switching her attention over to Cash. "And, how about you? What would you like?"

"Same thing sounds good," he said. "Except make mine medium well."

"You got it, darlin'," she said. "And you'd like fries too?"

"Yup," Cash said. "And maybe another can of beer."

"Will do," she said. "And would you like these on separate checks?"

"One check," Spyder replied, "and I'll take it."

"We'll get 'em right on," she said. "You're gonna love the food. We got a new cook and she makes everything just great."

"Lookin' forward to it," Spyder said, sliding his menu to the far end of the booth.

The waitress took the hint, smiled, and headed toward the order window.

Spyder parted the blind a bit and again examined the view from their window.

"Damn it!" he groused, "I can't see for shit outta this window!"

However, his whole scenario soon changed. He was barely halfway through his meal when a county patrol vehicle suddenly appeared outside the window that had so irritated him earlier.

"Well I'll be damned!" Spyder mumbled slowly. "There's those stinkin' cops we just ran into."

Cash spun around and took a look out of the blind to see what had captured Spyder's attention. "Damn," he said. "Are you sure that's the same cops we ran into out at the house?"

"Keep your voice down, you idiot," Spyder growled at Cash, as he leaned into him. "Of course it's the same car! How many cop cars would you expect to see on this little island? ... And those assholes are about to come in here! ... Are you carryin'? Drugs or guns? If so, go in the john and dump 'em right now. If it's a gun, wipe it down first, and then toss it. Flush any drugs. … These bastards might be after us."

"No," Cash replied. "I'm clean. *Totally* clean. My gun's still under the seat. You remember I put it there."

"Right," Spyder said nervously, "Mine's in the car, too. … Now, don't stare at them at all when they come in. Just eat your food and don't look at them."

"How 'bout you?" Cash asked his mentor. "You clean too?"

Spyder did not respond verbally—he simply flashed him a look of disgust. "They're comin' in," he said a few moments later. "Remember what I told you."

As Blake and Crandle headed toward the entry, Spyder and Cash each made their best concerted effort to focus attention on anything except for the two men of law enforcement.

"Maybe we should get outta here," Cash said.

"We would," Spyder agreed. "Except, I haven't got the check yet. Can't leave until I take care of that."

Spyder turned to get the waitress's attention, but she was preoccupied with explaining an order to the kitchen. Finally, the cook spotted him sending a signal and she pointed over at him for the benefit of their waitress. She immediately turned and walked over.

"Can I get anything else for you gentlemen?"

"We're good," Spyder said. "You can just bring me a check."

"How did you like your burger?" she asked. "Pretty good, wasn't it?"

"Absolutely terrific," he said. "We loved them."

"I thought you would," she said. "Our new cook is just marvelous. … I'll ring it up and bring your bill right back to you."

As Billie walked up toward the cash register, she stopped to greet the two county cops. She seemed very familiar with them, which made Spyder even a bit more wary of the whole situation.

Determined not to send the undesired signal, Spyder turned back to the few French fries remaining in front of him, dipped a couple of them in ketchup, and popped them in his mouth. "Remember what I tell you," he warned Cash, "do not stare at them."

"Uh oh," Cash said, with a wide-eyed glare directly at the man sitting directly across from him, "Don't look now, but I think our visitors are headed this way."

"Really!" Spyder exclaimed quietly. "If they are, just let me do all the talking—do not open your mouth. And do not talk to them."

"Excuse me, gentlemen," Sgt. Blake said, having walked up to their booth. Deputy Crandle had taken a seat at the bar and ordered two diet Cokes. After having ordered, the deputy took a long sip on his straw, and then turned half way around and began taking inventory of the conversation between the sergeant and the two men at the window booth. "Tell me, are you two residents of the island, or are you visiting?"

Spyder's first inclination was to tell him: *go to hell.* "What right has he got to be interrogating me without cause?" he asked himself. But, then he immediately thought better of it. "If I get hostile with this cop," he silently reasoned to himself, "all it will do is make him even more suspicious of me, this is one shittin' no-win situation, any way you look at it."

"No," Spyder said aloud. "We're up here to do some fishin'. Heard it was pretty good in the river. But I don't know anything about that yet. Do you?"

Before the sergeant could say anything else, Jack Handler walked in the door. Sgt. Blake saw him immediately, and said, "Well, wouldn't you just know it. If there is one person on the island who qualifies as an expert on the question on fishin' like that, he just walked through the door."

Sgt. Blake then turned to address Jack: "Hey, Handler, can you come over here for a minute? These fellows want to know where to go fishing on the island. Got any advice for 'em?"

"Yeah, Sergeant," Jack said, "I'm sure I can help. But, first, I need a few minutes of your time. If your friends here will kindly excuse us for just a moment. I'll get right back to them. Okay?"

"Excuse us, please," Sgt. Blake said to Spyder. "Jack will get right back to you in a minute. Just hang on, if you will."

"No problem," Spyder replied to him.

At that very time, Billie their waitress walked up and handed Spyder a check and thanked him.

Spyder thanked her and asked her to hang on for just a moment. He took one look at the check and handed her three twenty-dollar bills. "Keep the change," he said. Then he and Cash headed for the door.

"Hey, mister," Billie said, holding up the cash and calling out, "did you know you handed me three twenties?"

"Yeah," Spyder said to her. "We're good. The rest is for you. And you have yourself a great day."

"Thanks, mister," Billie replied with a big smile.

"Let's go," Spyder commanded Cash in a nearly silent voice, "and do not look back. OK, let's move!"

The two men moved as swiftly as possible out the main door and through the bar's parking lot on their way to their rented Toyota.

Just before they reached their car, Spyder barked his order again: "No matter what anyone says, do not stop or look back! We gotta get our asses outta here! And quick!"

Spyder hit the remote and unlocked the Toyota's doors, and they both got in.

For a second Cash could not resist the urge, and he spun his head around and took a quick look at the door they'd just exited out of.

"Damn you!" Spyder yelled at Cash—this time quite loudly. "You *stupid idiot*! What the hell have I been telling you? Don't you ever listen to me?! … Do *not* look back! Not until we're miles down the road. Just don't do it."

When Spyder pulled out of the bar parking area, he turned east on Sugar Island Road, instead of right toward the ferry. Cash wondered why Spyder had done that, but fear led him to resist the urge to open his mouth.

Spyder did not look back at all. Instead, he hit the gas with gusto and sped east until he came to Brassar Road, and there he turned south.

"He must be headed back to where the girls are staying," Cash said to himself. "That must be what he's up to."

As they progressed, it became more and more clear to Cash that he had called that move correctly. And when they turned back west on 6 Mile Road, all serious doubts about it were gone. But, he still feared to open his mouth to speak.

What could he have in mind this time? Cash wondered. *Why are we headed back there now? It's obvious that we are headed back to where the girls are staying. But why?*

Cash's mind was running at full speed, but he still dared not speak aloud.

Finally, Spyder had calmed down enough to convey his thoughts to Cash.

"This is what we do," he said. "First, we go back to the house where Liz is. We just left the cops at the bar. So, we know that they are not going to be at the house on the river—at least, if we move quickly."

What Spyder did not realize (because he had never seen Jack before that brief moment in the bar) was that at least for the short term he had a second advantage working in his favor. That being, if they acted swiftly, Jack, the man who posed the biggest potential problem for him, would not be at that house either. But, it did not register in Spyder's mind that the man they had just seen at the bar was living at the house where the girls were visiting.

"So," Spyder continued, "we scoop up the drugs they've got in that Traverse. We know that the cops *cannot* be there to hinder us for at least fifteen minutes. We'll just have to act fast, and then get the hell out of here."

"Well," Cash concluded, "how do you propose we get into that vehicle? It's a cinch that they'll have that Traverse locked up. Right? And, there's gonna be an alarm system. All cars have them nowadays. Right?"

"Yeah," Spyder admitted, after giving the question some affected attention. "Sure, they come with alarms from the factory."

"Should we create a distraction, maybe?" Cash suggested, a little hesitant to be suggesting anything.

"What are you thinking?" Spyder replied with a detectable chuckle, "Like, you setting the house on fire, while I rifle their car?"

"Not exactly," Cash replied. "But, you know what I mean, right?"

"I think we will take a little different tack," Spyder replied.

"Like what?" Cash inquired. He was just glad that his mentor was again responding to his comments in a serious fashion, instead of simply dismissing them out of hand.

"Here's what I have in mind," Spyder said. At that point they were still on Brassar, about one-tenth of a mile north of 6 Mile Road. "Here's how I think we do this. I don't think Liz knows what you look like, does she? Have you ever been introduced?"

"She ain't no friend of mine," Cash declared.

"I know that," Spyder barked, "But have you ever even met her? That's what I need to know."

"To my knowledge, I've never met her."

"Then, you're my backup plan," Spyder told him. "We'll slide in and get the VIN off the windshield. You know where that is?"

"Yeah," Cash replied.

"Actually, *I'll* get the VIN number," Spyder declared after he'd thought it through for a moment. "We'll park in the street—where I turned around before. I'll run in and get the VIN." He would have had Cash perform that task, but he didn't trust his helper to get the job done without screwing something up.

"Once I have the number," Spyder went on, "I have a buddy who can download the necessary info into this little beast." He reached into the center console and pulled out a Ziploc bag containing a strange-looking electronic device.

"This can be programmed to lock or unlock virtually any automobile remotely," Spyder told him. "I've heard that there are some makes and models that can't be compromised, but I haven't run into one of those yet. ... The only problem can be our connection. If I do not have good internet, it might not work. ... That would be when I would call on you to create a distraction. Because, if I have to enter that vehicle by force, all bets are off. I'm sure to trigger its alarm if I do that. So, get your ass ready to be useful."

"Sure," Cash replied, clearly a little apprehensive as to how he should go about it. "What should I do? To create that distraction? Do you have any good ideas?"

"Like I said," Spyder explained, "We will park where we turned around earlier. Plenty of room there. And it's right off the back of that house. You run up to the back door and tell them that there was an accident, and that your girlfriend is trapped in your car. And there was a fire. ... No, forget that shit. Someone at the house will call the fire department. We can't have that. Let me think about this for a minute."

And so Cash shut up for a bit and let Spyder think.

Just before they reached South Westshore Drive, Spyder blurted out, "This is how we do it. The first part stands—we'll park where I turned around earlier. That still works. But, if I need you to distract them, you will do this—you will tell them that your car is stuck in the sand, and that you could use a little help getting it out. *Not* a tow truck—just a couple people pushing. And you start walking over to our car. The power of suggestion. They are gonna want to see what sort of mess you got yourself into, and so they will follow you. They will get behind the car, and push. You will spin the tires a bit, and then drive out with a big smile and a 'thank you very much.' I will have the suitcases, or boxes, of merchandise out by the road. You will stop and quickly pick up me and the merchandise. And off we go.

"But, if we have a good internet connection, then all that will not be necessary. In either case, I will call you. Check, and make sure your cell is working. Check it now."

Cash retrieved his cell and turned it on.

"Is it ready to go, now?" Spyder asked.

Cash nodded in the affirmative.

"Then give me a call."

Cash did as he was told and Spyder's phone rang.

Careful to keep the Toyota under control, Spyder answered his phone and said, "Cash, do you hear me okay?"

"Yes," Cash said. "Looks like we've got a good connection. And we're almost there."

"This all should work fine," Spyder said as he turned onto Westshore Drive. Seconds later he pulled up and stopped at the Handlers' driveway. "You take it from here," he said to Cash.

Spyder pulled two large canvas bags out of his suitcase. "Drop me off here," he commanded Cash, "and you go over and park. Have your cell on and ready—I might need you. Be ready, and don't screw up."

Spyder took one last examination of his surroundings before closing the car door behind him, and then he quick-walked over to the girls' Traverse.

Holding the electronic entry programmer up by the windshield, he plugged it into his cell phone and carefully entered the Traverse's VIN on his cell. After he double-checked the correctness of the number, he hit *enter*. His heart was pounding—from his chest all the way into his neck. The processor thought about the command for about ten seconds, and then the word *Finished* flashed on his cell phone. At that point, two command lines appeared on the cell's screen: lock and unlock."Damn!" he declared.

"Ain't that just about as slick as shit gets?!"

He hit the *unlock* button. He heard a door unlock. Then, leaving the entry programmer on the hood of the Traverse, he walked around to the rear and tried the hatch. But it did not open.

"What the hell!" he muttered, as he returned to his programmer and hit the unlock button twice more. This time he heard all the doors unlock.

"That's more like it!" he said to himself. Walking back to the rear hatch he pressed the release button again. This time it opened. But, what he saw inside almost threw him into shock.

"That bitch!" he barked audibly in his most angry of utterances. "That damned thievin' bitch!"

Chapter 11 —

What had so thoroughly pissed Spyder off was what he discovered inside the Traverse when he popped open the rear hatch. Instead of the two huge travel bags that Liz had stolen from him, or anything comparable to them in size, all he found was one moderately large-sized satchel—a black rolling duffle bag. There was an absolutely overpacked jumbo-sized travel bag still missing.

To stoke even further the flames of his anger, Spyder discovered on examination that the bag that was missing contained the exclusively highly-priced cocaine, while the one that remained inside the Traverse, the duffle bag on wheels, was filled largely with the much cheaper fentanyl—the ratio being about 90/10. That meant that the bag missing comprised about ninety percent street value of the stolen merchandise.

Spyder grabbed the handle and started to slide the duffle bag out the hatch, but then he had second thoughts. He sat down in the back of the Traverse and reasoned, *I gotta get all my missing product, not just this cheap-ass China Girl shit. How do I do this?*

What's the best approach I could use?

Just seconds after sitting down to think, Spyder stood back up, shoved the duffle bag back to where it was originally, and he proceeded to close the hatch. He then called Cash and said, "Get your ass over here to pick me up. Stop on the road by their drive. Do not come up to the house. I'll meet you there at the road."

"Everything go as planned?" Cash asked.

"Just shut the hell up and do what I tell you," Spyder barked. "And do it now!"

Cash had left the engine running, so he would be able to slide out and pull up to the Handler driveway as quickly as possible.

Spyder closed the rear hatch, retrieved his programmer from the hood of the Traverse, and headed out to the road to meet up with Cash.

"Where is it?" Cash queried. "The ... merchandise. Didn't you get into their car?"

"Will you just shut the hell up for a minute?!" Spyder growled as he slid the bags into the rear seat, and the electronic key programmer back into his suitcase. In its place he retrieved a different, smaller electronic device. He checked it out briefly, and then headed back to the Traverse. This second unit was a compact, magnetic vehicle-tracking device.

When he reached the Traverse, he quickly slid around to the rear, knelt down and peered beneath the vehicle. He found an unobstructed section of the steel frame and allowed the super-magnet to attach the device securely to it. He then twisted it back and forth to be certain that it was firmly seated on the metal, and he then headed back to where Cash waited in their rented Toyota.

However, this last bit of commotion—probably when Spyder

closed the Toyota's door—had attracted Buddy's attention. With both ears standing at attention, he sprinted toward his favorite observation window at the front of the house. Sliding full speed up to it, Buddy planted both front paws on the windowsill and wiggled his nose between the curtains. As soon as he spotted Spyder scurrying back to his car, Buddy sounded his unique K-9 alarm.

The teenagers were altogether too busy to pay any attention to Buddy's resounding warning signal, but nothing ever escaped Kate's attention. She quick-stepped over to where Buddy had stationed himself.

"Hey, kiddo, what's up over here?" she asked, in her always-kind voice when communicating with her favorite four-legged friend. "You talking to someone out there? Or are you just looking for some attention? Whatcha got goin' on, Buddy?"

The dog anxiously pulled his nose out of the curtains, looked up at Kate, and whined quietly.

Kate then parted the curtains above him and took a look for herself.

"Oh," she said to him when she spotted Spyder, "I see what you're talking about. Looks like we've got a little company out there. … Wonder who that might be?"

She then walked over to the door, opened it and stepped out on the porch.

"May I help you?" she asked Spyder, in a pleasant but adequately loud and commanding voice.

Spyder just stopped in his tracks, and replied, "Oh, I have an Uber pickup, and I can't seem to find him. Supposed to pick him at the corner of 6 Mile Road and Westshore Drive. I guess I must have gone past it. Sorry for the inconvenience. You have a good day, and thank you."

Kate did not respond. She just stood there and silently watched as Spyder casually continued on toward Cash and the Toyota.

"I wonder what that was all about?" she said to a very attentive Buddy after she'd come back into the house and closed the door. "We don't get many Ubers out here—way too expensive and slow for us Sugar Islanders." She returned to Buddy's window and looked out of it with him.

And she didn't leave that station until Spyder had reached the Toyota.

"Just drive," Spyder growled, as he got in and slammed the car door closed. "And keep your stupid mouth shut! I gotta think! ... I can't be processing your dribble right now!"

And that's what Cash did—or, at least made his best effort to do so.

"What the hell was that all about?" Kate muttered in Buddy's direction. "That fellow got in the *passenger* side. Doesn't sound much like Uber-shit to me. There wouldn't be two people running around in an Uber, anyway. ... No money in that."

She did not have a clear view of the car, so she could not see a plate, but she was able to identify it as a late-model white Toyota.

For a moment Kate considered jumping in her car and getting a closer look at her visitor, but decided that it would be impolite to run out on her guests. And, one of those guests—the one named Angel—Kate considered to be of utmost importance to Jack and the boys. So, she instead grabbed her cell and called Troy, one of her friends who worked as an operator on the ferry. She asked him to have their guys keep an eye out for a late-model white Toyota headed off the island in the next half hour or so. "It might have two or more people in it," she informed him, "one of them a fellow in his late twenties. If you or one of your buddies were to spot the car, please, just jot down the plate number for me. And maybe take a close look at its occupants."

She then called her dad, and asked him, "Dad, where are you right now?"

"I'm on South Westshore," he told her. "Headed back to the house. Why? What do you need?"

"Keep an eye out for a late-model white Toyota with two or more people in it—at least one of them a young to middle-aged man. He'd probably be seated on the passenger side, front. ... No idea what the driver looked like."

She then explained to him what had just happened at the house, and that she didn't buy the man's story.

"Yeah," he said. "That does sound like a bit of a contrived bunch of bullshit—especially given the contents of that suitcase I saw on the video system. ... was your guy leaving *with* that case?"

"It did not appear like that to me," Kate replied, "or I would have stopped him. But, I am on my way out there right now to be sure he hasn't broken into one of our vehicles and ripped something off. ... Hold on for just a second."

As soon as she reached the driveway she confirmed to her satisfaction the belief that the 'Uber' passenger had not actually broken into any of the Handler vehicles. She then checked Angel's Traverse, and it, too, appeared intact and undamaged. So, she informed her father that "everything looked to be okay. But, it's highly unlikely that you will be running into them if you're headed home on Westshore. My guys would have headed west on 6 Mile Road. ... From there, who knows? But I doubt that you'll be finding them on Westshore."

"I'm sure you're right about that," he told her. "It's fortunate that you had no damage there. But, I don't think it'd be a good idea to question the girls about this—not at this time. Best to keep it between the two of us for right now. I'll explain it further when I see you. As it stands, if you were to tell the girls about your surprise visitor, they would probably hit the road. I gotta tell you, there's still much for us to learn about the motivations behind their visit. We can discuss the whole matter a little later… I'll still keep my eyes open for that white Toyota, and I should be home in ten."

At that moment, Spyder and Cash were just turning north on Brassar from 6 Mile Road. They had not even been aware that there was a more direct route through to Sugar Island Road, for had they been, it's quite possible that Spyder would have chosen Westshore Drive as his most direct method of escape.

So, as it turned out, the purely fortuitous fact that they lacked that little tidbit of information all but guaranteed that they would not be running into Jack on their way off the island. It's likely, in fact, that it might even have saved the two of them from meeting their end at Jack's hand of justice.

Cash remained mad as hell at Spyder for constantly talking down to him, but he had made up his mind that there would be no verbal confrontation with his protagonist at this time, on this trip. "We have an important job to do," he told himself, "I must avoid a duel of any kind. I must evade it at all cost—at least for the right now. But, when the ideal opportunity presents itself, down the road, I will put that bastard in his place. … Or, maybe I'll just get even with him. Whatever it is to be, it will have to be in my way, on my own terms, and in my own time. … Otherwise, if I do it wrong, that SOB will kill me on the spot. And I just know he would love to do that. … I will, someday and somehow, make it all right. And I will do it in a way that makes it clear to him that it was me doing it."

Cash consoled himself by forcing his pride to take shelter in that little, well-rehearsed narrative.

They hadn't gone far before Spyder began dumping his frustrations on Cash.

"That damned bitch didn't have all the merchandise with her in that Traverse," he said. "She stole two of my bags, and only one of them was in that car. And it was the cheap shit that I found in the car. Not the good stuff. … Not the gold. … That shit-ass bitch! I never did trust her. Somehow I knew she would end up pulling a stunt like this. She's just that kind of bitch. … Stupid. That's exactly what she is. Stupid. She should have known that I would kill her if she ever dared pulling a trick like this. Slit the bitch's throat and feed her to the dogs."

"Only one bag in their car?" Cash asked, finally daring to open his mouth.

"Right! And, like I said, it was the cheap shit."

"Maybe they took the other bag in the house," Cash offered.

"Hell no!" Spyder fired back. "That's bullshit! That could never happen. Think about what I told you. … That gal who jumped me in the driveway, I can tell you that she's not one to mess with. … That's got to be a fairly rich family that she's staying with. And, I could just tell that she—the one who lives there—she would not dare ever risking her reputation on that island by screwing around in the business with a lowlife bitch like Liz. I know that for sure.

"And I can guarantee you something else," Spyder continued.

"That woman, the one who lives there, she will be reading what that bitch Liz is all about very soon, if she hasn't already."

Spyder then realized that what he was saying might not add up to Cash, because Spyder knew how unwise it was for him to engage himself in a serious sexual relationship with any female he regarded as a "lowlife bitch." Cash was well aware that he had carelessly put up with Liz for quite some time.

So, Spyder was well aware that he ought to abandon that aspect of the matter without any further discussion.

"But," Spyder continued a few minutes later, but along a different vein, "I can now say that I'm pretty damn sure that I do know where the rest of my shit is."

After he had finished that sentence, Spyder just sat there for nearly another full minute without opening his mouth, and Cash was scared to open his.

"Really?" Cash finally asked timidly. "Where might that be?"

Again, Spyder delivered his car-mate an extended period of silence.

They were at that time approaching Sugar Island Road, and Cash flashed on his left turn signal.

"We heading back over on the ferry?" Cash asked.

"No," Spyder said. "Not right now. Let's stop in at that bar. That is, if the cops have left. I assume they will have. Never makes 'em look very good if their cars are spotted at a bar for very long at a time. ... That's what they have private vehicles for."

"Right," Cash replied. But he offered nothing further on that conversation.

"I don't see any cop cars here," Cash said, as he pulled into the Hilltop's lot. "What do you think? Shall we go in?"

"Sure," Spyder said. "Let's do it."

As they walked in the door they were greeted by the same girl who had waited on them an hour earlier.

"Hey, boys," she said, after having walked half a dozen steps toward them as they entered. "I'm surprised to see you back so soon. Everything okay?"

"Fine," Spyder said. "Everything's just fine. Loved the burger, by the way. We just have some time to kill and thought we'd get another beer. Got some Miller Lites left, I hope?"

"Oh, I think we might. One for each of you?"

"Sounds good," Spyder said.

He glanced over in the corner and saw that their original booth was open, and said, "Shall we go back to the same table where we were?"

"Sure," she said. "I wiped it down and it's all ready for you. ... Menus are on the table if you need one."

Spyder looked at her, smiled and nodded. And then the two men took their seats.

Cash had been wondering why Spyder would want to go back to the bar after he had just had a bit of a confrontation with the lady of the house where Liz was staying. But, he was hesitant to speak for fear of Spyder.

"You're probably pondering why we're stopping now," Spyder said, reading the question marks in Cash's eyes. "It just occurred to me that the woman at the house quite possibly suspects me of something. And, since there is only one way to get off this island, the ferry, she'll be calling them to be on the lookout for this Toyota. So, we're gonna hang out here at the bar for a while."

"Oh," Cash replied, "I get it."

"This is what I think happened to the merchandise," Spyder continued. "This must be what happened. ... It took them three days to get here. So, they obviously didn't fly. That was a good move on their part. They would have been nabbed at the airport. Bus or train would have taken too long. So, we can assume that they drove.

"I know that Liz didn't have a car. So, they must have rented one. And that Traverse ain't it—it has Michigan plates. They drove the rental over to where they had the Traverse stored, just like I laid out earlier. Probably someplace nearby—that's what The Coach told me was happening. Probably in the Soo, but at least some nearby place in the UP.

"And, when they switched cars, they must have left that other bag in the storage facility—where the car had been stored. ... I know it's convoluted, but it's the only logical explanation as I see it."

"Can we just go over there and pick it up?" Cash suggested.

"Not exactly, you idiot," Spyder said. "We have no idea where it is. ... and, even after we do locate it, if it's one of those typical storage facilities, there will be a gate, and it will be controlled with a card. Obviously, we don't have a card to get in. And they'll have cameras.

"It's possible that she had the vehicle stored at a private house, or a business. That's possible. Still, it would have been under lock and key all the same.

"It's just a simple fact, we will not only have to know exactly where it was that she stored it, but we will have to have a plausible method of entry. It will not be easy.

"Here's what we do. We can assume that the woman who came

out of the house to talk to me, she's gonna tell that Liz bitch that someone was snooping around her car. And she, Liz, is gonna want to do something with the merchandise they've been driving around with. And right away. She's not gonna want to wait around. That's what I think. And she, that Liz bitch, she's gonna have to go back and check on the other bag, and then probably put that other bag in their car for right now.

"Any way I look at it, there's just too much at stake here. She's gonna do *something* like that. ... And she can't just keep that shit in a 'borrowed' house. Something's got to be goin' down right away.

"Be nice if we could just somehow follow her," Spyder continued to lay it all out—as much for his own benefit as for Cash's. ... "And that's what we will have to do."

"What was that other thing you took," Cash finally got the courage to ask, "on your second trip to the car? Looked like some kinda electronic device. What was it?"

"Vehicle tracker," Spyder informed him. "I have an app on my phone to track it. As long as it doesn't move, I receive no alerts—not unless I initiate a status check. But when it moves at all, it lets me know. ... I'm thinking that it won't take long, and those girls are gonna have to do something."

"It could happen right now. Is that what you're thinking?"

"Exactly," Spyder confirmed what Cash was thinking.

"Do you boys want anything else?" the waitress asked. "Or, will these beers do it for now?"

The two men looked at each other, and Spyder spoke: "I think the beers will do it for us. Might want another, but we'll flag you down. ... But, could you leave a check for this round now—we might have to leave in a hurry. I'm expecting a phone call."

"Just like your first visit," the waitress said. "I'll drop a check off. And then, I'll be keeping an on you. In case you need something. Enjoy."

As soon as she was out of range, Cash asked, "How do we go about this? Gittin' the rest of the merchandise back, that is."

"We finish this beer," Spyder explained, "and maybe a second—we'll just see. And then we take the ferry off the island. I get an alert on my phone, and we find out exactly where they stored my shit—ideally, it will be at one of your regular run-of-the-mill rental places. We then rent ourselves a storage bin in the same facility as where the girls are. We rent one big enough to store a vehicle in. That way it will be in the same area as the one where they had the Traverse. Anyway, it will probably be near the island.

"We rent the storage garage, and that way we will get a card for the main gate, and be able to intercept them quite easily. ... I am convinced that the second bag has to be in their storage garage — *has* to be."

Cash sat waiting for Spyder to ask his opinion on the matter, but that request for help never came. In fact, neither of the men spoke for the next two or three minutes. Perfect quiet persisted between them.

He's just not interested in what I think, Cash silently deduced. And, to a large extent, his conclusion was correct. Spyder was a selfish, and thoroughly self-centered man. And he made no secret about his utter disregard for Cash.

Finally, Spyder's vehicle tracking device broke the silence.

"Holy shit!" Cash blurted out. "What the hell's that?!"

"That's our signal to get the hell outta here," Spyder replied. "Take a swig on your beer and let's go. ... That was even faster than

I expected. Come on. Let's get the hell outta here."

Cash immediately chugged down over half his Miller and then slid out from his seat.

Spyder quaffed a couple gulps of his drink, then he too stood to his feet. He got the waitress's attention, made sure she saw him laying a twenty on the table. He then flashed her a thumbs-up to let her know that the change was her tip, and the two of them bolted for the door.

They did not look back or utter a sound until outside, and then Spyder said, "I never expected them to be rolling on this so soon. We gotta get a move on if I'm gonna be able to get my entry card quickly enough after they get there. … Gimme the keys—I'm gonna drive from here."

Cash had no reservations about having Spyder drive. *I'm less likely to get yelled at with him at the wheel,* he was thinking.

"Be nice if we could catch a ferry right away," Spyder said as he tore out of the parking lot. "That could save us over twenty minutes—could make or break this part of the operation. Sure as hell be nice if we had the address of that storage rental. But, we're just going to have to follow them."

"I don't see any cops around," Cash said. "You're probably safe to floor it."

"Safe bet our buddies from before have left the island," Spyder said, as he hit the gas a little harder.

"Holy shit!" Spyder said, as they passed a sign indicating that South Westshore Drive crossed Sugar Island Road. "Wouldn't it be quicker to just take Westshore Drive next time? That should almost go right by their house. Right?"

"Hell," Cash said, reflecting a good degree of surprise. "I'd guess it would—same name."

"Nice to know," Spyder said. "But I suppose it didn't really matter before. We were just following the girls. But it would be good to know from here on if there is a more direct route. Might come in useful."

Spyder began braking the car well in advance of the ferry gate. But he still maintained the appearance of a highly motivated driver—one determined to make it on the ferry for this crossing.

And his plan worked. Their little Toyota was the last vehicle to board the ferry.

By the time the boat pulled away from the island dock, an equally eager silver Traverse could be seen speeding toward the already moving ferry.

"Sorry, Liz," Angel said to her friend. "But we're not going to make this crossing."

"That's okay," Liz said. "We tried. ... Besides, that strange visitor probably meant nothing. ... Probably some misdirected local. No reason to think that he was after my shit. I'm sure that it didn't mean a thing."

Angel began slowing down. Once stopped, she asked, "Anyway, what do either one of us have in our suitcases that would entice someone to travel all the way from San Francisco to Sugar Island, just to steal?"

Liz was anticipating this question, so she was ready with an answer.

"Be damned if I know," she said. "I ran off because he, Spyder, threatened to hurt me if I didn't keep doin' some of that crazy perverted shit that he liked. I was just sick of him. ... And I think he very well might have killed me. Probably would have. ... I've actually heard that he'd killed a man. Maybe more than one. He has people working for him—dangerous people. And they all illegally carry guns."

"Killed people?!" Angel asked in shocked disbelief. "What sort of crazy business is he in?"

"I've heard that he deals drugs," Liz said. "But I don't know that for a fact. I think it could be, but I don't know if it's true."

"Drugs!" Angel blurted out. "You gotta be kiddin' me. … Are you serious? Drugs?"

"That's what some people I know tell me."

"Is it possible that he thinks that you have drugs in your stuff?" Angel asked. "Could that be what he was after? Drugs?"

"Could be, I suppose," Liz responded, a little concerned about where this conversation might end up. "Could be drugs, I guess. But I don't have a clue how he might have got that idea."

"Holy crap!" Angel responded. "People kill people because of drugs. You know that. Right? It's a very dangerous business. Users die every day. … So do dealers—they die every day too. It's a very bad business to get mixed up with. … You're not mixed up with drugs, are you? … Right? You don't sell drugs. Do you?"

"No!" Liz said, denying it with some gusto. "I may smoke a joint now and then, but that's it. Like you. Sometimes you take a drag on mine. But that's it for the both of us. We don't use drugs. … And I sure as hell never deal it. … I have no idea what that bastard has in mind.

"And, most likely that was not him at your Uncle Jack's house. I'm probably a bit paranoid. It's just that when somebody threatens to kill you, you get that way. It's just gotta be some kinda coincidence, or something. I just thought it'd be a good idea to check up on my other suitcase, in case something like that was goin' down. It's all probably nothin', though."

Neither one of the girls was at all comfortable with the tone or content of their conversation. Liz, while she had considerable practice at lying, was not particularly good at it. She sensed that her friend might have detected her efforts to deceive, and she could not conjure up any reasonable way to make her story work in a convincing fashion. "Should I just come clean and admit what I've been up to?" she asked herself. "Or is there something that I could come up with that might put her at ease? Maybe get her off my ass a little bit?"

"Are the girls here?" Jack asked Kate as he walked through the door. "I don't see their car out there. Did they go someplace?"

"Yes," Kate replied. "They went to check on some of their luggage. ... Like I told you, we had a bit of a queer thing happen here while you were gone. It's been about ten or twelve minutes ago, now. ... That incident shook Liz up pretty good."

"You're talking about that visitor?" Jack asked.

"Exactly," Kate replied. "Her face turned pale, and the two of them took off immediately."

"Tell me about it again," Jack said. "And why you think it rattled the girls so much?"

"It didn't really shake Angel," Kate said. "But it certainly did get to Liz pretty good."

"What exactly happened?" Jack asked again. "Spell it out in detail for me. I think it could be significant."

And so Kate laid out for her father every detail of what had transpired—even the aspects that she thought inconsequential. When she had finished, he explained to her what he had earlier

viewed over their CCTV system. He told her how Liz had inspected one of the bags in the back of Angel's Traverse. "That's why I
wanted to catch up with Blake and Crandle," he told his daughter, "because what those girls are transporting in that Traverse
appeared to be a substantial quantity of drugs—*illegal* drugs, of
course. I did not want to have those drugs on our property without informing the authorities that it was there. Could have presented a substantial problem for us down the road."

"Drugs?!" Kate exclaimed. "You're sure?"

"I'm not wrong about this," he said. "There looked to be a lot
of fentanyl—a *lot* of it. And a fair quantity of what appeared to be
cocaine. Can't be too sure about that without getting a closer look.
… But, there is no doubt that it looked like cocaine, and that it was
packed in what looked to be kilo-sized bags. … I'd bet that's what
it was. Coke, or a damned great imitation. One of them's dealing.
… Take a look at the video with me. I know you'll agree."

"Holy shit!" Kate said, while Jack was running the video
through. "What have we got ourselves into this time? … How did
our buddies in uniform want us to handle this?"

"They gave me one day to get this ferreted out," he said. "After
that they would have to step in."

"I'm amazed they gave you any time," Kate said. "I guess they
are your buddies. … Kilo bags, you say—more than one—right?"

"I saw two," Jack said, pulling out his cell and setting it on the
island. "It's saved. … Where are the boys?"

"They're out working on Stanger."

"They don't need to be engaged in this mess," Jack said, as he
brought up the app. "At least not today."

"Here's where Liz goes out to their car," Jack said. "I'd guess that Blake and Crandle spooked her out a little bit. ... You can see that there is a lot of fentanyl in that one bag—a whole hell of a bunch. And there's a couple of those big bags. Probably enough fentanyl to kill off the entire state, if consumed in too high a dosage—wouldn't you say? If it's pure. .... But here she checks out these other bags—kilo bags of white powder. My guess is that those two bags contain coke. And, the street value of that shit would be double that of all the fentanyl—probably even a lot more than that. And, there might be more than just those two bags. But, I doubt it. I'll tell you why I suspect that there are only two bags of that white shit."

"Yeah," Kate said, fixing her attention on what her dad was saying.

"See how she carefully checks to inventory the kilo bags?" he asked. "I think that if there were more of them, she would have dug through the fentanyl to find them. But, she satisfies herself once she confirms that there are two bags of it.

"My guess," Jack said, "based on body language alone, is that she knows that the street value of the coke is substantial—much greater by volume than the fentanyl.

"And, that's the end of it. She immediately comes back into the house."

"That's when you left to chase down your two buddies—Blake and Crandle? You wanted to run it all past them. Right?"

"Exactly," Jack replied. "You were engaged with the boys, and I knew I'd have to quickly get on my pony and go after them ... if I was going to catch them before they got on the ferry. Luckily I spotted their car at the Hilltop. That's when they told me I had one day to do something."

"And did they view it pretty much the way we did here just now?" Kate asked.

"Just like we see it," Jack said.

"Okay," Kate said. "I'm beginning to get the picture. ... But, why do you suppose that after I told them about that character in the driveway, they then decided they needed to take a drive? What does that say to you?"

"Who was concerned about this?" Jack asked her. "Was Liz the one who was pushing it? Or Angel?"

"Totally Liz," Kate replied. "Liz had a big problem with that guy. ... But, it seemed to me, that Angel couldn't care less. She, Angel, was much more interested in catching up on stuff with me and the boys. But Liz, she was definitely troubled with the news about the suspicious visitor. ... And, like I told you, I didn't like it much either. I'm confident he was lying about his being an Uber driver. ... He wasn't even the driver of that car."

"Do you know where they were headed?" Jack asked. "The girls?"

"They told me that Angel needed to pick up something from a storage facility in the Soo," Kate replied. "I asked them if it was something that I might have, that maybe I would save them a trip if they could just get it from me. And Liz told me that Angel just wanted to go through some of her junk that got stored there. ... Angel asked me if it was still okay if they spent the night, and I assured them that they could stay as long as they wished. ... Just like I had told her before—same deal stood. ... That's how you and I had left it, too."

"Damn it all," Jack snarled, "I do not want to get those kids in trouble. But, they should know that you don't screw around with drugs—especially drugs in that sort of quantity. ... How the hell did they come by it, anyway? That is major dealer-sized volume. ... And they certainly did not put out the cash to buy it from a supplier. But, somebody sure as hell did. It just would not have been them. Impossible. ... They stole the drugs from someone. Truthfully, it's most likely that Liz stole the drugs. I doubt that Angel even knows that the drugs exist. Quite seriously, I doubt that Angel even suspects anything about the drugs. She might. It's possible, I suppose. ... But, my guess is she does not. She was way too relaxed to be hiding that sort of information."

Kate remained silent for a few seconds. She was thinking. Finally, she said, "Dad, I agree. Angel was too comfortable for a person to be knowingly toting around the type of package you're describing. I would agree with you—Liz is the only culprit here.

"Now, this is what we have to do. We've got to move on this. Regardless of who, or what, or however badly we want to protect Angel, we've got responsibilities here—our careers, the boys, and our own exposure. We cannot afford to even appear like we're trying to sweep this under a rug. This is one big-ass deal. ... It was good that you chased down those county cops and reported what you knew. ... We've both got enemies out there that would love to see us destroyed. And, if we don't handle this right, this could do it."

"So, what are you suggesting we do?" Jack asked. "Have you got a plan?"

"Not exactly," Kate said.

"Well," Jack followed up, "This is what I'm thinking. What if we just hang around here until the girls get back? And then check their car to see if that case, the one with all the drugs in it, to see if it is still in Angel's car. Could be that they might just want to unload it in that storage facility—now that they think someone maybe knows that they are staying here. Then, they might think it best to get all the drugs out of our house, and off our property. … It has to be that way, regardless. We can't have any drugs whatsoever on our property. Period."

"Don't you think," Kate suggested, "that the odds are great that we know where that storage garage is located? I would say that it's a virtual cinch that Liz has not contracted for a different one. … It is possible, of course, that Liz *did* sign for another one, so that she would have total control over those drugs. But, I don't think it likely. We could go there right now and check it out—confront them at the scene."

"No doubt that there are dozens of possibilities here in the Soo," Jack said. "But there really is no time to pursue it from that direction. It is my assumption too that there is only one garage, and it is the original one that we know about. … However, if Liz did rent her own, and we were to arrive on the scene by surprise, Liz would deny that there is a separate location, and we'd have no way to prove it. … And we would alienate Angel forever. … I think it might be prudent to give Liz a chance to leave that case at a location that is not on our property. Millie's storage garage is a good-sized area—big enough for anything. And then we could wait until they come back here. Best option available to us, I think. … But, when they come back for the night, we will have to—"

Right then, in the middle of Jack's sentence, his cell phone rang. He took a quick, concerned look at it, and said to Kate, "It's her! It's Angel!"

"Hey, girl. What's up?" Jack asked.

At first Jack could hear the loud shouting of a man's voice over the screams of a female. When Angel heard him answer, she was frantically crying.

"Uncle Jack, help us! Please, help us! They're gonna kill us! Help!"

Chapter 12 —

"They are going to kill us," Angel kept repeating in a terrified panic. "I know he means it. They're going to kill us! What can we do?! Nothing! We can't do anything! We don't stand a chance! *Please* help us!"

"Where are you?" Jack pleaded with her. "Tell me where you are."

"I don't even know the name of the street," Angel blurted out. "It's the place Aunt Kate told Mom about. She knows. And you know. Where the Traverse was stored. The one with the tall overhead doors. Over by my house! Oh God, please help me! Quick!"

"Come on," Kate said, as she grabbed Jack's sleeve, "It's the one we thought. Let's go!"

Kate had been standing close enough to Jack that she had heard what Angel had been saying.

Jack kept Angel on the phone as they bolted for Jack's already warmed up Tahoe. As they approached it, he handed his phone over to his daughter, and told her, "Keep Angel on the phone as long as you can. And get as much information as you can."

"You're inside the storage area right now?" Kate asked her.

"Yes!" Angel cried.

"They're outside?" Kate asked.

"Yes!" Angel said. "For now! Liz ran a rod through the track on the overhead door. And we have it locked. Don't know how long it will hold. Hurry! Please hurry!"

"We're coming," Kate told her. "We're on the way. Haven't got on the ferry yet. So don't know how long it'll take us. We'll get there as fast as we can. Do you know who it is that's after you? Do you know his name? How many are there?"

"Oh! God!" Angel blurted out in a muffled, frantic voice. "They're in! Oh no—"

"Use your phone and call the police," Jack told Kate. "Can't mess around with this. Tell them that a man is trying to break into a storage garage and kidnap your friend. That it's in progress right now. I just know we'll be losing too much valuable time on the ferry."

Kate covered the phone with her left hand and asked her father, "Should I mention the drugs with the police? I say no, because—"

"No!" Jack commanded. "It would only confuse the issue right now. Just get them on the way. Kidnapping attempt in progress."

Kate did exactly as Jack requested, and she kept Angel on the other phone while she was handling the dispatch. … At least, she made every effort to maintain communication with both. However, before she'd finished with local law enforcement, the call from Angel was cut off.

"Shit!" she muttered to Jack in disgust when she handed the phone back to him. "Angel got cut off. Just before it went dead, there was a loud crashing noise, and a lot more screaming—all Liz, most likely. Then I heard a man telling Angel to hang up the phone. Angel said 'Okay.' And then it all went dead."

"Then, he knows that she'd been on the phone," Jack said. "It'd be a given that he—they—won't be sticking around for very long.

They're going to be getting the hell out of there right now."

"That storage facility has cameras!" Kate said emphatically. "They all do. So, we should be able to get a good look at those boys right off. ... See what they look like. Maybe one of them was the same fellow that paid me that visit—that fake Uber driver."

"What kind of car was he driving?" Jack asked. "Your Uber driver. I know you told me already. But tell me again what you know about that car."

"I did not get a good look at it," Kate said. "It was parked behind some bushes out front by the road. All I know for sure is that it was a late model, at least a later model, white Toyota. Did not get a look at the plate. All I do know for certain is that there was a second person in the car, because the fellow on foot, the one I talked to in our driveway, he got into that car on the passenger side. He wasn't the driver. And they turned left on 6 Mile Road. ... They looked like they were in a hurry. Beyond that, I don't have any info."

As Jack and Kate approached the ferry it became very clear to them that they would have a bit of a wait, as the ferry was already in the middle of the channel on its way back from the Soo.

"Check my cell phone," Jack told Kate. "Find out if Angel was able to take her cell phone with her. Maybe she did. ... If we can see any movement at all after she surrendered to them, then she was able to squirrel her cell away and leave with it. We might still be able to trace her by using it. See what you get."

Kate retrieved Angel's phone number, and ran a trace on it using Jack's phone.

"There it is," Kate declared in a bit of a celebratory tone. "She's on 3 Mile Road, just west of Shunk Road. She's headed west. ... At least, her phone is headed west. Do you think it's possible that they left the two girls back at the storage garage, and just took her cell? Maybe trying to throw us off?"

"I suppose any damn thing's possible," Jack said, obviously perturbed because the ferry had not yet docked. "But, do you really think that these assholes are actually that smart? We can't know much at this point about them specifically, but experience tells me that most of these jerks are not very bright. I think that, in general terms, it's a good thing that she, or they, picked up the phone and took it with them. It makes it feel like she is still alive, at least for the right now. And, if one of them has survived to this point, probably they both have. Odds are still good. ... I just wish this damn boat would get a move on."

It would be another fifteen minutes or longer before the ferry would shove off. While not a long time, it felt like an eternity to Jack and Kate.

"How should we handle the tracking info?" Kate asked while they waited. "Think we should bring law enforcement up to speed?"

Jack heard what his daughter was asking, but he did not respond. He was, in fact, already calling the update in.

"This is Jack Handler," Jack said reporting in, "I've got an update on the attempted kidnapping I called in about six minutes ago—at the storage facility. We were on the phone with Angel at the time. She was the fourteen-year-old victim. We believe that the perpetrator broke into the facility, and kidnapped one, and possibly two, girls. We lost contact with the fourteen-year-old right after the perpetrators kidnapped her. We were able to track her cell phone, and it appears to us that the perpetrators have the girls and are on the move. We do not know that for a fact, but we are still able to track the girl's cell.

"Right now they appear to be still traveling west on 3 Mile Road. … Looks like they just turned on South Radar Road. Headed south. … Appear to be stopping at these co-ordinates: 46.45879, -84.38813.

"We're still stuck waiting on the ferry. Do you have more than one car responding? If you've got two on it, one of them might like to check out the 3 Mile Road location. Kate and I are headed straight to the storage area. What do you think?"

"We've got four units on this right now," the dispatcher declared. "Can you describe the vehicle they are driving?"

"Late-model white Toyota, we think," Jack said. "Or, they might be driving a late-model silver Traverse. The girls were driving the Traverse. The suspected kidnappers earlier were driving the white Toyota.

"It's possible that they have stolen a different vehicle, but those are the two we know might be engaged."

"The chief says he's going to get a helicopter up," the dispatcher said. "And he has notified the sheriff, and the State Police. He's hitting it hard."

"Great," Jack said. "I'll call in as soon as I get off the ferry. If you hear or see anything, you'll let me know—right?"

"We're on it with everything we've got," the dispatcher said. "We'll let you know what we find out."

Jack disconnected the call and turned back to Kate. He just sat there and looked into her eyes. She said nothing either. Jack was deep in thought about the horrible circumstances surrounding the gruesome death of Angel's lovely mother only months earlier.

In his mind, the whole tragic event involving the mother was his fault. And ever since the events of that tragic day, he had wanted to come to Angel's aid, but the girl was so distraught afterwards that all she sought to do was to separate herself from Jack and his family.

Now, with this latest episode of horror cascading down upon him and those close to him, Jack felt like his level of frustration was reaching a new, nearly unbearable, high.

"Dad," Kate said, interrupting the period of silence, "I just checked Angel's cell, and it looks like they pulled off 3 Mile Road. They went west past I-75, and turned into the gravel pit just west of there. And it looks like they've parked in the pit. Could that be?"

"Hey, Chief," Jack said after getting an idea and calling the police chief back. "Kate's telling me that these guys pulled into Northern Gravel, off 3 Mile just west of 75. This is what I'd like you to do. Call the car rental companies that service the airport, and have them locate a white, late-model Toyota—one that they rented maybe a few days ago. One that has been out by the gravel pit recently, and might still be out there. That could be the best way to find these assholes."

"They're not going to be at the gravel pit, are they?" Kate queried after Jack had disconnected from the dispatcher. ... "That was good thinking."

"It's possible that they might be hiding out there," Jack said. "But I doubt it. Good chance they found Angel's phone and dumped it at the pit just to throw us off. ... But, there can't be too many white rental Toyotas on the road around the Soo right now. Some, of course, but not that many. I'm sure the car rentals would not track it for us, but they just might for the chief of police, even without a warrant."

The actual ferry ride across the shipping channel takes only a couple of minutes—a fraction of the total time that the whole transaction takes. If there are no ore-carriers emerging from the locks to hold the ferry up, the trip is even quicker. Even though everything moved as efficiently as could be hoped for, both Jack and Kate were growing impatient with the process.

Finally, the ferry operators secured the boat at the dock, and opened the gate. One by one the vehicles were directed off the island. Finally, the Handlers were directed to drive onto the ferry. And they were soon on their way.

Even though the trip was as quick as it could have been, it felt to Jack and Kate like it took forever.

Just as they pulled out of the debarking area and turned south on Riverside Drive, Sgt. Blake called Jack.

"I've got some bad news for you, Jack," Sgt. Blake told him.

Chapter 13 —

Jack and Kate had traveled less than a quarter of a mile when they received the dire warning of 'bad news' from Sgt. Blake.

"Oh shit!" Jack blurted out in frustration. "What have you got for me?"

"We checked out those co-ordinates you gave us—for the gravel pit. We did find a cell phone, but no girls, and no car—just a cell phone. We collected it as evidence. … I'm sure you know what that could mean. … Any other ideas that might get us closer?"

"We anticipated as much," Jack replied. "We are having the chief see if the car rental companies might have some info on a white Toyota rental that might have been out in the area of the gravel pit, and see if they can track that Toyota right now. … Someone has to have that info. If we can just get them to release it to the chief without a warrant.

"Sergeant, does it look to you like there might be more evidence out there?"

"Doubtful," Sgt. Blake reported. "They just dumped the cell right here out in the open. Didn't drive over it, or do anything at all to disable it. It looked to us as though they meant for it to be found. … Like it was an effort to throw us off—send us down a blind alley. But, we will check out the entire area. Unless we find something else, or hear differently. … It looks to us like we've got ourselves a kidnapping in progress. The rental companies ought to comply with our request on that basis. That is, without a warrant. What did the chief think about it?"

"He's working on it," Jack replied. "But without comment. … Tell me, can you see their tracks there, and tell which way they went when they pulled out?"

"The last vehicle that exited the site appears to have turned north onto South Radar, but that doesn't tell us much. That road is pretty much a dead end road. There really exists no outlet heading south.

"We can make out with some certainty that the last vehicle turned north on South Radar, and then turned east on 3 Mile. At least, that's how it would appear. There is fresh dirt tracked up on 3 Mile, because of the gravel pit. But, once those vehicle tracks hit 3 Mile, nothing can be presumed, much less determined. Beyond that—the entrance onto 3 Mile—"

"Can you collect a tire print?" Jack interrupted. "There, where you found the phone?"

"We snapped some photos of the tracks," Sgt. Blake said. "But we did not take imprints. Need to get the lab out here to do that. … Of course, we got some shots of the tire prints … where we found the phone."

"Until we get some additional information," Jack said, "I'm going to head on over to the storage facility. That's where the chief sent his officers. They didn't find anyone out there either. …

I will check back with you. … Keep me up to speed. Okay?"

With that Jack disconnected from the Sgt. Blake call, and he addressed Kate.

"I think you should give our boys a heads up about what's going on," Jack said to his daughter. "They're probably still working on their car, but they should be warned that something appears to be going on involving Angel, and that they should be on a lookout for her, or anything unusual."

Kate had not waited for her dad to complete his directions to her before she rang Robby.

"Glad you've got your phone with you," she said when he responded. "We have a job for you. It involves Angel."

Kate then proceeded to fill the boys in on what was transpiring at the moment, letting them know that there was a potential problem lurking, and that it involved something as serious as a possible kidnapping of one or both of the girls. She instructed them both to keep their phones with them and handy, and to contact them—Jack or Kate—if and when they heard or saw anything from the girls, or anything else out of the ordinary.

"And, if something does come up," Kate went on to tell them, "just know that beyond a shadow of a doubt, that under no circumstance whatsoever, are either one of you boys to engage in *any* act of aggression. Should anything like that come up, be ready to call us. But keep *your* noses out of it! … Make sure Red gets this message."

Kate then disconnected from the call to Robby.

"Well, Dad," she said to her father. "Do you think that will do it? Could I have been any more clear?"

"Perfect," Jack said. "That will do it just fine, I should think—

as fine as it could be. … Of course, we both know, if anything goes down around them, they're both jumping in with both feet. But we did what we could to protect them."

Chapter 14 —

"W ho the hell was that callin' you?" Cash demanded. "We don't need anyone else stickin' their noses in our business."

"What the hell are you talking about?!" Spyder replied, expressing his supreme displeasure with Cash's crude and impudent comment. "I've warned you before to keep your stupid mouth shut when you're around me. I do not give a shit what you think! Your job is simply to help me—to do what I tell you to do. That's it for right now."

Cash was sitting in the passenger seat of the white rental Toyota—Spyder was driving. They had just found and loaded the travel bag containing mostly the fentanyl from Angel's Traverse over to the back seat of the Spyder rental. Cash and Spyder had bound and gagged both Liz and Angel, and stowed them away in the tiny trunk of the Toyota. Both girls were still alive, but Liz was unconscious and clearly having trouble breathing. Spyder had slugged her with a closed fist three times in deliberate, rapid succession, rendering her in the sort of quasi-comatose state commonly suffered in a serious automobile accident, or violent football collision.

He actually had not intended to make such solid contact with the side of Liz's head, but he knew he would have to live with the outcome. "Hope I didn't kill her," he said to himself, "not yet, at least."

Spyder and Cash had unceremoniously dumped the girls in the trunk of the Toyota after it had become clear to the two of them that someone had been monitoring at least the last fifteen minutes of their time at the storage garage. While they were able to find and load up the case containing largely Spyder's stash of the relatively cheap fentanyl, they did not locate the far more expensive huge bag of cocaine.

Spyder grew more and more angry. Even after they had stashed the two females out of sight in the trunk of their car so they could make their escape, the intensity of his anger did not subside at all.

"Is that guy you were talking to on your cell …" Cash said in a noticeably unpleasant tone. "Is he coming to Sugar Island to help us out? … I say we don't need any help. We got one whole case of your merchandise. I think we should just be happy with what we've got, and let it go at that. … Liz is not about to talk to you. That's pretty obvious to me. So, I say call that guy, whoever that was, call him back and tell him not to come out here. We just don't need him."

"He's already involved," Spyder told him. "He *lives* on Sugar Island—has lived there for years. He's the one who dropped off the guns for us—he's *already* involved. … In fact, we're headed to his house right now. So, what you're suggesting is out of the question. We have to follow through on this. I've got just too much at stake on it."

Spyder had tolerated all of Cash's mouth that he could handle. So he figured that he needed to get back across the channel if he was going to confront his underling, and there put him in his place once and for all. It was a challenge for him, but Spyder forced a smile onto his face, and addressed Cash several times in a highly affected manner, hoping to calm his helper's virtually belligerent state of mind.

"We'll discuss this further once we've crossed on the ferry, and drive onto the island," he explained to Cash. "You're absolutely right that we're going to have to do something definitive—and soon. We'll figure it all out after we pass the Hilltop. The Coach, he's our helper now. He has a house on the east side of Sugar Island by the river—right across from Canada, I'm told. He's right on the west side of Eastshore Road."

At that time they were just driving off the ferry and onto Sugar Island. Spyder was stewing in his anger. The longer he thought about Liz's obstinacy, the more furious he became about the whole situation, and the harder it became for him to control his temper.

"Are we gonna stop for a beer at the bar?" Cash asked as they approached the top of the hill. "It's right up here a bit."

"Hell no!" Spyder growled at his helper. "We got too much shit going on right now. ... We'll get over by the east side of the island, and find this other guy—this guy they call 'The Coach'. ... Like I said before, he lives on the west side of a street called Eastshore Road."

"Does he have any beer?" Cash wondered out loud.

Spyder flashed Cash a larger than usual frown—even for him in his worst of bad moods. But, he then quickly regained his composure and prepared to make his way to The Coach's house. "Gotta make for damn sure I obey all the laws over here on the island," Spyder said to himself. "Can't afford to get stopped with two half-dead bodies in my trunk. … Shit! What a farce all this has become! Damn it all! … Will it ever end?!"

Maintaining the speed at forty-five miles per hour, Spyder drove past the Hilltop Bar and continued on down Sugar Island Road.

"Then we aren't headed over to the house where we were before?" Cash asked.

"That was *Westshore* Road," Spyder informed him, his anger clearly growing. "The Coach lives on *Eastshore* Road. I'll show you up here. It's only ten minutes, or so. At least that's what it's supposed to be, I think."

Damn that guy! Spyder said to himself. *I am getting so damned sick of him. Just totally sick of all his stupid-ass shit.*

Spyder had the co-ordinates for The Coach's house, and he was just about to enter them into his cell phone. But he hesitated. "I think I have a different plan," he said to himself.

So when he arrived at the end of Sugar Island Road, instead of turning north onto South Eastshore Road, which would have taken him directly to the co-ordinates The Coach had given him, he turned south onto South Ross Road.

When he turned onto the 'wrong road,' Cash looked very confused. "I thought you said your friend lived on Eastshore Road," he said. "That's not where you turned. You're on somethin' like South Ross Road. I think that's what the sign said. … Did you make a mistake?"

"Probably did," Spyder said, in a feigned conciliatory fashion. "Anyway, we can take a quick look in on the girls first. We'll just pull down here on this little trail for a bit. I'll pull in and you can hop out and take a quick look."

"Where they gonna go?" Cash impudently responded. "The damn thing's locked tighter than a tomb. They couldn't get outta there with a crowbar. ... Why don't we just drive on down to your best buddy's house? Has he got a garage?"

"We'll just go back in the woods here and you can take a look," Spyder said.

"Oh, shit!" Cash barked, after they'd driven a couple hundred feet off the South Ross. "Gimme the damn keys and I'll check on them."

"I'll unlock it for you," Spyder said, turning the engine off and snatching the keys from the ignition. ... "Let's go."

Cash busted out and almost ran around to the back of the car.

Spyder, on the other hand, carefully surveyed his surroundings, making every effort to ensure privacy. "No lights, and no signs of life around," he said to himself. "Perfect," he said aloud, but not loudly.

Cash beat Spyder around the car and so was waiting for him when he got there. But, instead of reaching forward with the keys to open the trunk, he raised his right hand forward. In it, he produced a compact Glock 29 10mm.

Cash was totally shocked at that sight. "What the hell you doin'? You can't do that."

With those last words, Cash spun and tried to run, a move that totally exposed his left temple to Spyder. That's all he needed, even if for only a split second.

Shoving the Glock in even closer, Spyder squeezed off a round. And it was a good, clean shot, piercing the young man's temple and destroying both lobes of his traumatized brain. One round did the trick. Cash's body dropped like a stone to the earth. It was trembling, and his heart was still beating. So, while technically still alive, Cash was dead just the same.

Spyder, having done deeds like this before, considered putting another round into the fallen man's brain. But he thought better of it. "I know I took out both sides of that asshole's brain," he said to himself. "And I know for certain that he ain't never gonna get up again ... not even as a vegetable. So there just ain't no need to attract more attention out here. I'll grab his ID and get the hell outta here. ... all I can say is that my life's gonna be a hell of a lot better not havin' to deal with that stupid bastard."

After Spyder had acquired the fallen man's wallet, watch and jewelry, and looked for but didn't find any personal letters or notes on his body, he grabbed Cash by the legs and dragged him a few more yards off the trail.

I wonder if they got wolves up here on Sugar Island? he was thinking. *If they do, Cash's body ought to feed a pack for a day or more.*

As he was getting back into his car he glanced down and noticed that he was sporting streaks of blood on his left hand. At first it troubled him, but soon he became comfortable with the red smears, thinking that a little blood on his hands might make the girls more eager to tell him what he wanted to know.

"What the hell," he muttered. "I think I'll leave it right where it is."

As he prepared to restart the rented Toyota, he took another panoramic view of his surroundings, and he was absolutely amazed at just how uncluttered the whole view was. He got to thinking, *I'll bet I know just how my guy, The Coach, how and why*

he decided to move here—right on the border with Canada. I'll bet
he's actually a lot closer to the group that does business up here, than
anyone else. And talk about 'outta the way', nobody would find him
up here. Bet that's his plan.

Spyder backed out of the practically unused drive that was
now serving as Cash's final resting place, and turned nearly due
north on South Ross Road. He then caught South Eastshore Drive
at Sugar Island Road.

"Okay," Spyder said aloud, "what am I looking for now? That
new guy wouldn't give me an actual address. ... Let's see, I have to
plug these co-ordinates in ... I'll do that, and see what I get. Okay,
so here goes: 46.49214,-84.15004. That should give me a drive.
And then I measure the mileage from that drive, to the drive at
the house. That oughta work just fine. ... Hell, it could work out
fine unless I show up at the wrong house with blood on me. Now
that could be a problem—a *big* one."

Spyder physically observed his self-conversation and noted
that it was far more light-hearted than it had ever been when he
was actually driving Cash around with him. He amazed himself
at just how compassionless he had felt about that man. After having given their relationship some additional thought, Spyder said,
again to himself but aloud, "I don't think I will ever miss that bastard—not one bit."

"... And point five," he said, "this next drive should be the one.
... And, this house does fit the description. Should be the one."

Even though the house he was directed to did seemingly fit the
bill, he was hesitant to go to the door. So, he waited for a few minutes, and simply watched. Finally, just before he wheeled back out
of the driveway, a thirtyish-looking man opened the front door

and walked out through it. The young man then sat down on the front steps and just stared toward Spyder's car.

"Are you the guy I've been waiting for?" he asked Spyder, after he had eventually walked up and coaxed him to lower the car window.

"I could be the man you're waiting for. My name is Spyder. What's your name?"

"Me?" the man said through a smile and a bit of a chuckle. "My name is just *The Coach*. Ain't my legal name, of course. But, it is what I always like to go by. ... Does that work for you? If you call me by that name I'll always know who it is I'm talking to. ... That is, I'll at least know that you're not the law."

"Works for me just fine," Spyder said. "Expecting company or anything?"

"We're good until tomorrow," The Coach said. "I seldom get a regular visitor out here. That's one of the reasons I moved to Sugar Island. I figured no one would want to pay for a ferry ride just to talk to me—of course, unless it was important. Besides, I'm on the road all the time. I drive truck."

"Then give me a hand," Spyder said. "And we can drag one of these bitches in the house so I can have a little chat with her. Can you help me with that? She was feeling a little under the weather before, so we might have to carry her some."

"Sure. I'll give you a hand."

Spyder walked around and opened the trunk. The girls had heard the shot that took out Cash, and they knew enough to keep their mouths shut at this stage. They were terrified.

The odor of fresh urine hit both men like a slap in the face.

"Whoa," Spyder said through a snicker. "You two little animals have been messin' around in your stable. ... One of you is gonna be stayin' put for a while. I just want my little *thievin'* bitch for right now."

"Here," he said as he reached down to Liz, "I'll even give you a hand getting out, as long as you behave yourself and keep your mouth shut out here. Can you do that okay?"

As he helped lift Liz's quaking and stumbling torso over the edge of the trunk compartment and onto the ground, he looked down at Angel and said, "Don't worry none, darlin', daddy will be back for you later."

Angel squeezed her tear-filled eyes tightly closed as Spyder slammed the trunk closed.

"I'll get the door for ya," The Coach said, as he warily turned and walked off in front of his other two visitors.

As the three of them headed toward the house, Spyder glanced down to check out the damage he'd earlier done to Liz's face when he slugged her. After his cursory examination, he decided that, aside from the blood that had escaped out her nose and right ear—which, as it dried, left her face looking like a map of crooked country roads—he concluded that she really did not look to be much the worse off.

"Thanks," Spyder said as he entered the house, "Can you close that door behind me? ... And do you have a basement?"

"Straight ahead and through that door," The Coach said, pointing the way. "The light switch is there on the left just inside that door."

"Hey." Spyder helped balance Liz as the two of them made their way to the bottom. Once the two of them had reached the nicely finished off rec room, he turned and looked back at The

Coach who stood at the top of the steps. "Have you got some rope?" he said to him. "Or anything like it? Even a small extension cord would work. If you got somethin' like that, just toss it to the bottom of the steps for me."

"I'm pretty sure I got a rope," The Coach told him. "It's brand new clothesline. … I'll get it and toss it down to you."

It took the host but a minute to find the new rope and toss it down to Spyder. The Coach would probably have brought it down in person, but he thought better of doing it like that, because his *new master* had told him to "toss" it down, and he had no desire to cross his new boss. "After all," he said to himself, "that son-of-a-bitch has fresh blood all over his hands. … And, that one girl, she's been beaten up pretty bad. … I ain't gonna mess with this dude—no way. He'll get that damn rope any way he wants it."

As soon as the rope hit the floor, Spyder was all over it. He scooped it up, and returned to where he had left Liz on the floor. Once he'd lifted her to a standing position, he cut off a three-foot-long chunk of the brand new clothesline, stripped her down to her bloodied bra and panties, and then tied her hands together in front of her.

He then he tucked a second piece of rope over a water pipe that ran directly above Liz's head. He pulled the end of it through far enough to give him about ten feet, and then wrapped it a second time over that same water pipe. He pulled it through and then ran it down to secure it to the lash that bound her wrists.

Then, pulling the free end of the rope tighter and tighter, he not only forced both of Liz's hands up and above her head, he did so to the point that her toes were barely touching the floor. He then securely tied that rope off on another piece of permanent plumbing.

Liz was in terrible agony as she struggled to alleviate some of the pain on her wrists by pushing up with her toes.

After nearly half an hour of sustained, but unsuccessful, torture in his effort to coerce Liz into revealing to him where she had stowed the valuable portion of his drugs, Spyder summoned The Coach by shouting loud enough to be heard upstairs. He then tossed to him the Toyota's push button remote and ordered him to go out to the car and remove Angel from the trunk.

Because of his failure to force Liz give him the information he sought, Spyder thought that he might be able to use the younger girl as bait to draw out from Liz the info he wanted.

It was right at that time when the rental company had finally tracked down the car Spyder was suspected of driving. They came to that conclusion because they were the only car rental company who had one of their late-model white Toyotas take a run through a Sault Ste. Marie gravel pit on that specific day. And now, they had tracked that same white Toyota to a remote location all the way back to the far side of Sugar Island. While they could not state unequivocally that the white Toyota being surveilled was actually the one that law enforcement had targeted, they could conclusively testify that the car in question definitely had not only pulled into the gravel pit in question, but that the car they were tracking had lingered there fifteen minutes and twenty-two seconds before leaving. And then, after being on the road for over half an hour, had parked at a house on the east side of Sugar Island.

"Jack, we've got your car," the chief of police said to Jack. "The car rental communications office just called me and gave me the final word on that. Not only had their white Toyota spent nearly twenty minutes in the gravel pit in question, it has now traced that very same rental back across the ferry and onto Sugar Island once again."

"No shit!" Jack grumbled loudly. "Chief, where do you have them now?"

"They show that the car has been parked at the same place for twenty-seven minutes now. That is at a location just about three-tenths of a mile north and east of these co-ordinates: 46.49214,-84.15004. I know that area quite well, and your best chance at locating that house is going to be by spotting that white Toyota. And then following the tracks to the door. Otherwise it will be largely up in the air."

"I'm going to have to give my boys a heads up, one of them made a stop by my house earlier today, and he could be up to it again."

"I'll let the sheriff know what I learned and he will no doubt want to get someone over there as quickly as possible."

"Thanks for the heads up, Chief," Jack said as he disconnected.

Kate had heard Jack's side of the conversation, and so she was already calling Robby to warn him.

"You boys still at the house?" Kate asked.

"Yeah, we're working on Stanger. Where you guys at?"

"We're in the Soo right now," Kate replied. "We're trying to locate Angel and her friend. They appear to have run into some serious trouble over here in the Soo. You haven't seen them recently, have you?"

"Not since we came out here to work," Robby said. "Are they alright?"

"It would seem that they have been kidnapped by one of their roughneck associates."

"Kidnapped!" Robby said loudly enough for Red to take serious note of.

"That's right," Kate replied. "And Jack and I, like I said, are in the Soo, and will not be able to get over to the house in less than half an hour. So, mind your own business and keep your head inside. One of those guys apparently stopped by our house earlier today, and they might do it again. Be careful!"

"Stopped by our house?" Robby asked.

"That's right," Kate said. "They were apparently looking for something in Angel's car. And they didn't find it."

Red was writing something down on paper, and he showed it to Robby.

"Red has a question," Robby told Kate. "He wants me to read it to you."

"Fire away."

"Red wants to know if you can tell us where you think Angel is on the island."

"Well," Kate said, "it looks like they—by they, I mean the kidnapper and the two girls—they are at the following co-ordinates: 46.49214,-84.15004. That is clear over on the other side of the island, so it shouldn't be a problem for you boys as long as you keep your rear ends inside the house, and the doors locked. We have no idea just how dangerous this guy is, but I think you can be sure that he wouldn't be kidnapping our girls if he weren't dangerous. We want you to be very careful until your Uncle Jack and I get there to help. Got that?!"

"Okay," Robby said. "I guess we'll see you in a half an hour or so."

By the time Robby had disconnected from his conversation with Kate, Red had entered the co-ordinates Kate had given him and was in the process of tracing them out—an effort that took him only seconds.

Almost immediately Red was elbowing his friend trying to show him what he had come up with. While not able to talk, Red still had no trouble conveying his findings. Robby could see quickly that the location in question was barely six minutes away, and could be arrived at using only good roads.

"Are you suggesting what I think you are?" Robby asked his friend.

Red signaled that indeed he was, and he grabbed Robby by the upper arm and pointed toward their 1965 Yellow Mustang.

"You want us to go out and try to save Angel?" Robby asked. "That's what you're getting at. Right?"

Red nodded his head signaling a definitive, "Yes."

And off they went.

"Oh shit!" Robby complained vociferously, but he did not back down from Red's challenge.

Robby walked over toward the Mustang, but Red intercepted him and shook his head negatively. And then Red pointed toward the snowplow.

"Snowplow?" Robby gasped.

Chapter 15 —

S nowplow?!" Robby asked again, this time with a little more concern-induced volume. "You want us to take Uncle Jack's snowplow?"

It wasn't as though the two fourteen-year-olds didn't know how to drive Jack's brand-new Dodge Ram 3500 Diesel truck. Because that was the beast Jack bought exclusively to move snow around with, it was fitted year-round with a snowplow large enough to take care of county roads. And, both boys were well practiced at driving it because that was their wintertime job. Since plowing did not involve taking a vehicle onto a public road, Jack saw no harm in having his two underage drivers get up before school and make clear all of the resort's passageways.

From May through September the Ram rested quietly in the garage beside the boys' Mustang. But, to ensure that it would start when called upon, Jack had them keep a trickle charger on the battery, and then to start it up and run it for five minutes every Saturday morning. "That way we should have no surprises when that first snow falls," Jack told them.

Red headed for the plow with no hesitation. Robby, in spite of his confused demeanor, followed closely on Red's lead. Even though they were both adept at following blurred markings, and missing rocks and other vehicles, Red did not hesitate a bit—he grabbed the keys from the rack and jumped behind the wheel, an arrangement with which neither Robby nor Buddy had any problem, as both of them hopped in without hesitation.

After Robby had disconnected the trickle charger, he jumped in the passenger seat and snapped on his seatbelt. Red reached forward on the dash, and found and triggered the overhead door opener. "Well," Robby said, "looks like we are on our way. ... Do you have any idea what we're gonna do when we get to that house? Do we have a plan yet?"

Red offered no response as he proceeded to drive out of the garage and head for South Westshore Drive.

Red handled the big truck in a very comfortable fashion, even though he was not familiar with driving it on the county's roads. As soon as he hit 6 Mile Road, he handed his cell phone to Robby to have him get specific directions to their target house. Of course, while he was unable to spell it out in any detail to his foster brother, the two of them had so much in common that Robby knew in advance exactly what Red was requesting.

"Okay," Robby said. "Let's see what we got here. Looks like we have to get to 46.49214,-84.15004. That's where Angel is likely to be, according to Uncle Jack. ... And he said that it's gonna be over on the Canadian side of the island. That makes sense. Those co-ordinates look like they would be over there. I'll get this worked out in just a second. We should be able to just drive right up in front of the house, or barn, or whatever it is, by using these co-ordinates.

"Here we go, it's telling us to stick to 6 Mile Road. You picked that one right. We'll stay on that until it has us turn on Brassar. That figures. Turn north on Brassar, and take that to Sugar Island

Road, and then turn right on that.

"But, all that takes us back to 'what are we gonna do when we get there?' Uncle Jack and Aunt Kate are not gonna be wrong about this. If they're saying that this guy, whoever he is, if this guy has kidnapped Angel and her friend, then you can be sure that they are right."

Just then they reached Sugar Island Road. Red had not taken his time once he got on 6 Mile Road. Robby recognized that his friend was speeding, but he understood the reason for it, so he did not object. "Turn here," Robby told him. "Turn right, towards the river. Then it should be only about a mile and a little. Turn left when we get to the end of this. ... Now, Red, what are we gonna do when we get to the house?"

Of course, Red did not answer Robby's question, because Red did not talk. But Robby was used to his friend finding some way to communicate with him when called upon. That was not happening this time.

"You really don't know how you're gonna handle this yet, do you, Red?" Robby said to him.

Still, there was no reaction from Red.

"Whatever you decide to do," Robby told him, "I'm with you. No matter. But, it'd be nice to have a plan."

Red obviously understood what Robby was saying, but again, he did not react.

"Turn left up here," Robby instructed him. ...

"Red has not yet figured out how he is going to deal with Angel's kidnappers," Robby said to himself. "Otherwise he'd be about trying to explain his strategy to me. ... And, that's all fine. When he does have a plan, it'll be a good one. Red always has good ideas.

I trust him. It's just that we've never faced a situation quite like this before. We don't even know how many of them there are. ... There, Red threw me a look. He must have worked out a strategy."

"Okay, Red," Robby said, "I'm ready when you are. What would you like me to do?"

Again, Red did not present any plans to Robby.

Finally, Red checked his seatbelt and made sure it was securely latched. And he then signaled to Robby to do the same.

Robby got that message loud and clear, and had his harness on and secured for takeoff.

The house where they ended up was set off the road a substantial distance and was at the bottom of a slight gradient. Red shifted the truck into the low range. He then slid the automatic transmission into Drive, and hit the accelerator. He aimed the edge of the plow so it would just catch the left front corner of the house, and he hit it very solidly. Red kept his foot on the gas while small pieces of the wall went flying all over, with the rear wheels leaving the ground momentarily, while it glided in the air to the side. The momentum of the impact had knocked a sizeable section of the wall loose from off its foundation. The truck itself came down a couple feet to the left, but it kept on rolling slowly.

When the boys reached a safe location off to the south of the house, Red turned the truck around. He raised the plow high enough so that it would protect them somewhat against rounds from Spyder's pistol should he opt to strike back. And then Red took another run at that same corner of the house. This time he caught it a little higher on the front plow. This time his strike dislodged the corner of the house, discernably separating the front wall from the side. And, again, Red kept his foot on the gas, and so he bounced off the building a bit and he was able to drive the plow back up the little hill and out to South Eastshore Road.

"Two successful runs!" Robby exclaimed aloud, "one hundred percent success so far!"

Red then turned the plow around on the road, and he pulled back into the front yard of the home. By that time, Spyder had come outside to confront "the crazy man who was trying to knock The Coach's house down."

At first Buddy barked loudly, but when Red, in his own inimitable way, scolded him for carrying on, Buddy lay down on the seat and waited patiently for Red to have his fill of the *fun*.

By the time he was ready to have another run, Red spotted a semi-auto 10mm in this strange man's hand, and so he signaled for Robby to remove his seatbelt and to get down on the floor of the truck. And Robby took his friend's advice.

As Red was making his third run at the house, Spyder was standing at the front door preparing to fire at him.

Red did not back down or let up. Instead, he zeroed in on that same corner, only this time he chose to clip it more in a parallel line with the east/west outside wall. In fact, he had the truck almost totally in line with the end of the house. And his speed was topping thirty miles per hour when he struck the building the third time. The second he made contact, he cranked the wheel sharply to the left. The reason Red did it that way was because he wanted to make the most of his truck's inertia and so to allow it to bounce off the wall, and not be stopped by it. It worked. Not only did the truck change directions slightly upon striking the wall, because he had cranked the wheels upon impact, the force of the blow barely slowed the truck down, while it essentially launched a small section of the wall close to fifty feet.

Robby remained virtually glued to the floor of the truck, because Spyder had now totally exited the house, and was actively firing rounds from his 10mm on every one of Red's runs.

This next time, the boys were to come at the house from the rear. Red had driven the plow entirely past the house, and had turned around behind it. He decided not to run at it from the southeast any longer because his strikes had already opened a gaping hole below the main floor which was at that point clearly exposing the basement. Actually, Red was afraid to batter the house any further on that southeast corner for fear of having the plow drop through to the basement.

Now, he had made up his mind to this time run at the house from the rear—that is, the southwest corner of the house. That is, he would strike the same corner of the house, but from a different angle.

Realizing that he would this time be driving up a small gradient in his approach, Red dropped back an additional fifty feet. He did that in order to ensure the likelihood that he would be able to strike the wall with adequate speed. And again, Spyder stepped away from the house a few feet and prepared to fire at the truck as it bounced off the corner.

Red, in the meantime, was beginning to feel confident with what he was doing.

He sized up the project at hand, and spun all four tires as he jetted the truck toward the house. The very instant that the front of the plow made contact with the building, he readied his reflexes to crank the custom-made steering wheel to the right so that the truck would bounce clearly away after the impact, and not get hung up on the foundation. And that's precisely how he did it.

At exactly the same moment he made impact, he hit the accelerator and spun the wheel to the right. As a result of his quick actions, he was able to maintain a good amount of momentum after making contact, and by continuing to floor it, he actually increased the plow's speed until he neared the road. And that's where he turned around and prepared for yet another run at the house.

A myriad of unrelated thoughts raced through his mind as he looked down at Robby and Buddy to be sure they were still okay. His psyche had become so drenched with adrenalin he had not even seen the muzzle flashes of Spyder's semi-auto, nor did he hear the bullets bouncing off the plow. Still, he realized that they had yet again been under heavy fire.

However, he realized that another run at the house would not be necessary. During those few minutes of attack, Red charged and hit the kidnap house six times—all of which were successively effective. Not only had Spyder abandoned the two kidnapped girls in the basement, he now had also exhausted all the rounds he had with him … and the two boys still had the plow functioning as an effective battering ram (no pun attempted but may be applied).

Just as Red had sat there preparing to take that seventh run at the house, the two men—Spyder and The Coach—bolted from the house. They both jumped into the rented white Toyota, spun it around, and headed south down Eastshore Drive.

Robby looked up at Red to see what was going on. And when he saw his friend's eyes following something, or someone, heading south on the road, his curiosity overwhelmed his desire for self-preservation, and he elevated his line of sight to a plane above the bottom of door glass.

"That's that damn Toyota, ain't it?!" Robby barked out. ... "I'm right, ain't I?!

Both boys realized something major was happening, but neither one of them recognized what it was. So, for over a minute they just sat virtually motionless waiting for their minds to catch up with them.

"What might that crazy man's next move be?" they asked themselves. But, once they observed that Toyota disappearing on Eastshore, and then heard it turn west on Sugar Island Road, it became clear to them that this issue had been settled, and totally in their favor.

It was at that time that they took a deep breath, and began to relax in the confidence that the three of them—Red, Robby and Buddy—were safe. Now the big question was, "How about Angel and her friend?" It seemed obvious to them that while the two girls were no longer under threat, were they still alive? They had both heard screams earlier, so they knew that at that point, which was barely nine minutes ago at the longest, both girls were still alive. So they were very hopeful.

Red shifted into Drive and drove the Ram 3500 back down to the house. But, instead of ramming it again, he parked beside the front door, and both boys bailed out and ran inside.

"Angel," Robby yelled at the highest volume he could muster. "Angel, Liz, where are you?"

Initially there was no response from the girls.

The two boys ran to the top of the basement steps, and yelled again, "Angel, where are you?"

"Robby. That you?"

"Yes!" Robby shouted. "Where are you?"

"We're down here," Angel replied in a weak, quivering voice. "Oh! Thank you, God. ... Liz and I are both down here. Can you help us? We're tied up and can't get away."

Red bolted down the stairs first. There he found each of the girls bound by her hands, with the rope that bound them tied off above their heads onto a cold water pipe. Red tried to untie the rope on Angel's hands, but he could not free her because the knot was too tight. Robby witnessed his plight, so he found an old box cutter knife that was lying on a small workbench, and he cut Angel's hands loose. When he freed her, she lost her balance and started to collapse on the basement floor. Red caught her before she reached the concrete and helped her to the couch.

Still, no one had heard a sound coming from Liz's swollen face.

While Angel still had her top and pants on, the wound on her neck had bled down and stained her clothes.

Then, the two boys worked together on freeing Liz. Robby cut her hands free, while Red prepared himself and caught her before she collapsed.

"Check her hands out, Red," Robby said. "Is she still alive? Her hands have been tied with the blood shut off for a long time, it looks like. Do you think they're gonna be okay? ...Is she still alive?"

Just then Liz began to realize that the two boys had saved her, and she began to open her eyes and move a bit.

"She's alive!" Robby announced in a spirit of joy. "They are both alive! ... I'm gonna call Uncle Jack. We need to see what he thinks we should do. ... Liz's hands look pretty bad to me."

"Hi, Aunt Kate," Robby said, when she answered Jack's phone.

"Wanted to let you know that we found Angel and her friend, and they're both sort of okay. Both beaten up pretty bad, but both are coming around."

"Where the hell are you?!" Kate asked in horror. "I told you to stay home! Where are you?!"

"Well, we came over to that house—you know, the one you gave us the address to. Over here by the Canadian side. ... That crazy guy had them tied up in the basement of that house. Red and I cut them loose, and I *think* they're gonna be okay. Liz's hands look really rough, though. Probably should see a doctor right away. Whereabouts are you and Uncle Jack? Will you be on the island soon?"

"What did you boys do?" Jack said, taking possession of his phone. "You've seen the girls—Angel and Liz?"

"Yes," Robby answered. "We plugged in the co-ordinates Kate gave us, and we drove over here."

As Robby was providing Jack and Kate with a few details about their exploit, Red helped the girls slip on a couple of men's flannel shirts he found hanging in the laundry. After he'd given them the shirts, which fit them like housecoats, he scrounged up some socks and helped them put them on. He considered shoes, but there was nothing around the truck driver's house that would work to walk far in. So, he just appropriated two additional pair of the truck driver's socks and gave them to the girls to keep their feet somewhat dry while walking out to the plow.

"You drove on the county roads without me? You're not *supposed* to do that. You know better."

"Sorry, Uncle Jack," Robby said. "We were worried about Angel. It sounded like she needed some help, so we just did it."

"Are you guys okay? Did you get hurt?"

"We're fine," Robby said. "And, we think the girls are okay too. … We hope they are. We're just a little worried about Liz's hands. That guy had her hands tied off so they weren't getting much blood like they should have. We think Liz should see a doctor pretty soon. Are you going to be home right away?"

"Kate and I are just driving off the ferry right now. We're headed up the hill by the bar. We'll head straight there right now. See you in about ten minutes."

"Perfect," Robby replied.

"You drove the Mustang over there—right?" Jack asked. "Is that what you drove?"

"No," Robby said. "We drove the snowplow."

"The snowplow?" Jack queried. "Why the plow?"

"Red thought it would be good to have the plow," Robby said. "We both thought the plow was the right move … since we were having to deal with a kidnapper and all. And, everything worked out well. That guy was a real jerk. He actually shot at us a bunch of times. Didn't hit either one of us—or Buddy. But, he did bounce a few rounds off the snowplow. … And, they actually put a few holes in the truck. The windshield is shattered—when he missed the plow and hit the glass. I actually think it might have been a ricochet. … But, whatever, like I said, he didn't hit either one of us. I think he emptied his Glock, and had to quit shooting. Pretty intense for a few minutes, but it all worked out pretty good. He finally gave up and took off. And the girls are still alive."

"Neither of you were hit, though?" Jack asked as reassurance. "Or injured in any way? Like hit by shattered glass?"

"We're fine," Robby said. "We both got hit by some broken

glass. But not in the eyes, or anything like that. ... Honestly, Red and I are fine. Need a shower when we get home, but I think that's it."

As providence would have it, Jack and Kate were so incredibly distracted by Robby's call, they both failed to notice that detested white Toyota when they met it as they drove east on Sugar Island Road. It's an absolute certainty, had they encountered that vehicle before Robby's call, one of them would have spotted it, and a fierce, and most certainly fatal, pursuit would have ensued.

"I'll get the sheriff over there right away and let them check it out," Jack said. "How will we find you? Can we see you from the road ... from Eastshore Road?"

"Oh yeah," Robby said. "After we get the two girls loaded up, we'll put the plow where you can see it. I think Red's gonna park it up at the road, then you can easily find us."

Red nodded in agreement, and while Robby finished talking to Jack and Kate, he led Angel out to the snowplow and situated her in the rear seat of the Ram. Afterward, he helped Liz walk out to the truck and placed her in the front passenger seat. His thinking was that both of the girls were chilled and needed to get warm, and he believed their best chance at that would be in the snowplow with the engine running.

Besides, Red was not totally sure that the crazy men would not return. And, if that were to happen, he was more confident in his ability to drive evasively than he was in successfully dodging bullets.

He'd considered having the two girls bundle up in blankets, and then wait for the authorities to interview them inside the house, but the boys had beaten the cabin up so badly with the snowplow that they did not trust the plumbing or electrical to not create problems for them.

"It'll just be safer for the girls to wait in the plow," the boys agreed. "Safer and possibly even more comfortable."

"Hang on a second, Robby," Jack said. "I think Kate has a question for you. She wants to know if the kidnapper is still on scene, or if he bolted. What can you tell me about that?"

"There were two of them—two men," Robby replied. "They stuck around until it started to look like their house was going to collapse, and then they took off. ... They left in a white small car. Looked like maybe a Toyota. They headed back toward the ferry. You had to have passed them on your way here. That is, if they were headed back to the Soo."

"We did meet a small white sedan right after we got off the ferry," Jack said. "Could have been them, I should think. But I was on the phone with you at the time. ... Well, if it was them, at least it wouldn't appear as though they were heading back to our house. Bet you didn't arm the alarm system, did you? I probably wouldn't have thought of it either. Kate's going to call it up and arm it right now. ... Well, I'll let you go. We're just about to turn onto Eastshore, by you. I think I can see the plow already. Good job, boys. Kate and I are proud of you both."

"Thanks, Uncle Jack," Robby said. "I can see you comin'."

Jack and Kate pulled in behind the plow. And when they did, Angel turned to greet them with a friendly wave. Jack walked directly over to where the boys were standing, while Kate opened up the front passenger door of the crew cab and checked in on the status of the girls.

"Hi, Aunt Kate," Angel said, throwing her freezing arms around

Kate's neck and hugging her. "Am I ever happy to see you. I hope you know that these two boys are both heroes. They saved our lives. ... That Spyder creep, he kept telling us that he was going to kill us if we didn't tell him where his 'shit' was. His word not mine. I just knew that I had no idea what he was talking about. I don't think Liz knew what he was asking about either. ... We were both scared to death, and there was nothing we could do to make him happy. He was just going to kill us. That's what he told us. 'Tell me where my shit is, or I'm gonna kill you!' That's what he kept saying.

"And then, what comes *exploding* through the wall but this big red truck. It shook the whole house when it hit it. ... And it kept ramming the house. *Bam. Bam. Bam. Bam.* Liz and I had no idea what was happening. And neither did they—the two men. They looked scared too. The whole house just kept shaking. I thought it might fall down every time the truck hit it. We didn't know what was happening.

"And then, Spyder got his gun and he went outside. When they would crash the truck into the house, Spyder would start shooting at them. *Bang. Bang. Bang.* Every time the truck would hit the house, Spyder would shoot his gun some more. I did not know at first that it was Red and Robby out there. I couldn't see anything. All I knew was that somebody was running into the house with something big and noisy.

"I didn't know it was the boys until after Spyder and his friend took off. Right after they ran away, Red and Robby came in looking for us. They found us, and then they got some shirts and socks for us to put on. We were very cold. I'm *still* cold. They put us in here and turned the heat on. Then they found some warmer clothes for us to wear—they don't fit at all, but at least they cover some of the goose bumps. I don't think I will ever get warmed up. Liz is freezing too.

"Kate, do you have any idea what all that was about? Liz and I—"

By that time Jack and the boys had walked up behind Kate and were listening to their conversation. After Angel's last comment, Jack interrupted, "What exactly did they ask you for? The two men who kidnapped you. What did they want?"

"I only heard one of them talk," Angel said, "and he was the one we knew from San Francisco, the one named *Spyder*. He kept asking us where his *shit* was. Neither one of us had anything to say. We didn't know what he was talking about.

"That's when he took a knife out and poked it into my neck until I started to bleed. I just had to give up. He was asking me for something I had no idea about. Neither did Liz. We didn't know what he wanted, so we couldn't help him. … He was going to kill us. And there was nothin' we could do to stop it. Absolutely nothin.'"

At that point, Jack took a few steps away from the truck and called Sergeant Blake of the Sheriff's Department. "Are you headed to Sugar Island?" Jack asked.

"We are waiting to get on the ferry right now," Sgt. Blake replied.

"We suspect our kidnappers just might be on that ferry as we speak. You should check out carefully every vehicle driving off it. And maybe wait out a couple of cycles before you get on. There's nothing you can do here anyway. … I think you should just wait for them to drive off of the ferry, and then safely take them down. Might want to get some backup, too. My boys leveraged the girls from them, and did it without injuring anyone, or getting themselves hurt. But I would recommend backup to take the guys down. They had a head start on us."

Liz was still seated in the front seat. Her hands were swollen and purple. Her lips were purple as well.

When Kate opened the front door of the truck she caught a quick glimpse of Liz's swollen fingers. "Let me check out those hands of yours," she said to her as she more carefully examined them. "Looks to me like your abductors had your wrists tied up pretty tight, and it cut off circulation. Let me see if we need to get you some immediate medical help. ..."

"You're lucky that the boys got those ropes off your wrists when they did," Kate finally said, trying to reassure her. "Much longer and you could have lost your hands. You're a pretty fortunate young lady because I think they're starting to get some blood through them now. But, I'll bet they get pretty sore over the next week or so.

"And, I even think they're starting to warm up a bit," Kate said after she had rubbed Liz's hands with her own for a couple minutes. "That's very good news. ... Where'd the boys find that blanket? That's got to feel a little better to you."

"Yes," Liz agreed. "Red found it someplace in the basement. But I didn't see where exactly he got it from. He cut me loose and I fell on the couch. That guy, Spyder, had poured cold water on my bare skin. I was freezing. Never in my life have I ever been that cold. And he kept—"

"He, that Spyder guy," Kate said. "He kept asking you where his shit was. Right?"

"Yeah," Liz answered.

"Well, where was his shit?"

Liz did not respond to Kate's question. So, sensing that her years of experience as a detective were about to kick in, Kate said, "Liz, grab your blanket. You and I are going to go sit in Jack's Tahoe. We're going to have a little conversation. Just you and me. … Jack, you can entertain these folks for a little bit while Liz and I have a woman-to-woman chat. Okay?"

"Go for it," Jack said. "You ladies should have a little time before the sheriff gets here—depending on what he finds at the ferry. See what you can figure out."

Jack knew exactly where Kate was headed with her "little chat" with Liz, and he was seeking to lay some groundwork for her to build upon.

When they reached Jack's truck, Kate helped Liz get squared away in the front passenger seat, while she slid in behind the steering wheel. Kate started the engine, and turned the heater blower on circulating warm air around Liz's still-chilled body.

"There," Kate said. "That ought to help a little. … Okay, Liz, time is running out. I want you to tell me the truth from this time on. I am going to need the truth if I'm going to be able to help you. First of all, we know that you girls brought a sizeable quantity of illegal drugs from California to the UP. That was not a question—we know that to be the truth.

"We know that you had a suitcase in your car with a large quantity of fentanyl and coke. It is safe to assume that the suitcase contained the 'shit' that this associate of yours, the one you knew as Spyder, that he was asking about. The sheriff also knows about it, and they are going to be driving up here anytime now. And they're going to be wanting to get some answers.

"I'm not sure just how much about this you might or might not know, but the PHC, that's the Public Health Code, Act 368 of 1978, states that possession of 1,000 grams or more of those drugs warrants a fine of one million dollars, and a prison sentence of not more than thirty years."

Liz did not respond. She knew that what she was up to was against the law, but she had never before heard it so stipulated by people who seemed legitimate.

"Now," Kate continued, "if you noticed, I was not asking if this was true or not. We know this to be the case. We know that's what you had in Angel's car. And so does the sheriff, at this point. He knows. … That means, if you are going to be able to help yourself, and to let us help you at all, then you need to act decisively. I am not sure just how much you know about us. But I am a lieutenant homicide detective in New York City. And Jack, my father, he's a retired Chicago homicide detective. We have both worked hand in glove with the feds for years and years."

Liz was panicked. "What, exactly, are you suggesting?" she asked.

"I'm suggesting you work with us," Kate said. "That is with me, the sheriff and my father, and we will see what sort of a deal we can come up with for you. It other words, you won't be totally on your own. But, you will need to act quickly."

While seeking a path through the legal malaise Liz had created for herself did present Kate with a challenge that she abhorred— i.e. charting a course for a suspect that bordered on shrewd, it was not as though she was totally without experience in that area. After all, she had started out her professional career as a very cunning criminal defense attorney.

"What can you get me?" Liz asked. "As far as a deal—do I have a legal way out of all this … crap?"

"Look," Kate said, "All I can tell you is that right now, as we speak, the sheriff is likely taking down your guy at the ferry. That would be that guy named Spyder, I believe that's what you call him. So, our time is limited. Sgt. Blake will be driving up any minute, and the time to make a deal will be over."

"What kind of deal are you talking about?" Liz asked, after thinking for a few seconds.

"Where are the drugs?" Kate asked. "Right now, as we speak. Where are they?"

Liz was growing weak. She was sick of playing games, and so was totally open to seeing what might be available.

"Right now, he's got most of them—Spyder. He's got the fentanyl with him in the car he's driving. And some of the coke."

"Are there more?" Kate asked. "Are there more drugs than what Spyder has with him right now?"

"Yes, a lot more."

Chapter 16 —

T here's more drugs?" Kate asked, more than a little disappointed with the information. "Then, where would
they be?"

"Last I knew, they're in with Angel's stuff, in her storage area.
… But Angel doesn't know anything about it. I switched it out
while she was getting her car started."

"Can you take me over to it?" Kate asked. "Like right now? Do
you feel up to showing it to me right now?"

"Well, sure," Liz said. "We could do that right away, if that's
what you want. … You're gonna need Angel's card and key. Maybe
not the door key—I don't know if the door is locked or not. But
the gate will be locked—that's automatic. But you will need the
card to get past the gate."

"Then let's go do it," Kate said. "And, I have another question
for you. This has to do with Angel. Exactly what does she know
about the drugs? Starting from when you gals were in California.
You just said that she did not know about the drugs that are still
in the storage area. Spell out to me what you are saying. Exactly.
What does Angel know, and how is she involved? I need the truth,
and all of it."

"Honestly," Liz said. "Angel never knew anything about the
drugs. Nothing, as far as I know. She never bought or sold any

drugs. And I never saw her use drugs. I was the damn fool who was going into the business, and I am the one who loaded up Spyder's shipment for us to drive back east. ... But Angel never knew anything about it. And now, she *still* doesn't know about it."

Kate was not happy with what Liz had just shared with her, but she did not let on that she was displeased.

"Do you have any on your person right now?" Kate asked. "Drugs, that is."

"No, but I don't even have any real clothes on," Liz quipped. "All my extra clothes are in Angel's car. ... And, there are no drugs in my purse or in my pockets. I promise. The only drugs I know about are going to be in one of two places. They're going to be in Angel's stuff in the storage area, or in Spyder's car. The car he had over here earlier. That's gonna be it. And that's the truth, as far as I know."

Under most circumstances, Kate would have been highly skeptical of such a declaration of innocence by a cornered suspect—and Angel's friend was definitely trapped. But, in this case, because Liz had just been so miraculously rescued from the very precipice of death, Kate tended to believe what the young lady was telling her.

"Then, let's start off by seeing what we can do about her storage area," Kate said. "Are you game to attack that now? The sooner the better, I can promise you that. There is absolutely no time to waste."

"I feel like crap," Liz responded. "But I can do it now, if that's what you want."

"I'm going to go explain what we're doing to my dad," Kate said. "And I'll be right back. I'll grab Angel's storage room pass card. ... You think she has it with her?"

"Spyder didn't strip her. ... She should have it with her, or it will be inside the house here. You'll have to ask her about that."

Kate then walked back over to where her dad was waiting with Angel. After she'd collected Angel's facility gate pass card, and her padlock key, she said to her father, "Dad, can I talk to you for a minute?"

"Sure," he said. "What's up?"

"Let's slide over here. I have something to run by you."

So, the two of them walked over to where they were out of earshot of Angel and the boys, and Kate said, "We've got a bit of a challenge here, Dad. Liz informs me that there still could be a stash of drugs at Angel's storage facility. She said that she hid it there herself. ... Good chance that the sheriff is taking down that Spyder character, possibly at the ferry dock. It's possible, actually, that it's going down right now as we talk.

"But, whatever the case, this Liz gal tells me that there are likely more drugs at the storage facility. They could present problems for all of us, and they've got to be dealt with immediately. ... On the positive side, she told me that Angel knows nothing about the drugs. According to Liz, only she was ever aware that this whole thing had been about drugs. And I tend to believe her.

"That part of this whole drama might just be my heart talking. ... But that's what I think. I'd like to take Liz over there right now and get the drugs out of Angel's storage garage. ... If there is any way at all that we can legally protect Angel, and help her get through this, that's how we ought to proceed; that should be our goal."

"Whoa there, daughter of mine," Jack said. "Just how smart

would that be? You get busted dumping those drugs, and they've got you—even your slick talkin' old man would not be able to talk your way out of that one."

"Dad, here's the deal," Kate explained. "Angel never knew that Liz was transporting drugs. Still doesn't, as far as I know. Liz is a very sneaky young lady. She pulled that part of the whole caper off very well. ... That means, as it stands right now, Angel could be in more trouble than Liz is, because the drugs are either in Spyder's car—that's the dude that kidnapped the girls—or, they're in Angel's storage garage. Basically, Liz could be home free. But, our Angel is quite exposed. And, except for perhaps her bad taste in friends, she's most likely *totally* innocent. I've got to see what I can legally do to clear her. Even if that means that Liz is allowed to skate as well—and it could. ... After all that fourteen-year-old has been through, we owe that to her. ... Anyway, I need to give it a shot. Given our history with that young lady, I think we owe her that much."

"Kate, I get what you are going for here," Jack said. "But you are playing with fire. I'm with you all the way. So, give it a go and see what you can do. Anything I can help with—I'm here. ... Just remember, this whole thing could turn on a dime."

"Where's the sheriff on this?" Kate asked.

"I'll check up on that end of it," Jack said.

"Liz and I are going to be outta here," Kate said as she walked away. "We'll take the Tahoe, if that's okay. I'll talk to you later. ... Let me know what you hear from the sheriff."

Jack smiled and nodded his agreement with her requests.

Kate then walked back to the Tahoe and slid in behind the wheel. "Ready to go do it?" she said to Liz. "Sooner we get this done, the better off we will all be."

"Yeah," Liz said. "We need to get it done. I suppose the cops are gonna be all over his shit real soon. They probably are already. The sooner we get that stuff resolved, the better our chances. ... Do you think the cops already have it? Are they at Angel's storage space? That's where the missing case is. Actually, the drugs are no longer in the case itself. I took them out and packed them in one of Angel's boxes."

"I'm not sure what we're gonna find there," Kate replied, as she started up the Tahoe and checked for traffic.

"Aunt Kate," Robby said, running up to the driver's window. "Where are you goin'? Can Red and I go with you?"

"I would rather have you boys stay with Angel and Dad," Kate replied. "They might need you. And I think that they are going to have to wait around for the sheriff to check this house out. Plus, somebody is going to have to explain about the bullet holes in the RAM. That's going to have to be you and Red. ... We'll see you fellows later this evening. Okay?"

As they pulled out and onto Eastshore Road, Liz asked, "Do you know where Spyder is? He has to kill me now. I know too much about him."

"Good point," Kate agreed. "I'll check with the sheriff and see if he's chased that Spyder fellow down. ... *and* with the city—the chief. We haven't talked to him in a while."

By the time they had passed the Hilltop Bar, Kate had confirmed that the sheriff had missed engaging Spyder at the ferry dock. "He must have left the island before you reached the ferry," Kate said. "Don't you suppose that's how that went down?"

Sgt. Blake agreed with her assessment.

Liz was monitoring Kate's phone call, and after she had disconnected her conversation with the sheriff, Liz asked her, "Where's he gonna be—I'm talking about Spyder. Do you think he will be at the storage facility?"

"That's a very real possibility," Kate replied, "although I doubt it. The city police might be there as well. Don't really know what to expect in that regard. ... Just know that having those drugs packed away with Angel's belongings presents a big problem for her—regardless of what you have to say about it. That's the issue I'm seeking to solve right now."

"Like I said, Angel doesn't know anything about the drugs," Liz said.

"I get that," Kate said. "But you saying that does not significantly affect her vulnerability here. Courts like to keep it as simple as they can. If those drugs are found inside her storage area, that's going to be a problem for her—*and* for you, for that matter. ... Not sure what we could do to mitigate the situation if local law enforcement finds it before we get there. But, I would like to see the both of you walk away from this with nothing hanging over you—that is absolutely *nothing* hanging over either one of you. ... It could still go down like that. We'll see what we find when we get there."

"Who are we dealing with?" Liz asked. "Is it the sheriff or the local police?"

"If it has to do with Sugar Island," Kate replied, "then we're likely looking at the Chippewa County Sheriff. If we're talking about Sault Ste. Marie, MI, that would be in the city itself, then it would be the city police—Sault Ste. Marie Police Department. ... I think it could get a bit muddled up if this is viewed as a Federal matter. But, my gut tells me it's going to be both city and county. … I think that's just about what it's likely to look like. We'll see shortly."

As Kate and Liz were driving off the ferry, both of them scrutinized carefully the approach leading onto the ferry from the Soo, and neither of them spotted anything unusual—no law enforcement vehicles of any description were waiting to get on the ferry.

"So far so good," Kate said as they pulled off the approach and onto Riverside Drive. "Another twenty minutes and we'll know what the scoop is. … Do you remember how you left Angel's storage area? Was it locked up or open? Do you remember?"

"Angel and I both left there in the trunk of that white Toyota. I have no idea if it was locked up or wide open. I just don't know."

"We'll soon see," Kate said as they drove up to the outside gate.

Both Liz and Kate checked out the facility to see if they should even entertain the feasibility of gaining entry.

"I don't see any cops on site," Kate said as she drove up to the card reader at the gate. "Let's give it a go."

The gate system employed a prox reader for entry. The first time Kate presented Angel's card, the reader rejected it. So, she tried it twice more, and her third effort was successful and the gate opened.

"So far so good," Kate said as she drove through the open gate. "Now, how do I find Angel's locker? I haven't been here in months."

"Go straight down this drive," Liz replied, "and it's down quite a ways. It's the one down there with the trash by it. If you just pull up at that trash, I'll check to see if the door got locked from when we were here earlier."

Kate drove right up to the overhead door, and Liz got out to check it.

"It's not even got a lock on it," Liz said, as she opened it up. "It appears to be totally unsecured."

Kate jumped out of the Tahoe and they both entered the locker.

Liz immediately went over to the area where she had switched out the contents of one of Angel's boxes, and she found three of Angel's storage containers emptied and ransacked. It took her about a minute to determine that the drugs had already been removed.

"Spyder must have been back here already," Liz said. "He must have figured out that I'd hidden the contents of that last suitcase here in the storage locker, and he recovered it. ... So, that means that Angel doesn't have to worry about getting caught with the drugs. Spyder's got it all back."

"That's not all that Spyder has done over here," Kate said, as she discovered the body of a young man casually tossed upon some of Angel's boxes. "Liz, do you recognize this fellow?"

Liz walked around in front of the Tahoe and took a look at the discovery Kate had made. "Oh my God!" she exclaimed. "That's the guy Spyder called 'The Coach.' ... That house we just left on Sugar Island, the one your boys—Red and Robby—took apart. That was his house. ... Do you think he's dead?"

"He's dead alright," Kate said. "Shot twice in the head. *Definitely* dead. ... We're going to take one more look through Angel's stuff. Just to be sure. Because, I'm going to have to call the cops, and they'll be asking more questions."

"Are you pretty sure that I can come out of this okay?" Liz asked. "If I just tell the truth?"

"Maybe," Kate replied. "But, I can promise that both of you ladies will have a big problem if you talk too much, or get caught in even a little lie. We've got a murder here. That's a big deal. First in line as a prospective suspect is your friend from San Francisco. He, Spyder, would be the first person I would like to question. But, I'm not doing this investigation. That being the case, my principal interest here is in ensuring that Angel gets a fair shake. ... Now, that having been established, from what you tell me, she is or is not associated in any way with anything illegal?"

"Angel's done *nothing* wrong," Liz replied. "She has done nothing illegal at all, as far as I know."

"Okay," Kate said, "let's just leave it that way. ... Now then, that brings us to you. I'll put it to you again: do you have in your possession any illegal drugs—any at all?"

"No," Liz said. "There is something that you might not be aware of. I believe Spyder has a storage area here under his name. Not sure what he has it for, but I overheard him talking about it with one of his dealers from the Bay Area—a man known as Cash. ... I think Spyder might have murdered him as well. When we left here, Spyder had Angel and me locked in the trunk of his car, and about fifteen minutes before he got me out of the car and took me into that house, Angel and I heard a gunshot—maybe two. And then, when he got me out and took me inside, Cash was no longer there. That's when we met this new guy—the dead guy over there, the fellow named The Coach. My guess is that there is also a body back there on Sugar Island—ten or fifteen minutes from that house."

"I've got to call the local police," Kate said as she dialed them. "I'm going to do that right now. They're going to want to know about your involvement. We'll talk about that after I get them on their way."

"This is Kate Handler. I want to report a fatal shooting. I am at the storage facility where we had sent you earlier today. I am back there right now, and we have found a dead body in the storage area rented by our young friend, Angel Star. I think my father filled you in on our success in locating and freeing Angel and her friend Liz. Well, not all is well. We, Liz and I, returned to the rental storage area, and we found the body of a young man—apparently a murder victim. We will remain here and talk to you. … Thanks."

"Okay, Liz, they will be here in a few minutes. You need to get your story straight right here and right now, because it's not going to be easy to convince them that this Spyder guy followed you all the way from California because you turned him down for a date. … I think that you *could* beat this thing, but you are going to have to come up with something a lot better than a jilted lover story. … What can you tell them that will be both significantly disturbing, *and* believable?"

"Should I tell the truth?" Liz asked after pondering Kate's request for a long moment. "Should I say that I stole Spyder's drug shipment and brought the whole thing to Michigan?"

"Let's think a little more about this," Kate suggested through a skeptical smile. "First, let me ask you a question, and I do want the truth here; did you remove any of the drugs from the suitcases? And I do mean *any* of it at all."

"Remove?" Liz answered. "Did I remove any of the drugs? The answer is no—absolutely no. There was a lot of fentanyl, and a whole lot of coke. … But I don't use drugs. I might smoke a joint now and again, but nothing regular. And nothing stronger than an occasional joint. … Everything that was in those cases when I started out in San Francisco was still there the last I knew. … And, as far as Angel is concerned, she never even knew what was in those suitcases to begin with. So, the answer to your question is no—I never removed any of Spyder's drugs … aside from repacking that one suitcase. But I did not remove any of the product."

"Then," Kate said, asking another question, "tell me this: did you handle any of the contents of those suitcases? By 'handle', I mean physically touch without a glove?"

"No," Liz said. "Not aside from repacking that one suitcase, that one time. And I wore gloves when I did that."

"Help me out here," Kate said. "Are you saying that you never physically touched any of the contents of those suitcases?"

"I never did," Liz replied. "Spyder taught me that. I always put gloves on when I looked inside the cases. He always wore gloves, and told me that *anyone* who handles bags like that needed to do the same."

Kate's major concern was in protecting Angel from any repercussions resulting from the whole affair. While her years as a big-city detective did not render her impervious to negative situations, it did provide her with an uncommon level of confidence as to how to avoid detection.

"Okay," Kate offered, "Liz, let's see if this flies. You and this fellow known as Spyder were lovers. Is that true?"

"That is true. I'm not proud of it, but it's true."

"He followed you to Michigan because you left him without an explanation as to why you left. True or false?"

"True," Liz answered, "at least in part."

Kate, troubled by Liz's answer, told her, "Don't volunteer anything beyond the basic truth. Try this: 'Spyder followed me to Michigan because I left him without an explanation. We were lovers.' Would that be true or not?"

"Yes, it is the truth."

"And he kidnapped you and Angel and held both of you captive. True or false?"

"True."

"Now, this is where it could get tricky," Kate told her. "I want you to tell me this—am I correct in stating that at no time did your hands physically touch anything that belonged to this Spyder fellow?"

"That would be true," Liz said, after a few moments of thoughtful silence. "And, it could not be proven that I did. ...Angel would back me up on that too."

"Here's how this has to go," Kate said after weighing Liz's words. "You will need to have an attorney. I'll see that you get one—a good one. And then, you will need to refuse to talk to anyone without that attorney present. I'll talk to the local law enforcement, and give them what they are going to need. I can be confident that there are no illegal materials in your luggage, and certainly none at our house. Is that correct?"

"That is correct," Liz said.

"Good," Kate said, "I need to bring my father up to speed before the locals arrive."

And that's what Kate did. She called her father and filled him in on the salient details regarding there being at least one dead body, and probably two. She also informed him that he should advise Angel not to talk to law enforcement except through legal representation, that it should be a different lawyer than that used by Liz, and that she, Kate, would go over the important points with him regarding this whole issue when she saw him later that evening.

"Oh," Kate then said to him, "About that *second* body—the one I just mentioned. Liz just informed me that it, that second victim, is likely to be out by the house where the girls were found. Liz thinks that it will be about a fifteen-minute drive from that house. She said that the two of them, that is Liz and Angel, were locked in the trunk of Spyder's car, and that he stopped about fifteen minutes from that house. She thinks that it will be there that he, Spyder, shot somebody they knew as *Cash*. He would be the second shooting victim."

"Okay," Jack said. "Here's how I'll handle it. The car rental place can probably give the chief the exact location of where that car stopped. And that's where that body would be. That is, if there even is a second body, and if it hasn't been moved. … I'll get him on it. We'll talk more this evening."

Chapter 17 —

That evening, after the sheriff had declared the house on the east side of Sugar Island an official crime scene, and after Jack and the chief, with the help of the car rental folks, were able to track down Spyder's Toyota to the location of Cash's body, Jack finally was able to convince the two boys to hit their beds, and then to find the opportunity to engage Kate in their long-awaited conversation.

"What do you think, Dad?" Kate pressed her father. "Do you agree with what I was seeking to accomplish with the girls?"

"I'm pretty sure I know where you were going with it," Jack said. "Not so sure I would have taken the same route, but I get what you were doing."

"What don't you like about my approach?"

"Oh," Jack said, "I respect what you're attempting to accomplish, it's just that I think I might have been a bit more cut and dried. I might have just turned Liz over to the sheriff, or the chief, and let whichever one of them might want her—to let the law deal with her. I understand what you're doing. Your approach was arguably the more humane—particularly with respect to Angel. And I admire you for that."

"In my mind," Kate explained to her father, "the most critical problems to be dealt with are, first of all, protecting Angel from any undeserved recrimination for the actions of this Spyder character. In my view, he's the one true bad player here. ... And I think Angel has had enough bad luck in her life already, she doesn't need any more. ... And so, whatever I can do to help put an end to bad fortune for that young lady, I would like to give it a shot.

"My second goal is to provide an escape hatch for Liz. ... I confess that I don't know if she deserves one, or if she's even smart enough to know what one would look like if it walked up to her and shit on her shoe. ... But, if possible, I would like to leave for her a possible path out of this mess—a way to avoid repercussions, should she have the desire to change her ways, and seek a way out.

"It seems to me like Liz is young enough to put her life back together, and turn it all around. ... I might be wrong in that assessment. But, quite possibly, she is not beyond salvation. Of course, we have to make sure that we do not allow her to ascend to a position where she could drag Angel, or us, into this insane malaise. ... As long as that can be avoided, I would like to see her have a shot at escaping."

"Well," Jack said, "lofty goals for sure. Do you think you've accomplished what you have set out to?"

"I don't know," Kate replied. "In fact, it could be years before I find out definitively—maybe longer. Perhaps I will never know.

"One of the most critical issues to be dealt with is to be sure that there are never any drugs kept on our property. That we have to diligently, passionately, guard against. ... As it stands right now, I am relatively confident that there are no drugs at our house.

"How about it, Dad? What do you think? Do you think it could be pulled off? Or, even if it should be?"

"I'm not *exactly* on the same page with you," Jack replied. "Not one hundred percent. But, if I'm not on the same page, I'm probably in the same chapter."

Jack then gave his words a few moments to sink in.

"But," he then continued, "I do think we have to be very careful with just how much fluidity we allow when it comes to dealing with the sort of serious legal issues we are now dealing with. ... Do you get my train of thought here?"

"Totally," Kate replied. "As I see it, nothing about this whole case is yet settled—everything—and I do mean *everything*—is still up in the air. Right?"

"That's right," Jack said. "And, we are going to have to be very careful what we say about this to anyone. We've got some good friends here—on all levels. But—"

Kate laughed out loud as she interrupted.

"The key word being 'here.' We do have good friends around *this* area. But that would not be an accurate statement to make when you take in the East Coast."

"Agreed," Jack said, smiling in agreement. "And this issue is most likely to be one that gets resolved right here in Michigan's Upper Peninsula. If we play it right. ... We would do well to keep the Feds out of it, if you know what I mean."

"And that's going to be our challenge," Kate replied, "Playing it right."

The two of them were sitting at the table in the kitchen. Red and Robby had gone up to their bedroom. No doubt the boys would be up half the night talking about what had gone on that day, with Red turning on the lights momentarily every half hour or so in order to write down the thoughts he was seeking to convey on one topic or another. But, it was understood that they would not be coming down to the kitchen again unless the house was on fire.

In like fashion, Angel and Liz had eaten and showered, and they as well had been tucked in for the night. It was understood between the two girls that all their conversations regarding what had just transpired, ought to take place only in the presence of their respective attorneys.

And, as far as Liz sharing any details regarding drugs, she was under strict orders from Kate not to discuss the matter with anyone.

So, with very little to talk about, the two girls quickly fell asleep for the night.

Later, as Jack and Kate sat alone at the dining room table, he queried his daughter about her thinking as to just how sincere Liz actually was about straightening her life out. "Do you think that there might be something to it?" he asked her.

"God, Dad," Kate said, looking up from her Coors Lite and leveling her gaze into his eyes. "I only wish I knew. ... I don't. I truly *hope* we are not wasting our efforts here. But I don't know if it's going to work with her. ... I really think that she is very sick of all the crap that has been coming her way of late. And I do think that she is pretty smart—smart enough to know that she has brought it all on herself. She has to know that.

"This is how I think it might go down," Kate said. "At least, how I *hope* it goes down. ... I would like to keep both of those young ladies around for at least the short term. I will take my vacation as soon as I can arrange for it, and spend it here with you and the girls."

"That would help," Jack said. "I could certainly use some help."

"I've got some time coming," Kate said. "I think can make it work. ... This is what I would be looking at, for the short term. I am not a psychologist, but I would like to see if Liz can avoid dwelling on the dark side, especially with Angel and the boys. Any sign of that, and she's gone. We'll buy her a ticket and stick her on a plane back to California."

"Makes sense," Jack observed.

"Keep them both right here under our roof," Kate said. "But, that would be for the short term—*only* the short term. I would want to see how Liz adjusts to this new life. See if she really *wants* to turn it around. ... She might not have it in her to straighten her life out.

"The truth is, we do not even know that girl—that young woman. We need to get to know how she thinks—how she deals with problems. Who she really is. ... We will need to see how she reacts to problems, large and small—see what her character brings out of her.

"If we did it like that, we could be relatively sure that we would be able to keep Angel here with us, at least for the short term. I would like to see if we can get her on her feet. She doesn't have a lot of friends here in the Soo, but she does have our boys. ... I'm not so sure that we can get her back to being fourteen. But, I am quite sure that would be best for her, if she could do that.

"So, Dad, what say you? Do you think that we could give this a shot?"

Jack did not verbalize an answer to his daughter, but he did offer her an extended, sincere smile. And she knew exactly how to interpret that response.

The message her father was sending to her was this: "Neither one of us knows how all of this is going to work out. Hopefully, we will be able to get both of these young ladies on their own two feet. But, we do both know that nothing in life is ever guaranteed before it has a chance to work itself out. So, this is what we have to do. We have to give each of these two young ladies the best chance we can to make something out of their lives. And then we stand back and observe."

And, that is exactly how they approached it.

The next morning, as Jack would have predicted, Red and Robby were the first members of the Handler clan to make their presence known down in the kitchen. They were there to eat breakfast, and hear all the stories emanating from the adventures of the previous day. And, they were both eager to share their exploits/stories with the girls, and with Kate. That was not so much the case when it came to explaining to their Uncle Jack all the bullet holes in his practically brand new RAM 3500. But, even though they were not too sure what his reaction was going to be, they both knew better than to stretch the truth, or make excuses with him.

Then, there was the confusing matter of what those two young ladies had been up to. Neither one of the boys had any notion that illegal drugs had been involved in many of the convoluted transactions of the day before. And, while they did correctly suspect that no one was ever going to share with them the parts of the story that might unnecessarily jeopardize one of the young females in her ability to put her life back together, they also knew that the best opportunity they would ever have to learn about what had gone on would most likely be during breakfast that morning. And they were ready to find out everything they could.

Jack was actually the first one up, but he did not initially join the boys for breakfast. As he most always did, after he had put on the morning's coffee, he secured himself away in his office in order to quietly peruse the overnight events on his computer. And then, hearing activity in the kitchen, decided to go up and join the scrimmage. As he walked up the steps from his office, he heard Robby talking with Kate, and knew that she would be seeking her father's wisdom in order to deal with some of the questions that were sure to come up. However, just before he reached the top of the steps, he received a phone call.

"Who the hell would be calling me this early?" he asked himself. He looked down at his phone and saw that the call was from the Chippewa County Sheriff's Office.

"Yes," he said, lingering near the top step, "this is Jack Handler. What can I do for you?"

"Jack, Sgt. Blake here. Crandle and I'd like to stop over and talk to you this morning. Would that be okay?"

"Well, sure," Jack replied. "I just put some coffee on. Come on over. ... But tell me, can't we do this over the phone?"

"I need to talk to you in person," the sergeant said. "Have some questions I will have to run by you face to face. I'm on the ferry as we speak. So, I'll only be a few minutes. Just wanted to give you a heads-up. I trust that will be okay?"

"I'm here," Jack said. "And I will have some fresh coffee."

"Thanks. See you in a few."

Jack then continued up the steps and on into the kitchen.

"Did I hear your phone ringing?" Kate asked.

"You did," Jack replied. "We're going to have some company in a few minutes—Sgt. Blake and Deputy Crandle. I think he misses us. It's been at least seven hours since he talked to us last."

Jack then addressed Red and Robby: "Good morning, boys. You fellows are looking pretty chipper for this early in the morning. Hope you both got all your beauty sleep."

"Good morning, Uncle Jack," Robby said. "Yeah. We got a good sleep."

"What's the sheriff need to know?" Kate asked.

"No idea," Jack said. "Sgt. Blake didn't want to talk about over the phone. … Might just want a cup of my coffee. … Probably better doing it like this, anyway. He's a pretty good guy."

"Should I get the girls up?" she asked.

"I'd say not yet," Jack answered. "I think we should think long and hard before giving any agency access to those girls. I don't think either one of them needs to be talking to law without benefit of an attorney."

"Exactly," Kate said. "The same might extend to these two as well, don't you think?"

"Let's just see what the sheriff's after," Jack said. "And then we can make that call on the fly."

Neither of the boys expressed any interest in talking with Jack or Kate about the night before. They had each hung around with the Handlers long enough to know that a person never learns anything when he's the one wagging his tongue.

Jack knew what was going on with them and just thought it prudent to keep his own mouth shut and his antennae up.

It was just a little more than ten minutes later that the doorbell rang. Jack looked over and smiled at Kate, and then walked to the door. After taking a peek through the side window to be sure whom he was dealing with, he opened the door and said, "Gentlemen, could I share with you some of my wonderful morning brew? Nothing like it on Sugar Island."

"Would love some," Sgt. Blake said, "but first I'd like to get your thoughts on some news that you're probably not yet aware of. Could you step outside on the porch for a minute or two? And then we'll take you up on that coffee. Can we do it like that?"

"Sure," Jack said. "I'd be happy to hear what you have to say."

As soon as Jack had closed the door, Sgt. Blake began to talk: "We received some disturbing news from the western part of the state last night … from the State Police. This is what they told us. Just west of Powers, on Highway 2, the State Police pulled over a white Toyota for a routine traffic stop, and it turned violent. There were two troopers involved in the stop, and a lone driver in the Toyota. That lone driver immediately opened fire on the troopers. That shootout resulted in the deaths of the perp, and one of the State Troopers."

"Oh my God," Jack muttered. "That's terrible … about the loss of the State Trooper. That's just awful. … You say that the shooter was alone in his vehicle?"

"He was alone," Sgt. Blake said. "The shooter appears to reside in San Francisco. … And, get this. The State Police report that they found over one hundred pounds of illicit drugs in that shooter's car."

"Holy shit!" Jack said. "That's a small fortune. Do you know what he was up to? And why he was headed this way?"

"He wasn't headed this way," Sgt. Blake said. "He was headed west on Highway 2 when he was stopped."

"Headed west, you say?"

"That's right," Sgt. Blake said. "But, it gets even more interesting. Police here in the Soo tell us that the car in question was the same one that you had been dealing with earlier in the day. It's the same car that the rental company placed at that house on the island where your boys had that run-in with the kidnapper. ... And the same car that seems to have been involved in the fatal shooting at the storage building here in the Soo, and the other shooting out here on the island."

"That was one very busy son-of-bitch that you are talking about," Jack said. "It's just a damn shame that that trooper had to lose his life. Did he have a family?"

"It was a damn shame," Sgt. Blake agreed. "Just terrible. ... And, yes, he was a veteran of fourteen years, and the father of three. But, as I understand it, the whole story boils down to the drugs. ... That's why the Feds are taking over the case. They do that all the time, you know, when there are a lot of drugs involved."

"Damn," Jack said, not at all pleased to hear about the Feds getting involved. "What is it that I can do for you?"

"Not sure, at this point," Sgt. Blake said. "But, I can tell you for sure that it is about to get rather busy around here. The Feds are already throwing a fuss. They're gonna want to talk to all the parties involved. And that would include you, your daughter Kate, your two boys, and, I'm sure, even those two girls. ... It's obviously out of our hands now, but I wanted to give you a heads-up that the Feds are now involved. ... So you can prepare yourself for whatever awaits. ... Can we take you up on that coffee offer now? And, if you and your daughter have any questions, we'd be glad to help wherever we can. ... But, like I said, this whole case is now out of our hands, so we won't be of much help in that respect."

By the time Jack and the two county cops had joined Kate for coffee, both Angel and Liz had found their way downstairs to the breakfast table as well.

As the three men approached her, Kate smiled and greeted them, "Coffee all around?" she asked, through her customary good morning smile.

"Sounds perfect to us," Jack replied. "I see she's going to tempt us with some of those Katz's Deli Desserts. ... Kate lives and works in New York—Lower East Side Homicide. She makes sure we don't run out of these little rolls. What do they call them? *Rugelach*? Come in cinnamon and chocolate. Take your pick. I prefer the cinnamon."

"New York Homicide?" Sgt. Blake said. "I think we knew that already. But, aren't you a long way from home?"

"You could say that," Kate said. "I guess I do spend a lot of time up here on Sugar Island."

"What precinct is that you work out of in New York?" Sgt. Blake asked.

"It's the 7th Precinct" Kate replied. "It's located down there on 19 1/2 Pitt Street. ... Of late, however, I've actually been working on a special task force—one that I don't talk much about."

"These are really good," Sgt. Blake said as he tried one of the cinnamon rolls Kate gave him. "You bring these all the way from New York? How do you get them here?"

"I pick them up from Katz's Deli on Houston, freeze them, and then pack them in my luggage when I fly home. The boys like them especially. ... And Dad. I have to admit that I like them as well."

"Where's Houston?" Sgt. Blake asked. "Isn't that down there by the Williamsburg Bridge? Or close? I don't really recall. Haven't been to that city in years."

"Right," Kate answered. "Not far at all. I work out of the 7th Precinct a fair amount—that's down by the bridge as well—the Williamsburg Bridge."

"Our friends here have some interesting news for us," Jack said, sensing that Kate could use a bit of a heads-up warning. "They just found out that our buddy, you know, the Spyder Man, he was just involved in a shootout with some Michigan State Troopers over by Escanaba, and it turned out bad for both. A trooper lost his life, and so did Spyder-Man. … And, a lot of drugs were found in Spyder-Man's car. Enough to push it well beyond the limit, and the Feds have now taken over the case. … Big news, I'd say. Wouldn't you?"

Kate looked up and her jaw dropped open. She then looked over at Liz, and asked her, "Did you hear that? They think Spyder was shot and killed … west of here a couple hundred miles."

"Holy shit!" Liz exclaimed, with an equally surprised expression. "Is that pretty much a sure thing? That Spyder is dead?"

"I'm sure that there's not been a conclusive forensic identification made at this point," Jack said, "but, from what my friends here have expressed to me, I think it looks like there's a pretty significant likelihood of that being the case."

"Does that mean," Robby began, "that the jerk who was shooting at Red and me last night is dead? Is that what that means, Uncle Jack?"

"A very good chance that would be correct," Jack told him. "But, we won't know for certain for a while."

"Damn," Liz said, after laying her rugelach roll down on a paper towel in front of her. "This just gets weirder and weirder by the minute."

She ran her eyes around the room, catching contact with Kate and then Angel. No one spoke for a few seconds. And then she and Jack began speaking at the same time. "How does this affect me?" she asked over Jack, as he yielded to her question. "If Spyder is *really* dead. Does that change anything?"

"Well," Kate started, "I think that there is very little chance that Dad, and these officers, that they are mistaken. I would think that there would be very strong odds that Spyder is no more. I would be very surprised if that did not turn out to be the case. Right, Dad?"

"I would agree with that," Jack said. "Correct me if I'm wrong, Sergeant, but I am assuming that you, or the State Police, used the car rental company to trace where that white Toyota was yesterday, and that it has been accurately traced to the house over on the east side of the island. And we know that Spyder-Man had that car at that time, and it's only logical that he was the one driving it last night. So, I would agree with the conclusion that you've reached. It's not yet been conclusively demonstrated to be factual, but I think that there are strong odds—bankable ones—that our conclusion *is* correct."

"That should be good news for me, don't you think?" Liz asked.

"It's definitely not *bad* news," Kate replied as she stood and walked away from the table and toward the pantry. "Come with me for a minute and give me a hand with this."

Kate was trying to get Liz away from the group in order to explain to her in private what was happening.

"Can you give me a hand?" she asked a second time.

Liz immediately stood this time, and followed Kate.

Once in the pantry, Kate explained to her. "This business about the Feds does put a whole different wrinkle on the matter. Now, we must be even more diligent in how we move forward. ... As it stands, with the death of this Spyder-Man character, your potential for involvement in the issue has probably been removed a fair distance from you. And, I think that if you are very careful about keeping it like that, you should be the better off, if not entirely in the clear. ... At the very least, you now have a much better chance at coming out of this virtually unscathed."

"What does that mean?" Liz asked, wearing a confused expression. "How do I go about *keeping Spyder at a distance?* If he's dead, what can I really do to make a difference?"

"Off the top, it has become even more important that you *never* answer any questions without a lawyer with you," Kate explained. "It's *absolutely* got to be that way from here on out. Even just sitting here with us today, with these county law enforcement officers, Jack, Angel, the boys and me, we *all* want to see good things happen in your life. But, unless you start right now keeping your mouth shut unless you have an attorney with you, and advising you every inch of the way, there could be problems—big problems.

"You see, the Feds are now almost certain to be totally in charge of the case, and they are always harder to deal with than local authorities. ... Do you understand what I am saying to you?"

"Not totally," Liz replied. "But I think I kind of get it."

"And you are good with it?"

"Yeah," Liz replied, now convincingly more sincere. "... But why is it now going to be so critical for me to keep quiet? With Spyder being dead, and all?"

"Because the Feds are going to be thoroughly checking out

every single detail," Kate explained. "When that happens, and I think you should assume it already has started, you will find that very smart people will be pulling at you from all directions—*very* smart people. ... And, if you are to come out of this intact, you absolutely must start being very careful all the time. Take nothing for granted.

"Here," Kate said, "take these rugelach rolls out and place them on the cupboard beside the refrigerator. We will give them to the officers when they leave. Let's go out now. Ready?"

"Yup," Liz replied.

As they walked back to where the rest were, Liz took a moment to scrutinize the two county cops. And both Jack and Kate observed her reaction.

Jack immediately addressed the matter for Liz's benefit: "These two friends of ours from county, they've both been around the block more than once, and they are fully aware of what you've been through. They know that you are the victims here."

Jack then looked over at the officers and asked, "Right, gentlemen?" His purpose in doing that was to encourage them into making that call along with him. ... And, it worked.

"That's how we see it," Sgt. Blake agreed. "And I'm sure I speak for the both of us. The two of you have been through a lot, and we're just glad you came out of it as good as you did. ... Of course, this case will undoubtedly be taken over by Federal authorities, and we don't speak for them. But, as far as we're concerned, we agree with Jack, you two are just two more of this killer's victims."

"The same is true with Kate and I," Jack said. "If you keep your nose clean from here on out, we see no reason why you should not be able to pull through this intact."

Kate was nodding her head in agreement when she turned her attention to Angel and said to her, "Do you understand what we have been telling your friend, kiddo?"

Angel nodded her head in agreement, and then started to say, "All I know about that Spyder fellow is—"

"Now would be a good time for you to shut your mouth as well," Kate said interrupting. "Because, you could be called on to testify against your friend here. You, Angel, need to keep your lips sealed totally unless you are accompanied by an attorney—and it should not be the same one that is representing Liz. Your Uncle Jack and I must not be privy to information that could be detrimental to either one of you. Because, we could be called in to testify, and we are going to tell the absolute truth—no matter who it hurts."

"I get it," Angel said. "At least I think I do."

"That's good," Kate said, "because it's very important that both of you really get a handle on this. ... Innocent people have been convicted of crimes before. You both need to take this whole matter very seriously, starting right now."

Jack then interjected his thought at the moment: "The FBI is very good at its job. And, something else to be aware of here, you can rest assured that they will investigate the roles both of you girls have played in this case. And that costs money. ... Here's the rub on that. When the Feds spend money, they like to justify it. If they believe that developing a case against you two young ladies will help them to justify the time they spend on you, then they just might charge you with some crime—real or imagined. And they have a very good record with juries. So listen to what your Aunt Kate is telling you. Keep your mouth shut, all the time."

Sgt. Blake and his friend did not take issue with anything that had been proposed around the breakfast table on that day. Both Jack and Kate knew them to be upstanding officers of the law, which meant that the Handlers were convinced that if the girls were as innocent as they appeared to be, and if they both kept their mouths shut and their hands clean from that day forward, then they stood a pretty good chance of avoiding prosecution. Kate could not have sought a more effective venue for demonstrating her point.

With that, Sgt. Blake wiped his hands and face with a paper napkin and pushed his chair back. "Well, Jack," he said, "I'm glad you could make time for us this morning. ... We definitely agree with what you and your daughter have suggested. We do not see anything wrong with the way these young ladies have comported themselves throughout this whole unpleasant situation. We are just very pleased that neither one of them suffered serious injury. ... But, I think it's time we got back to work.

"Loved those little rolls. What did you call them? Rugelach? Never had anything quite like it before. ... Anyway, they were very tasty. The next time you come out here, from New York, you can drop a few of them off at your dad's for his friends in uniform. That would be us, of course. ... Just kidding with you—but they are very good. ... And if you do get the urge to visit that deli before flying west, it would be fine with us."

With that, Sgt. Blake and Deputy Crandle politely excused themselves and walked out the door—mission accomplished.

Once Jack was certain that Blake and Crandle were on their way, he poured himself, Kate, and Liz a fresh cup of coffee. He took a healthy sip of his, and began addressing the whole group.

"Here's the scoop on what just went down. For all intents and purposes, city and county law enforcement are no longer major players in this matter. From here on out it will most certainly be the Feds running the whole show. That could work to our advantage, if we handle it right. Or, if we don't, it could magnify the problem."

Kate silently looked down into her hot cup of black concentration, while the other four stared wide-eyed at Jack, intently following every nuance of his directives.

"If we approach this properly," he said, "we stand an excellent chance of coming out the other end in good shape. We can all be winners in this. ... Here's what we do. Boys—Red, Robby—it is absolutely critical that you do not talk to anyone about what has gone down over the past few days, unless I'm with you. And I will not allow any interviews without Jeremy being with you. You all remember Jeremy? He was the lawyer I hired for your custody hearings? We all liked him, so he will represent you boys throughout."

While Jack was still talking, Red started writing a note. When he had finished it, he slid it over for Robby to look at. After Robby nodded his approval, Red then passed it over to Jack.

Jack looked at it for a few seconds. He then smiled and read it aloud to the whole group: "Are Robby and I going to be in trouble for knocking that house down with the plow?"

"Not at all likely," Jack responded, maintaining the beam on his face. "But you never know. ... Just make certain that all conversation about last night passes through me or Jeremy—preferably both, with me first, when possible. If we all do that and we can make this work out for all of us. ... Do you boys understand?"

Both Red and Robby nodded agreement with their *Uncle Jack*.

"Great," Jack said, again flashing a confidence-building smile. "Now, Angel and Liz, this is how I would like you two to handle this. For the next few days, *everything* regarding either one of you needs to pass through Kate. She can stay around here long enough for us to get a good attorney for you. Jeremy's wife is named Anne, and she is also an attorney, and at the same firm. With your permission, Angel, she will represent your interests in this whole matter. Is that agreeable to you?"

"Yes," Angel nervously agreed.

"Great," Jack said. "She will be coming over here as well, and we can see how that goes. ... Of course, you can do whatever you wish. But, I can assure you that there are huge repercussions lurking for both you and Liz if you do not use wisdom. This is how I suggest you deal with it.

"First, Angel, you can talk to Anne, and if you like her, and she's willing to take you on, we can see what she would recommend, and ask her if she would recommend an attorney who would be able to represent Liz. Or, what she would recommend there. What do you think of that, Liz?"

"I have a question," Angel interjected before Liz could respond. "May I ask you a question?"

"Sure—fire away."

"I think I remember that Aunt Kate is a lawyer," Angel said. "Couldn't she represent all of us?"

"Fundamental rule of being a lawyer," Jack said with a smile. "A good lawyer never represents himself. Kate is too intimately involved in this case, if there is one, to ever consider representing any of us. Do you get what I am saying?"

Angel did not speak, but she did nod in agreement.

"Mr. Handler," Liz replied. "I have no money for a lawyer."

"Not a problem for right now," Jack said. "I have a hunch that Anne will represent Angel, but that she might suggest a different attorney to work with you. I will tell you that whatever she recommends would be what I would like to see happen. Both she and Jeremy have spotless reputations, and you will be in good hands with them. … And, as far as legal expenses, I will be picking up the tab for now. If and when I need to have you look elsewhere, I will let you know well in advance. Does this sound okay to you?"

"Yes," Liz said. "Thank you, Mr. Handler."

"And, Kate," Jack said, addressing his daughter. "How does all this sound to you? What do you think?"

"Well, Dad," Kate said, "I think your advocating caution is wise, for all of us—critical, actually. … And the attorneys you recommend I know to be competent. So, I am one hundred percent in agreement. … And, with what's at stake here, I will also be represented in this by my attorney. I do not think that we can be too careful."

"Then," Jack suggested, "with all that decided, let's take a drive into the Soo, and have a little talk with the legal team. What say you?"

"Can we just do that?" Liz asked. "Don't we have to make an appointment?"

"Already have one," Jack replied. "Let's finish breakfast, and take a drive into town. I really look for the Feds to take this whole thing very seriously—and real soon."

Jack had plenty of reason to be concerned. His numerous run-ins with the Feds had practically put him on the Government Watchlist. It seemed to him that virtually nothing he did, on any level, ever seemed to go un-scrutinized.

It even occurred to him that the two girls might be better off were he to step aside and let them fend for themselves. However, on the advice of Melanie, his personal attorney, Jack instead decided to procure excellent legal representation for all involved. "Otherwise," she advised him, "because of their association with you, you can be assured that they will somehow fall foul of the law and end up being indicted for something." As was always his practice, Jack took her advice seriously.

Later that morning, the six of them left the house and were headed into the Soo to meet with their lawyers. As they passed the Hilltop Bar, Kate caught sight of a small plane flying in from the northwest. It looked to her to be only about two hundred and fifty feet above them. "Dad, where do you suppose *that's* coming from? Looks like it might be coming across from Canada, maybe? What do you think?"

Chapter 18 —

J ack was taken aback by the appearance of the flying machine that had just entered their field of view. But he was particularly puzzled that by the time he was able to spot the plane it had already flown directly over his vehicle and was by then at his ten o'clock, and headed almost directly south. "That's not a real plane," he said, "can't be. I'd say it's some sort of drone. … It looks to be very large for a drone, but that's what it is. … Where the hell do you suppose it came from? Canada—do you think?"

"Makes sense," Kate replied. "Don't see anything like that around here. … And it looks to me like it's starting to drop altitude."

Jack slowed and started looking for a place to pull over on the side of Sugar Island Road.

"Can't be up over a hundred feet now," he said. "And it looks to me like it's going in pretty damn low—maybe it's landing over there?"

"By our house," Robby said. "Isn't that over by our house?"

"Sure as hell is," Jack agreed.

By that time all six of them were straining their necks to see out a window.

"Whoa!" Robby exclaimed. "Did you see that?! It looked like it shot a rocket or something. Did you guys see that?"

No one replied verbally to his question, so Robby looked over at Red to get his friend's reaction. Red was intently trying to follow what was going on outside, but he did affirmatively react to Robby's question by slowly nodding his head.

Neither Jack nor Kate responded verbally either. Instead, he and his daughter just sat there stoically with the engine running, but neither talking. Finally, he looked over at her with a very concerned expression on his face. But still, neither one of them uttered a single word as the plane disappeared behind the trees.

And then, after only another twenty seconds or so, the plane remerged right in front of them. It was at that point ascending rapidly and heading directly north. It continued on that path until it disappeared from their view.

"It is *absolutely* headed to Canada," Jack said. "What the hell do you think that was all about?"

"Did you see it fire something?" Kate asked Jack. "If it did, I missed it."

"I think Robby has a point," Jack replied. "Couldn't really see much, because of the trees, but that little bastard looked like it fired something like a Hellfire missile just before it disappeared. … Something about that size, I'd say. … And now it's headed back to where it came from—Canada, most likely. … Almost certainly it's headed to Canada."

"If that's what happened," Kate said, looking back to where the missile was supposed to have been fired, "shouldn't we see a cloud of smoke, or something?"

"I should think so," Jack cautiously replied, first turning his eyes toward his house, and then back to follow the little plane as it disappeared over the trees to the northwest. "We need to go home and see what that was all about. … Altogether too damn close to our house for my liking."

"How about you, Red?" Kate said, addressing him as Jack whipped back onto Sugar Island Road, "did you see it fire a missile like Robby said?"

Red looked at her and nodded his agreement.

But, before they had even turned onto Brassar Road, Kate blurted out, "Holy shit! That cloud looks to be right about over by our house! Somebody's house is on fire, and it sure looks like it could be ours!"

Even though Jack was picking up speed, he still allowed his eyes to search out what Kate was pointing at. And, even though he did not verbally react to her comment, he did silently concede to the apparent accuracy of her observation.

He was now driving faster than he would have liked to. So, when he reached his intersection, he had to exercise a near high-speed maneuver to complete his right turn onto the southbound stretch of Brassar Road. After successfully rounding the corner, he trained his eyes to the southwest and again stepped on the gas.

"Should I call the fire department?" Kate asked. "Would be good to get them there as quickly as possible, don't you think?"

"Do it!" Jack barked. "Might not be our house that's burning. But it doesn't matter at this point. It's obvious that somebody's building's on fire—so just do it! They'll find it just fine."

Kate immediately called County Dispatch, only to be informed that they had already been contacted by a neighbor, and by an emergency alarm system. "We've got equipment on the way," they told her. "… And, the address we dispatched to was that of Jack

Handler. It was his house, according to the alarm system."

When Kate relayed that message to her father, all he could say was, "Oh shit!"

While it seemed an eternity, it took them less than ten minutes to arrive at the house. And, sadly, they found that the dispatcher was correct—it was their house that was totally engulfed in flames. As soon as Jack got a good look at it, he shoved the Tahoe into reverse, and backed it south down Westshore Drive until it was well out of the way.

"Nothing we can do at this point," he said. "The fire department is definitely going to need to get in there as close as possible. These trees could catch on fire and end up burning half the island."

After Jack had backed onto 6 Mile, he then turned around and headed toward the water. There he pulled fully onto South Laramie, and parked. A growing crowd had questions for Jack, but they all also knew better than to try to engage him right at that time. So, all six of them in the Tahoe just sat silently watching as their house burned down.

Finally, Jack's cell rang. He did not recognize the calling number, but did note that it was area code 202—so he answered it.

"Hello," he said.

"Jack Handler, I presume," said the female caller, delivering her greeting in a heavy but confident Beijing accent.

"This is Jack."

"Well, well, Mr. Handler," the female caller said. "My name is Zheng Pingru, and I am calling to see if you are enjoying the little show we have created just for you?"

While the call caught him totally by surprise, Jack quickly discerned the source and rationale behind this attack on his home, and so he took a deep breath and calmly responded, "Might have been better at night, and perhaps with some popcorn. But, all told, I'd give it four stars."

"Happy you are taking it all in stride," Ms. Pingru said. "I would say that was the only appropriate approach for you. After all, we could have raised the screen on our show eight hours earlier. ... I'm sure you are aware of what that would have meant—all those beautiful ladies and children. The results would not have been pretty. ... If you decide to rebuild, Mr. Handler, I would strongly recommend that you install a sprinkler system."

For the briefest of moments, Jack considered issuing his own brand of warning, but thought better of it. "That would be testosterone speaking," he told himself, "not wisdom." Instead, calmly he said to her, "I'm pleased to see you're sounding so well. Last I heard, you'd developed a bit of a chest problem hiking in the woods outside Shanghai. Perhaps we can get together after I build my new house. Will you do that with me?"

"Sounds fun," she said. "Call me later. Okay?"

And then she disconnected the call.

"Who was that?" Kate asked. While she could not make out much of what the other party had said, Kate was able to detect that the caller was a female who communicated through a significant accent, and that her father had assumed a posture not commensurate with the dire situation confronting them.

"That, my dear daughter," Jack responded. "That was the beautiful Ms. Zheng Pingru—at least that's what she called herself. She wanted to make sure that we were enjoying the theatrical presentation she had provided for us."

"Okay," Kate replied with a bewildered expression gripping

her whole face, "Now say that again—this time in English."

"What we just experienced here," Jack explained, now beginning to surrender to his anger, "was a hit job. That drone flew in from Canada, but was dispatched from somewhere else altogether. It was not intended to harm us physically, merely to cause us distress. You know what I'm saying—she wanted to get our attention."

"Who is this she that you are referring to? That Ms. Zheng Pingru," Kate inquired, seriously mispronouncing it, "Do I know her?"

Everyone in the Tahoe was eager to hear Jack shed a little light on what was going on.

"Ms. Zheng Pingru," Jack explained, "she was a very beautiful Chinese spy during the Second Sino-Japanese War. Unfortunate for her, she was executed in 1940 after a failed assassination attempt on the life of a feckless Chinese security chief."

While intensely interested, no one else in the Tahoe dared venture forth into the conversation—they all understood that, at this point, talk must remain strictly between Jack and Kate.

"Okay," Kate said again, "I think what you're telling me is that the drone attack on the house was part of a larger plot. … Do you actually understand what this is all about? And would you care to share it with me? … And, are you sure we're safe up here in the UP?"

Jack chuckled a bit at her question, and said, "Well, I don't think that we will be spending another night at that house. … But, it should be clear that, as it stands right now, had Ms. Pingru wished us dead, you and I would not be having this conversation."

Kate thought about what her father was saying and nodded her agreement, and then turned her face to watch the flames shooting out of the windows of her favorite house in the world.

Angel and the two boys were beginning to make conversation with one another in much the same fashion as one would expect of any group of fourteen-year-olds that was deeply engrossed in watching their house burn down.

Liz, however, exhibited a different set of emotional packaging. She was not relating well to Kate, and not at all to Jack. She could think of nothing, at this moment, that she shared in common with the three teenagers. And they, the teenagers, were even less interested in relating their thoughts or concerns to anything she might be thinking.

"Damn it all," she said silently to herself. "What the hell have I got myself into? … Not only do I not have any of the product I worked so hard to steal, I've even lost all the clothes I brought with me from San Francisco. I do not even have a stupid toothbrush. … And now, they're telling me that I cannot even talk to another human being unless I do it through an attorney. What kind of a shit life will this be?"

The six of them sat there in Jack's Tahoe for nearly ten minutes, while the only ones talking at all were Angel and the two boys. Finally, two fire trucks arrived on the scene, and they began throwing water on what remained of the house, and on nearby buildings.

"They might as well let the house burn," Kate said. "Nothing there that can be saved at this point. … Be nice to keep the fire out of the garage—got the plow in it, and the boys' Mustang. Looks like they will be able to save them."

But before Jack could respond to his daughter, a late-model

black Buick pulled right in front of them, and another blocked them from the rear. At the same time two men in suits got out of each of the Buicks, and they approached Jack's Tahoe.

"What the hell is going on here?" Jack blurted out. "Those guys look like Feds to me. What are they doing here—at my house?"

One of them immediately approached Jack's door with his Glock drawn. He knocked on the driver's side window, and commanded Jack to step out of the vehicle. No sooner had Jack opened the door to grant him access, than another man opened Kate's door. He also had his Glock drawn.

"I need all six of you to step out of the vehicle immediately," said the agent who had approached Jack.

The agent proceeded to order all six of those riding in Jack's Tahoe to stand up beside their Tahoe, and to then lean on that vehicle with hands raised above their heads. Then, one by one, he and the other agents placed all six of them in handcuffs.

"I would like to see your warrant," Jack barked angrily.

"I already tucked yours into your jacket pocket," the agent dealing with Jack said. "Here, I'll read it to you."

After the Fed had finished reading the short warrant aloud, Jack repeated several times the only significant section: "Aiding and abetting. Aiding and abetting. Aiding and abetting."

He then stared coldly into the agent's eyes, and said, "I assume you know that three of us are minors. The two boys and the girl— Robby, Red and Angel, they are all fourteen. Are you sure you are intending to place them under arrest as well? You might want to rethink that."

"Let the kids go," the agent commanded the other agents. "Search them for weapons, and then remove the handcuffs. Hold them in the back of one of our cars. Put the three adults in the other … and leave them cuffed."

"Remember what we told you," Jack said to the three kids as they were led away. "Do not talk to anyone until you have talked to your lawyers. And I mean *anyone*. You'll know your real lawyers because they will have the password I gave you—absolutely no exceptions."

Liz was overwhelmed with what had just gone down in front of her. As the three adults and Buddy were being led over to one of the Feds' other vehicles, and were out of range of being overheard, she asked Jack, "When do I get to meet this lawyer you told me about?"

"Soon enough," Jack replied. And after a short pause, he continued: "And remember, the same warning goes for you. If you want to exercise your best shot at keeping your rear end out of prison, listen carefully to what I tell you. Keep your mouth shut until you've talked to him—to your lawyer. And make sure you listen to and do whatever he says."

"Then, do I need to know the secret password like the boys?" she asked.

"There is no password," Jack threw back at her. "I said that to the boys for the agents' benefit. … Passwords are just too easily stolen or otherwise circumvented. My boys are smart. They will know when the right lawyer talks to them. … So will you."

"Got it," Liz emphatically replied after a few moments' thought, even though she actually had no clue as to what this guy named Jack was getting at.

Kate took one long last glance back at her beloved cabin in the woods as she prepared to face what lie ahead. "Damn, I am going to miss Bungle and Baloo," she silently said to herself. "I wonder if that sculptor—the one who breathed life into those huge logs in the first place—I wonder if he could be convinced to create an identical set. ... Well, I suppose if there's anyone on the planet who could convince Rafael to do it again, that would be my dad."

As Liz was led away, it seemed to her like a thousand divergent thoughts had descended on her mind like a thick, angry cloud. Initially, she set about trying to process the tangled mess that seemed to have captured her whole being, but she quickly concluded that such a feat lay far beyond her reach.

She opened her eyes even wider in a final, frustrated effort to take it all in, perhaps for one last time—the burning cabin, the boys' classic Mustang, Angel's unfeigned innocence, and Buddy. And then she quite audibly muttered a single word: "SHIT!"

Disclaimer

LIZ is not a true story. It is a work of fiction. All US characters, locations, names, situations, and occurrences are purely the product of my imagination. Any resemblance to actual US events or persons (living or dead) is unintentional and coincidental.

The Cast
of Main Characters in this and Earlier "Jack Handler" Books

(Characters are listed in a quasi-chronological order.)

To date, there are sixteen books in the evolving Jack Handler Saga—*seven* in each of the two first series, and two now in the third series. The title of that new series is *Jack Unchained*. The name of the first series was the *Getting to Know Jack* series, and the second was called *Jack's Justice*. It is intended that each series will contain seven Jack Handler books when complete.

While many of the characters encountered in this book might already have made appearances in one or more of the previous Jack Handler books, if you want a deeper understanding about how a character thinks, you can refer to the chapter called *The Cast* to help answer quickly some of your additional backstory questions.

Main characters include:

Who is Jack Handler? Jack is a good man, in his way. While it is true that he occasionally kills people, it can be argued that most (if not all) of his targets needed killing. Occasionally a somewhat sympathetic figure comes between Jack and his goal. When that happens, Jack's goal comes first. I think the word that best sums up Jack's persona might be "expeditor." He is outcome driven—he makes things turn out the way he wants them to turn out.

For instance, if you were a single mom and a bully were stealing your kid's lunch money, you could send "Uncle Jack" to school with little Billy. Uncle Jack would have a "talk" with the teachers and the principal. With Jack's help, the problem would be solved. But I would not recommend that you ask him how he accomplished it. You might not like what he tells you—if he even responds.

Jack is faithful to his friends and a great father to his daughter. He is also a dangerous and tenacious adversary when situations require it.

Jack Handler began his career as a law enforcement officer. He married a beautiful woman (Beth) of Greek descent while working as a police officer in Chicago. She was a concert violinist and the love of his life. If you were to ask Jack about it, he would quickly tell you he married above himself. So, when bullets intended for him killed her, he admittedly grew bitter. Kate, their daughter, was just learning to walk when her mother was gunned down.

As a single father, Jack soon found that he needed to make more money than his job as a police officer paid. So he went back to college and obtained a degree in criminal justice. Soon he was promoted to the level of sergeant in the Chicago Police Homicide Division.

With the help of a friend, he then discovered that there was much more money to be earned in the private sector. At first he began moonlighting on private security jobs. Immediate success led him to take an early retirement and obtain his private investigator license.

Because of his special talents (obtained as a former army ranger) and his intense dedication to problem solving, Jack's services became highly sought after. While he did take on some of the more sketchy clients, he never accepted a project simply on the basis of financial gain—he always sought out the moral high ground. Unfortunately, sometimes that moral high ground morphed into quicksand.

Jack is now pushing sixty (from the downward side) and he has all the physical ailments common to a man of that age. While it is true that he remains in amazing physical condition, of late he has begun to sense his limitations.

His biggest concern recently has been an impending IRS audit. While he isn't totally confident that it will turn out okay, he remains optimistic.

His problems stem from the purchase of half-interest in a bar in Chicago two decades earlier. His partner was one of his oldest and most trusted friends—Conrad (Connie) O'Donnell.

The principal reason he considered the investment in the first place was to create a cover for his private security business.

Many, if not most, of his clients insisted on paying him in cash or with some other untraceable commodity. At first he tried getting rid of the cash by paying all of his bills with it. But even though he meticulously avoided credit cards and checks, the cash continued to accumulate.

It wasn't that he was in any sense averse to paying his fair share of taxes. The problem was that if he did deposit the cash into a checking account, and subsequently included it in his filings, he would then at some point be required to explain where it had come from.

He needed an acceptable method of laundering, and his buddy's bar seemed perfect.

But it did not work out exactly as planned. Four years ago the IRS decided to audit the bar, which consequently exposed his records to scrutiny.

Jack consulted with one of his old customers, a disbarred attorney/CPA, to see if this shady character could get the books straightened out enough for Jack to survive the audit and avoid federal prison.

The accountant knew exactly how Jack earned his money and that the sale of a few bottles of Jack Daniels had little to do with it.

Even though his business partner and the CPA talked a good game about legitimacy, Jack still agonized when thoughts of the audit stormed through his mind. This problem was further complicated when Conrad was murdered in what was thought a botched robbery. Connie's lazy son, Conrad Jr., inherited his father's share of the bar.

A year earlier Jack had been convicted and sentenced for attacking a veteran detective, Calvin Brandt. The day that his conviction was overturned, an attempt was made on his life inside a federal prison camp (*Assault on Sugar Island*). He believed at the time, and still does, that Calvin Brandt had been responsible for contracting the Aryan Alliance to carry out the hit.

Fortunately for Jack, Chuchip (Henry) Kalyesveh a Native American of the Hopi tribe, who was also an inmate at the prison camp, came to his rescue.

Who is Kate Handler? Kate, Jack's only daughter and a New York homicide detective, is introduced early and appears often in all the Handler books. Kate is beautiful. She has her mother's olive complexion and green eyes. Her trim five-foot-eight frame, with her long auburn hair falling nicely on her broad shoulders, would seem more at home on the runway than in an interrogation room. But Kate is a seasoned New York homicide detective. In fact, she is thought by many to be on the fast track to the top—thanks in part to the unwavering support of her soon-to-retire boss, Captain Spencer.

Of course, her career was not hindered by her background in law. Graduating Summa Cum Laude from Notre Dame at the age of twenty-one, she went on to Notre Dame Law School. She passed the Illinois Bar Exam immediately upon receiving her JD, and accepted a position at one of Chicago's most prestigious criminal law firms. While her future looked bright as a courtroom attorney, she hated defending "sleazebags."

One Saturday morning she called her father and invited him to meet her at what she knew to be the coffee house he most fancied. It was there, over a couple espressos, that she asked him what he thought about her taking a position with the New York Police Department. She was shocked when he immediately gave his blessing. "Kitty," he said, "you're a smart girl. I totally trust your judgment. You have to go where your heart leads. Just promise me one thing. Guarantee me that you will put me up whenever I want to visit. After all, you are my favorite daughter."

To this Kate replied with a chuckle, "Dad, I'm your only daughter. And, you will always be welcome."

In Murder on Sugar Island (the first Jack Handler Thriller set in Michigan), Jack and Kate team up to solve the murder of Alex Garos, Jack's brother-in-law. Beginning with this book, all or most of the subsequent Jack Handler Thrillers also at least start out on Sugar Island, which is located in the northern part of Michigan's Upper Peninsula (just east of Sault Ste. Marie, MI, and south of Canada). Because Kate was Mr. Garos's only blood relative living in the United States, he named her in his will to inherit all of his estate. This included one of the most prestigious pieces of real estate on the island—the Sugar Island Resort. And that's where Jack and his two foster boys now call home.

Who is Reginald Black (Reg)? In *Jack and the New York Death Mask (Death Mask)*, Jack is recruited by his best friend, Reg (Reginald Black), to do a job without either man having any knowledge as to what that job might entail. Jack, out of loyalty to his friend, accepted the offer. The contract was ostensibly to assassinate a sitting president. However, instead of assisting the plot, Jack and Reg worked to thwart it. Most of this story takes place in New York City, but there are scenes in DC, Chicago, and Upstate New York. Reg is frequently mentioned throughout the series, as are Pam Black and Allison Fulbright. Pam Black is Reg's wife (he was shot at the end of *Death Mask*), and Allison is a former first lady. It was Allison who contracted Reg and Jack to assassinate the sitting president.

Who is Allison? Allison is a complex and captivating character in the fictional world of this Jack Handler series. A woman of considerable intelligence and determination, she possesses an aura of sophistication that comes from her years in the political limelight. As a former first lady with her own presidential aspirations, she exudes an air of ambition and strategic thinking that few can match.

Tall and graceful, Allison carries herself with a regal poise that commands attention whenever she enters a room. Her steely blue eyes seem to hold a wealth of secrets, and her perfectly coifed blond hair frames a face that can seamlessly transition from warm smiles to icy glares. Her impeccable fashion sense reflects her status and attention to detail, always wearing tailored power suits in rich hues that accentuate her authoritative presence.

Despite her public persona, Allison is no stranger to the ruthless world of politics. She has a keen understanding of power dynamics and isn't afraid to use her intelligence and charm to manipulate situations to her advantage. Although she's a master at maintaining an image of elegance and grace, underneath the surface lies a calculating mind that never rests.

Jack Handler, the protagonist of the series, finds himself often at odds with Allison. While she fears Jack and the potential disruptions he might bring to her carefully crafted plans, she is equally fascinated and intrigued by his resourcefulness and audacity. Their interactions are a delicate dance of veiled threats, psychological maneuvers, and verbal sparring.

Allison's annoyance towards Jack is driven by her need to control every aspect of her world, a trait that has served her well in her political endeavors. She's not above using her influence and connections to subtly interfere with Jack's activities, casting shadows of doubt and uncertainty over his endeavors. Her actions are never overtly malicious, as she refrains from causing physical harm to Jack or his loved ones. Instead, she prefers to operate in the shadows, undermining Jack's efforts just enough to make him question his own decisions.

As the series unfolds, Allison's character evolves, revealing layers of vulnerability beneath her façade of power. Readers catch glimpses of her past, her motivations, and the sacrifices she's made to climb the political ladder. While she remains a formidable adversary to Jack, her complexity and inner struggles make her more than just a one-dimensional antagonist. Allison adds depth to the series, challenging both the protagonist and the readers to consider the blurred lines between ambition and morality in the pursuit of power.

Who is Roger Minsk? Roger Minsk is one of the readers' favorite characters in Michael's book. Roger is a friend and confidant to Jack Handler. In his 50s, this distinguished Secret Service agent stands tall and exudes an air of confidence befitting his years of experience and expertise. His chiseled features and a lifetime of dedicated service have etched a timeless handsomeness into his face. With striking, steely eyes that have seen it all and a commanding presence, he easily commands respect and assurance from those around him.

His hair, once a rich shade of dark brown, has now matured to a distinguished silver hue, giving him an air of wisdom and sophistication. It crowns his head in a manner that complements his distinguished appearance, serving as a testament to his long years of service protecting the nation's most esteemed leaders.

His immaculate, tailored suits drape over his well-toned frame, enhancing his strong and lean physique. Every movement he makes is measured and precise, a reflection of his unwavering dedication to his duty. Years of rigorous training and countless hours of service have honed his skills to perfection.

Beyond his striking appearance, he possesses a genuine warmth that sets those around him at ease. Despite the high-stakes environment in which he operates, he is known for his calm demeanor and ability to remain composed even in the face of adversity. He has a knack for connecting with people, be it fellow agents, White House staff, or even the former President and First Lady themselves, forging bonds built on trust and mutual respect.

To the former President and First Lady, he is not just a guardian, but a confidant, someone they can trust with their lives. His loyalty knows no bounds, and he treats their safety as his sacred duty, going above and beyond to ensure their protection at all times.

This seasoned Secret Service agent is the epitome of a dedicated professional, and his service extends beyond just a job. It is a calling, a passion, and an honor to protect those who have led the nation and safeguard their legacy for future generations. His commitment to duty, his remarkable looks, and his silver hair are but outward reflections of the depth and strength of character that lies within, making him a truly exceptional member of the Secret Service.

In "To China with Love" you will find Roger working with Jack carrying out a daring mission that literally breaks all the rules.

Just as they were about to make their fateful decision, a chilling whisper drifted through the air, a voice from a time long past, warning them of the consequences of their choice. The expedition members exchanged hesitant glances, realizing that their daring adventure had brought them to the edge of a precipice from which there might be no return.

And there, with the fate of the world hanging in the balance, the book's final page turned, leaving readers with a heart-pounding cliffhanger, urging them to continue the expedition's thrilling journey in the next volume. As they close the book, they can't help but wonder what lies beyond that final moment of choice, and what untold dangers and revelations await in the China Sea and the Island of Serenity. The expedition's epic tale is far from over, and readers are left yearning to discover what incredible adventures and perils await them on down the road.

Who is Red? This main character is introduced in *Sugar*. Red is a redheaded fourteen-year-old boy who, besides being orphaned, cannot speak. It turned out that Red was actually the love child of Alex (Jack's brother-in-law) and his office manager. So, Alex not only leaves his Sugar Island resort to Kate, he also leaves his Sugar Island son for her to care for.

Red has a number of outstanding characteristics, first and foremost among them, his innate ability to take care of himself in all situations. When his mother and her husband were killed in a fire, Red chose to live on his own instead of submitting to placement in foster care.

During the warmer months, he lived in a hut he had pieced together from parts of abandoned homes, barns, and cottages, and he worked at Garos's resort on Sugar Island. In the winter, he would take up residence in empty fishing cottages along the river.

Red's second outstanding characteristic is his loyalty. When put to the test, Red would rather sacrifice his life than see his friends hurt. In *Sugar*, Red works together with Jack and Kate to solve the mystery behind the killing of Jack's brother-in-law (and Red's biological father), Alex Garos.

The third thing about Red that makes him stand out is his inability to speak. As the result of a traumatic event in his life, his voice box was damaged, resulting in his disability. Before Jack and Kate entered his life, Red communicated only through an improvised sign system and various grunts.

When Kate introduced him to a cell phone and texting, Red's life changed dramatically.

Who is Robby? In the thrilling world of the "Jack Handler Series," meet Robby, a captivating 14-year-old with a mop of dark, curly hair that seems to have a mind of its own. Robby's life takes a mysterious and heart-wrenching turn when his father, a passionate diver, goes missing in the depths of Lake Superior, leaving Robby and his mother in a state of uncertainty and sorrow.

Robby is not one to let life's challenges break his spirit. Despite the turmoil surrounding his family, he remains a beacon of resilience and determination. With a pair of bright, inquisitive eyes that seem to hide secrets of their own, Robby navigates the complexities of adolescence with unwavering strength.

His closest confidant and best friend, Red, is another 14-year-old with whom he shares an unbreakable bond. Together, they've faced countless adventures and challenges, their friendship forged in the fires of shared laughter and shared tears. Red's presence in Robby's life has been a constant source of support and camaraderie.

But when Robby's father goes missing under mysterious circumstances during a fateful diving expedition in the enigmatic waters of Lake Superior, Robby's world is turned upside down. With his mother struggling to cope with the loss, Red's foster family graciously extends their welcoming arms to him, providing a lifeline of stability in an otherwise turbulent sea of emotions.

As Robby embarks on his quest to uncover the truth about his father's disappearance, he carries with him the strength of his friendship with Red and the newfound support of his foster family. Together, they unravel the mysterious clues that lead them deeper into the shadows of Lake Superior's secrets, all the while facing the challenges and perils that lie ahead.

In the whole of the "Jack Handler Series," Robby's unwavering determination, tenacity, and his loyal friendship with Red, form the beating heart of a suspenseful tale filled with intrigue, mystery, and the unbreakable bonds of youth. Join him on his journey as he uncovers the truth about his father's vanishing act and confronts the secrets lurking beneath the serene surface of Lake Superior.

Who is Buddy? Buddy is a very special member of the Handler team. He is the two-year-old Golden Retriever who, after having been introduced into Red's life in Murders on Sugar Island, immediately melted the hearts of not only Red, but that of every other character highlighted in Michael's books—except, of course, those belonging to those malefactors intent on doing Red and Robby harm. But, wouldn't you agree that those nefarious culprits are largely heartless to begin with?

Who is Sheriff Bill Green? Bill Green stands as the unwavering guardian of Chippewa County, Michigan, in the pages of the Jack Handler novels. As the county's dedicated sheriff, he exemplifies the very essence of integrity and honor. Bill's knowledge runs deep, an intricate tapestry woven from years of experience, his education enriched by the halls of Lake Superior State University. Born and bred in the rugged heartland of Michigan's Upper Peninsula, every contour of the landscape is etched into his soul, every story of its people etched into his memory.

At 40 years old, Bill's gaze bears the weight of both the years he's seen and the unseen burdens he carries. The tragedy that etched its mark upon his life, the cruel loss of his beloved wife in a heart-wrenching revenge plot, has left an indelible scar. A man of solitude, he walks a path marked by sacrifice, his heart an altar to his community, his dedication a testament to his devotion.

Bill's blue eyes, like polished stones, reflect the wisdom of one who has witnessed the ebb and flow of life in this close-knit corner of the world. The lines etched into his weathered face tell stories of countless struggles and victories, each chapter leaving its mark. In a place where the past threads seamlessly into the present, Bill's unwavering presence is a beacon of stability, a reminder of the enduring spirit of the UP.

Though he walks among shadows cast by the tragedies of his past, Bill remains a pillar of strength. The absence of children serves as a reminder of the life he once dreamed of, a life that was tragically stolen from him. Yet, rather than succumbing to despair, he channels his grief into his duty, each step a testament to his unyielding commitment to protect and serve.

Bill's moral compass is steadfast, guided by the book of law he clings to like a lifeline. In a world that often dances in shades of gray, his actions shine with a stark clarity, a testament to his unshakable belief in justice and order. With each sunrise, he takes up his mantle as guardian, a solitary figure against the vast expanse of the Upper Peninsula's wild beauty, his resolve unbreakable, his purpose unwavering.

Who is Captain Spencer? Captain Spencer is a central character in the Jack Handler novels, serving as the head of the New York City Police Department's precinct. He is a seasoned and dedicated law enforcement officer with a long and storied career in the force.

Physically, Captain Spencer is a tall and imposing figure, known for his strong, commanding presence. His salt-and-pepper hair and distinguished features highlight his years of experience in the field. Despite the graying hair and lines on his face, his piercing blue eyes reveal a sharp mind and an unwavering commitment to the job.

One of Captain Spencer's defining characteristics is his intense sense of duty and responsibility towards the precinct and his team. He's well-respected among his peers and subordinates for his unwavering dedication to the safety of the city and his unwavering pursuit of justice.

However, what truly sets Captain Spencer apart is his relationship with Kate, the novel's protagonist. Kate is his protegee, and he takes her under his wing from the moment she joins the police force. He recognizes her potential and is determined to see her succeed in her career. This mentorship goes beyond just professional development; Captain Spencer cares for Kate like a father figure, and their bond is built on trust and mutual respect.

The Captain has been planning his retirement for years, but

he seems to harbor a deep fear of leaving the department until he is certain that Kate's career is fully developed. He knows that he has a responsibility not only to the city but also to her. He wants to ensure that she is well-prepared to take on the challenges of her role as a police officer and potentially even follow in his footsteps as a leader in the precinct.

Captain Spencer's struggle to let go of the job he's dedicated his life to is a central theme in the Jack Handler novels. His character brings depth and emotion to the story as he grapples with the tension between his personal desire for retirement and his unwavering commitment to Kate's success and the safety of the city he loves.

Who are Paul Martin and Jill Talbot? Two new characters do emerge in *Sugar Island Girl, Missing in Paris (Missing)*. They are Paul Martin and Jill Talbot. They do not appear in subsequent stories.

Who is Legend? Legend is a pivotal character in the thrilling sixth installment of the captivating series, *Wealthy Street Murders*. In this gripping narrative, Legend emerges as a central figure, intricately woven into the web of mystery and intrigue that envelopes Jack and Kate, as well as their determined allies, Red and Robby.

What sets Legend apart is the enigmatic aura that surrounds him, an aura borne from a traumatic event that unfolds at the end of *Wealthy*. Having endured a harrowing experience of being bound within a rug and left for dead, Legend's survival is nothing short of miraculous, thanks to the unwavering support and assistance of a loyal companion, Buddy.

As the story progresses, Legend's character takes on an even more significant role, transforming from a victim into a key player in the intricate puzzle of "Ghosts." His resilience, determination, and newfound sense of purpose propel him forward, making him an indispensable asset in the quest to solve the series of mysterious murders that haunt the streets of *Wealthy*.

As readers delve deeper into the world of *Wealthy*, they'll find themselves captivated by Legend's complex persona. His journey from near-death to pivotal involvement in unraveling the mysteries that unfold not only adds depth to the plot but also serves as a testament to the resilience of the human spirit. Legend's presence in this enthralling narrative is sure to leave an indelible mark, as he embarks on a journey of self-discovery and redemption, ultimately becoming an emblematic character in a tale that transcends mere storytelling.

Furthermore, the rumor is that Legend just might make some more appearances in the pages of the Jack Handler saga yet to receive ink.

Who is Mrs. Fletcher? Mrs. Fletcher, one of the caretakers at Kate's resort on Sugar Island, progressively plays a more prominent role as an occasional care-provider for the two boys. And, of course, she becomes embroiled in the intrigue.

Unfortunately, Fletcher and her husband are murdered in an earlier segment of this series: *Dogfight*.

Who is Sheriff Griffen? The sheriff first appears in *Murders in Strangmoor Bog*. He is sheriff of Schoolcraft County, which includes Strangmoor Bog, and Seney Wildlife Preserve.

Who is Angel Star? Meet Angel, a 14-year-old girl whose journey through life has left her feeling like a lost soul. Having tragically lost her mother, Angel finds herself alone in the vast landscapes of Michigan, grappling with the weight of her grief. Despite the hardships she faces, there is an undeniable beauty about her, both inside and out.

Angel's physical appearance is captivating. Her long, flowing strawberry blonde hair is often pulled up in a messy bun, an outward reflection of the chaos and confusion within her heart. Her delicate features and piercing blue eyes hold a hint of sorrow, as if they have witnessed more than their fair share of pain. Yet, there is a softness and vulnerability in her gaze that draws people in, as if she carries a piece of ethereal tranquility within her.

In this vast and sometimes desolate world, Angel yearns for a respite from the sadness that permeates her surroundings. She seeks solace in the small moments of beauty that Michigan has to offer. As she wanders through the tranquil forests, she finds solace in the whispering leaves and the rustling of wildlife. The gentle sound of a babbling creek or the sight of a vibrant sunset dipping below the horizon provide fleeting moments of peace in her tumultuous existence.

But it is not just the external world that Angel seeks to find solace in; she is on a personal quest for inner tranquility. Through her journey of self-discovery, Angel strives to heal her wounded soul. She seeks out the wisdom of books, the melodies of music, and the inspiration of art, all of which offer her a temporary escape from the harsh reality she faces.

Though Angel may feel lost and alone, she possesses a strength that is both innate and cultivated. Despite the pain she carries, she holds onto a glimmer of hope, an unyielding belief that one day she will find her place in this vast and often sad world. With every step she takes, she moves closer to uncovering her purpose, forging her own path, and finding the peace that she so desperately seeks.

In the face of adversity, Angel's resilience shines through, inspiring others to see the beauty in their own lives and to find strength in the midst of darkness. She is a reminder that even in the saddest corners of the world, there is always the potential for healing and finding peace.

Who is Millie Star? In *Strangmoor Bog*, the seventh and last book in the "Getting to know Jack" series, another new main character is introduced: Millie Star.

Even when considered all by herself, Millie is a captivating character within the Jack Handler series, as she is known for her impressive accomplishments, and her unwavering determination to navigate life as a single mother. As the mother of Angel, her 14-year-old daughter, she exemplifies strength, resilience, and a fierce commitment to providing a stable and nurturing environment for her child.

With her striking strawberry blonde hair cascading down charmingly from a lovely up-do, Millie's appearance was enhanced by her natural beauty that radiated both elegance and approachability. Her features were always complemented by a warm smile that reflected her kindness and favorable nature, making her someone people are naturally drawn to.

Millie's success in various aspects of her life showcasesed her as a super achiever. Her accomplishments serveed as a testament to her determination and work ethic, proving that she was more than capable of taking charge of her life. Even without the presence of her daughter's father. she managed to create a fulfilling life for herself and her daughter, establishing a strong foundation built on her ambitions and dedication.

Jack, the series protagonist, found himself captivated by Millie's magnetic personality and inspiring approach to life. Her natural beauty and determination resonated with Jack's own sense of purpose, forging a deep connection between the two of them. Millie's ability to balance her responsibilities as a mother and her personal aspirations intrigued Jack, creating a bond that went beyond mere attraction.

As the two characters grew closer, Millie's role as a love interest brought a new dimension to the whole Jack Handler saga. Millie's presence in Jack's life encouraged him to strive for his own goals while also providing a source of emotional support to the woman.

Millie's character added depth and complexity to the Jack Handler series. Her multifaceted personality, striking appearance, and determined spirit created a dynamic counterpart to Jack's own journey, enriching the narrative with themes of love, ambition, and the challenges of single parenthood.

Who are Lindsay Hildebrandt and Calvin Brandt?

These two significant new characters are introduced in *Ghosts of Cherry Street (and the Cumberbatch Oubliette)*. Lindsay, a rookie detective in the Grand Rapids Police Department, quickly becomes a special person in Jack's life. If you were to ask her if she is dating Jack, Lindsay (who is about two decades younger than

Jack) would immediately inform you that people their age don't *date*. But she does admit that they are good friends and occasionally see each other socially.

They have in common the fact that they both lost their spouses in a violent fashion. Lindsay's husband, also a Grand Rapids detective, was shot and killed several years earlier. This crime has not yet been solved.

Calvin Brandt, a veteran Grand Rapids detective, does not get along with anyone. And that is especially true of Jack Handler. Jack would be the first to admit that he was not an innocent party with regard to this ongoing conflict.

Who is Chuchip Kalyesveh? The single principle character contribution of *Assault on Sugar Island* was the introduction of Chuchip Kalyesveh, also known as Henry (You will be reading a lot about Henry in most of the Jack Handler books yet to be written).

As life would dictate, it was early in his life that Chuchip determined to unofficially change his name to "Henry" because he found most people butchered his Native American first name.

Jack first met Henry in a federal prison camp, where both were serving hard time. They became good friends when Henry saved Jack's life by beating up four other inmates who had been contracted by Jack's enemies to kill him. Jack has said many times that he has never met another man as physically imposing as his friend Henry.

Now that both are free men, Henry works for Jack at the Sugar Island Resort in the role of the "Man of Many Talents". And, sometimes, he partners with Jack (unofficially, of course) to help Jack out with some of his tougher private security cases; in so doing, Henry has absorbed more than a couple rounds intended for his boss.

Physical Appearance: Henry is described as a tall, wiry man with weathered features that reflect a life spent in the rugged landscapes of the Upper Peninsula. His skin is tanned from exposure to the sun, and his piercing gray eyes reveal a depth of wisdom and experience.

Personality: Henry is known for his quiet yet strong presence. He possesses a deep knowledge of the island and its mysteries, making him an invaluable resource to the series' protagonist, Jack Handler. He has a reputation for being resourceful, self-reliant, and fiercely protective of the island and its secrets.

Background: Henry's past is shrouded in mystery, and he is reticent to share much about his personal history. However, readers gradually uncover tidbits about his life, including his deep connection to Sugar Island, which is more than just a physical place for him—it's a part of his identity.

Role in the Series: Henry's role in the series goes beyond being a mere character; he serves as a symbol of the island's history, its untamed beauty, and its enduring secrets. He is an integral part of the community on Sugar Island, and his interactions with Jack Handler often reveal crucial clues and insights that help unravel the mysteries in each book.

As the series progresses, Henry's relationship with Jack deepens, evolving into a friendship that transcends words. Jack comes to rely on Henry's guidance and wisdom, especially when faced with complex and dangerous situations. Their dynamic adds depth and richness to the overall narrative.

Significance in "Assault on Sugar Island" and Beyond: In "Assault on Sugar Island," Henry's knowledge of the island's hidden past becomes instrumental in solving a critical mystery. His willingness to share information, albeit cautiously, sets the stage for the book's intriguing plot.

Throughout the subsequent books in the series, Henry's presence continues to be a source of intrigue and fascination. He becomes a character readers eagerly anticipate encountering, as his wisdom and connection to the island play pivotal roles in the unfolding stories.

As readers delve deeper into the Jack Handler series, they will undoubtedly appreciate the complexity and depth that Chuchip Kalyesveh, or Henry, brings to this captivating world of murder mysteries and Upper Peninsula adventures.

Who is Aunt Halona? Aunt Halona is a striking embodiment of wisdom, grace, and the timeless beauty that seems to emanate from her very soul. Her journey across the country to be with her nephew, Henry, speaks to her deep love for family and her adventurous spirit. She has made her new home on Sugar Island, Michigan, and the island's natural beauty seems to mirror her own.

Aunt Halona has weathered the years with a poise that only time and experience can bring. Her face is etched with lines that tell the stories of a life richly lived, yet her eyes remain bright and full of vitality. High cheekbones frame her gentle smile, which seems to effortlessly put those around her at ease.

Her long, silver hair cascades down her back, a testament to her connection with nature and her respect for her Native American heritage. She often adorns her hair with beaded ornaments and feathers, each piece carrying a story of its own. Her attire blends tradition with practicality. She frequently wears traditional beaded moccasins and intricately designed shawls, but she's equally comfortable in jeans and a cozy sweater when the island's weather turns cool.

Aunt Halona's presence exudes warmth and kindness. She's a skilled storyteller, recounting ancient legends and family tales by the fireside. Her voice, soft and melodic, carries the wisdom of generations. She has an uncanny ability to listen, making others feel heard and valued in her company.

Living on Sugar Island has rekindled her spirit of adventure. She loves exploring the island's lush forests, pristine beaches, and crystal-clear lakes. Her knowledge of the island's flora and fauna is extensive, and she's more than happy to share her insights with Henry, who is eager to learn from his wise aunt.

As Henry and Aunt Halona spend more time together, their bond deepens. They embark on new adventures, from canoeing on the island's rivers to hiking through its forests. Aunt Halona is the guardian of ancestral knowledge, passing down traditions and teaching Henry about their Native American heritage.

Aunt Halona's presence on Sugar Island has brought a sense of continuity and love to Henry's life. Her beauty isn't just skin deep; it radiates from her character and her love for family. Together, they are poised to embrace the adventures that await them on the island, strengthening their family ties and creating cherished memories along the way.

Who is Emma? Emma stood a well-proportioned five feet

nine, and was viewed by all as strikingly beautiful. Always impeccably attired, and possessing the flair of a professional model, her very appearance in a room would draw all eyes to follow.

Most every evening after seven would find her dressed in a long black dress with spaghetti straps and a side slit to the middle of her thigh. She would typically be wearing dark stockings with tall leather three-inch-heeled boots. Slung over her right shoulder she'd be carrying a Versace patent leather tote. It was large enough to carry her weapon of choice for any given assignment.

Emma would have her dark brown hair pulled up in a top-knot with face-framing wispy bangs cut to lash length, tapered to cheekbone length, and blended with jawbone length layers. Huge golden hoop earrings accented the stylish coiffure. When outside her living quarters, she'd always have her eyes fringed with dark thick eyelashes, and highlighted by tastefully applied smoky eye shadow.

However, those who knew Emma well were totally aware that her apparent affinity for the runway was by design not designers. Put simply, elegant Emma, was a professional assassin. Yes, Emma (Legs) is a very attractive thirty-something-ish contract killer. Emma made her first powerful appearance in *Dogfight*. "You should expect to see her again," Michael suggests.

Who is Detective Greggory Townsend? Detective Greggory Townsend is a remarkable individual hailing from the picturesque Upper Peninsula of Michigan. He grew up surrounded by the region's natural beauty and developed a deep appreciation for the great outdoors. As a young man, Greggory set his sights on attending Lake Superior State University in Sault Ste. Marie, MI, known for its excellent criminal justice program.

During his time at the university, Greggory was a dedicated and diligent student. He excelled in his studies, absorbing knowledge about the intricacies of law enforcement, criminal investigation techniques, and the complexities of the justice system. It was evident from an early stage that he had a natural talent for unraveling mysteries and solving intricate puzzles.

After four years of rigorous education, Greggory graduated with a well-deserved degree in criminal justice, ready to embark on his professional journey in law enforcement. His dream came true when he joined the police force as a young detective, where his skills, intellect, and intuition quickly made him stand out among his peers.

One of Detective Townsend's most notable accomplishments was his role as the lead investigator in the gripping book "To China With Love." The case took him on a thrilling and dangerous journey, pushing his investigative abilities to the limits. In working closely with Kate, the daughter of the protagonist of the famous Jack Handler series, she proved to be an unexpected but captivating presence in his life.

Physically, Greggory Townsend was undeniably attractive, with dark, lustrous hair that framed his face handsomely and mesmerizing green eyes that seemed to hold a thousand untold stories. However, what truly made him stand out was his unwavering commitment to justice and his dedication to solving even the most enigmatic cases.

Despite being known for his tough and serious demeanor on the job, when it came to Kate, Greggory found himself more than infatuated. She brought out a softer side of him, showing his capacity to care deeply for someone beyond the call of duty. Their connection added an element of romance and vulnerability to his life, something that he didn't often allow himself to experience amidst the rigors of being a detective.

Overall, Detective Greggory Townsend was a complex and intriguing individual, with a mix of intelligence, determination, and charm that made him a captivating protagonist in his own right. Whether he was delving into the depths of a challenging case or exploring the nuances of human emotion, he left an indelible mark on the hearts of readers and those who crossed his path.

Who is Liz? Liz is a 26-year-old woman whose striking beauty often turns heads as she walks through the gritty streets of Los Angeles. With her long, blonde hair adorned with shades of pink and magenta, she adds a splash of vibrant color to the otherwise drab surroundings. Her petite frame carries an air of elegance, though her appearance belies the complexities of her life.

Liz's journey has taken a perilous turn as she's become entangled with some unsavory characters in the underbelly of LA. One of the most prominent figures in her life is Spyder, a heavily tattooed and weathered man known in the criminal world as a drug dealer. Spyder's life has been a perpetual cycle of run-ins with the law, making him a dangerous and unpredictable presence in Liz's life.

But despite her involvement in this dark and chaotic world, Liz has decided that she wants out. She yearns for a life beyond the constant danger and illicit activities that have ensnared her. It's then that she stumbles upon Angel, a remarkable accomplice.

Angel's story is as compelling as Liz's. She left behind her home and life in Upper Michigan after a tragic event – her mother was shot, leaving her with no choice but to escape the harsh reality of her past. Angel and Liz find solace in each other, two souls seeking redemption and a chance to start anew.

Together, they hatch a plan to break free from the clutches of their destructive environment in LA. Their partnership is a glimmer of hope amid the darkness that surrounds them. Liz's beauty may have initially drawn attention, but her resilience and determination to change her life for the better, with the help of Angel, make her a remarkable figure in a world filled with unsavory characters.

Who is Spyder? In the gritty underbelly of San Francisco, there exists a figure known as Spyder, a shadowy character whose existence thrives in the realms of the illicit and dangerous. He navigates the city's dark corners, orchestrating a life filled with crime, deception, and a touch of desperation.

Spyder's appearance reflects his hardened lifestyle. He often dresses in worn-out clothing that's seen better days, a deliberate choice to blend into the city's urban chaos. His tattooed face and intense eyes betray a history marked by struggle, a testament to the harsh reality he has endured.

At the heart of Spyder's operations lies a network of drug dealing and the production of illegal identification documents. He's a craftsman in his own right, creating fake IDs that serve as tickets for those seeking a fresh start away from the authorities. In addition to possessing a well-cultivated streak of meanness, Spyder was known for his ability to fabricate very believable phony identities, and the credentials to support them. In fact, even after creating and selling nearly one hundred full sets of new identities over a ten-year period, Spyder still had never had one of his creations successfully challenged. His skills in this arena have earned him a degree of notoriety among those who require such services, further cementing his position in the criminal underworld.

However, Spyder's relationships are far from stable. His interactions with his drug suppliers are characterized by a palpable tension, a constant push-and-pull of power dynamics. He's known to be ruthless, eliminating dealers who dare to challenge him or threaten his business. This reputation for violence ensures that others think twice before crossing him.

Amidst the chaos of his criminal pursuits, Spyder's personal life is a chaotic mess. He's a loner by choice, with few genuine connections in his life. The weight of his chosen path has left him emotionally scarred, causing his caustic demeanor and a lingering distrust of others. He lives in the shadows, haunted by the choices he's made and the consequences that loom over him.

As the city pulses with life around him, Spyder remains a symbol of the seedy underbelly that thrives beneath the surface of San Francisco. His existence is a reminder that, even in a place of beauty and innovation, darkness can fester and give rise to individuals who navigate the thin line between survival and self-destruction.

In order to keep his dealers in line, Spyder had a well-documented penchant for cruelty, if not outright torture. When it came to dealing with the drug dealers who worked for him, on more than one occasion he had been suspected of terminating them if they persisted in getting on his nerves. Bottom line, even though still in his late twenties, he had spent more than one year in prison.

One of his signature identifying features was his labyrinth of frightening tattoos. Virtually every inch of his visible skin was intricately painted by some of the best artists in the California prison system.

Here are the Amazon Links to all Michael's Previous Jack Handler Books:

Jack and the New York Death Mask:	http://amzn.to/MVpAEd
Murder on Sugar Island:	http://amzn.to/1u66DBG
Superior Peril:	http://amzn.to/LAQnEU
Superior Intrigue:	http://amzn.to/1jvjNSi
Sugar Island Girl Missing in Paris:	http://amzn.to/1g5c66e
Wealthy Street Murders:	http://amzn.to/1mb6NQy
Murders in Strangmoor Bog:	http://amzn.to/1osAjJ8
Ghosts of Cherry Street:	http://amzn.to/1PvWfJd
Assault on Sugar Island:	http://amzn.to/2n3vcyL
Dogfight:	http://amzn.to/2F7OkoM
Murder at Whitefish Point:	http://amzn.to/2CxlAmC
Superior Shoal:	https://amzn.to/2pbM89v
From Deadwood to Deep State:	https://amzn.to/330eElx
Sault:	https://amzn.to/3gq21Dj
To China with Love:	https://shorturl.at/jpvBU

www.ingramcontent.com/pod-product-compliance
Lightning Source LLC
Chambersburg PA
CBHW020544020726
47494CB00006B/1910